Laura wasn't going to like what he was about to suggest.

Not one bit. But then, Devlin wasn't exactly thrilled with the idea, either.

"I can't guarantee Timmy's safety unless you live here with me," he stated baldly.

"Live here with you?" She glanced up at him in astonishment.

"It's the only way...."

"I...I understand." Her face bright red, she tipped her chin up defensively, as if readying herself for the worst. "So...what kind of... arrangement do you have in mind?"

"Under the circumstances, I thought marriage might be the best arrangement."

Dear Reader,

Welcome to another month of fabulous reading here at Silhouette Intimate Moments. As always, we've put together six terrific books for your reading pleasure, starting with *Another Man's Wife* by Dallas Schulze. This is another of our Heartbreakers titles, as well as the latest in her miniseries entitled A Family Circle. As usual with one of this author's titles, you won't want to miss it.

Next up is *Iain Ross's Woman* by Emilie Richards. This, too, is part of a miniseries, The Men of Midnight. This is a suspenseful and deeply emotional book that I predict will end up on your "keeper" shelf.

The rest of the month is filled out with new titles by Nikki Benjamin, *The Wedding Venture;* Susan Mallery, *The Only Way Out;* Suzanne Brockmann, *Not Without Risk;* and Nancy Gideon, *For Mercy's Sake.* Every one of them provides exactly the sort of romantic excitement you've come to expect from Intimate Moments.

In months to come, look for more reading from some of the best authors in the business. We've got books coming up from Linda Turner, Judith Duncan, Naomi Horton and Paula Detmer Riggs, to name only a few. So come back next month—and every month—to Silhouette Intimate Moments, where romance is the name of the game.

Yours,
Leslie Wainger
Senior Editor and Editorial Coordinator

Please address questions and book requests to:
Silhouette Reader Service
U.S.: 3010 Walden Ave., P.O. Box 1325, Buffalo, NY 14269
Canadian: P.O. Box 609, Fort Erie, Ont. L2A 5X3

THE WEDDING
VENTURE

NIKKI
BENJAMIN

Silhouette®
INTIMATE™MOMENTS®
Published by Silhouette Books
America's Publisher of Contemporary Romance

SILHOUETTE BOOKS

ISBN 0-373-07645-2

THE WEDDING VENTURE

Books by Nikki Benjamin

Silhouette Intimate Moments

A Man To Believe In #359
Restless Wind #519
The Wedding Venture #645

Silhouette Special Edition

Emily's House #539
On the Whispering Wind #663
The Best Medicine #716
It Must Have Been the Mistletoe #782
My Baby, Your Child #880
Only St. Nick Knew #928

NIKKI BENJAMIN

was born and raised in the Midwest, but after years in the Houston area, she considers herself a true Texan. Nikki says she's always been an avid reader. (Her earliest literary heroines were Nancy Drew, Trixie Belden and Beany Malone.) Her writing experience was limited, however, until a friend started penning a novel and encouraged Nikki to do the same. One scene led to another, and soon she was hooked.

When not reading or writing, the author enjoys spending time with her husband and son, needlepoint, hiking, biking, horseback riding and sailing.

For my dear friend Jennifer Stevens (aka Jimmy's mom), with thanks for always being there when I've needed you. I couldn't have juggled writing and raising a son without your constant support and encouragement.

Chapter 1

"Just keep on driving," Devlin Gray muttered to himself. "Otherwise you're going to end up ruining your reputation by doing a good deed."

Any minute now, someone else would come to the woman's rescue, he reasoned. But who? The late-spring rainstorm seemed to have sent everyone with any sense scurrying for shelter.

Hoping he'd see someone, *anyone*, besides the woman huddled half on the curb and half in the rain-washed gutter, he slowed the Jeep to a crawl and peered through the windshield as the wipers clicked rhythmically across the glass. Unfortunately, the narrow cobblestoned street was just as deserted as it had been when he'd turned onto it a few moments earlier.

Although he hadn't actually seen her fall, he assumed that was what had happened. A canvas bag spewing books and papers and an umbrella, now turned inside out, lay beside her on the sidewalk. From the way she sat there, hunched into herself, clutching her ankle as the steady downpour drenched her, he was also fairly sure that she'd hurt herself.

Cursing quietly, Devlin pulled over to the curb. There was no telling how long she'd been out in the rain. And, since the storm showed no sign of letting up, he doubted anyone else would be venturing down the quiet side street anytime soon. Still, he knew that if he had any sense at all, he'd get out of there as fast as he could.

For the past three years he'd done his damnedest to distance himself from the other residents of San Pedro, Mexico. In fact, he'd gone out of his way to establish himself as being rather... reprehensible. Lending the woman a hand would be strictly out of character. And while he doubted one random act of kindness would blow his cover, he'd really rather not risk it.

Yet, much to his surprise, and to a certain extent his relief, he hadn't actually *become* the cold-hearted bastard he'd wanted everyone in the small town to believe he was.

Shifting into Neutral, he set the parking brake and switched off the engine, eyeing the woman intently. Since he'd first caught sight of her, he'd had the strangest feeling that he knew her. Not personally, of course, but—

As if sensing his assiduous scrutiny, the woman glanced up at him. Then, a look of utter dismay on her face, she quickly ducked her head again.

"Aw, hell," Devlin swore softly.

Of all the women in San Pedro, the one he'd come upon sitting in a gutter in the midst of a rainstorm, injured and alone, *would* have to be the one he'd forced himself to avoid at all cost almost from the first day he'd arrived in town.

"Laura Burke."

Grinding out her name, he fingered the key in the ignition, more than half tempted to restart the engine and be on his way.

Although he hadn't spoken more than a dozen words to the woman in the time he'd used San Pedro as his base of operations, he knew quite a bit about her. She, too, was an expatriate American, a widow in her late twenties. Along with her young son she'd resided in the old colonial town, tucked into a mountain valley two hundred miles north of Mexico City, for about five years. She taught English at the convent school, lived quietly in a modest house and, aside from spending time with one or two close friends, kept mostly to herself.

He had no idea why she'd come to San Pedro in the first place. Nor could he imagine what had made her choose to stay. She didn't have any family there. And she certainly didn't fit into the American community—a group made up mostly of artists, aging hippies and retired senior citizens—any more than he did. She was an attractive woman, and she seemed to be more than moderately intelligent, as well. Burying herself in a small town in central Mexico seemed like an unusual thing for her to do. Unless she was hiding from someone.

The more Devlin had thought about it, the more he'd come to the conclusion that was exactly what she was doing. But he hadn't allowed himself to use the resources at his disposal to find out why. He'd figured he was better off not knowing what kind of predicament she'd gotten herself into. He had enough to worry about already without twisting himself into knots over a woman who'd more than likely, and very wisely, want nothing at all to do with him.

Instead, he'd gone out of his way to give her a wide berth. He couldn't afford to pursue a personal relationship with anyone in San Pedro, especially a beautiful young woman with a five-year-old son. Not after what had happened to his wife and daughter. After Carly and Melissa had been killed, he'd vowed never to endanger anyone else as he had them. And although the work he was doing in San Pedro wasn't nearly as hazardous as his work in the small Central American country of El Norte, that was one promise he intended to keep.

A sudden gust of wind shook the Jeep, jarring Devlin from his reverie. Realizing that several moments had passed since he'd switched off the engine, and aware of how miserable Laura must be feeling, he shoved the door open and stepped out. He'd chosen to work for the United States government more than fifteen years ago, and though he might not like living with the limitations that choice now put on his personal life, he certainly had no reason to resent them. He'd learned the hard way that in his profession one was better off alone; it was a lesson he wasn't about to forget.

As he ran through the pelting rain the icy drops quickly drenched his hair and his plain white cotton T-shirt. Though he tried to avoid the deeper puddles on the narrow sidewalk, water sloshed into his sneakers and soaked the legs of his faded jeans. He'd probably end up with pneumonia, but what the hell? It wasn't every day he had a chance to rescue a damsel in distress, he mused, a shiver stealing up his spine as he came to a halt beside a very bedraggled Ms. Laura Burke.

"Here, let me give you a hand," he said as she glanced up at him fearfully.

Without waiting for her permission, he bent and scooped her into his arms in one economical movement, turned, then headed back to the Jeep.

"Oh, no, please," she protested. "I'm all right. Really, I am."

"Yeah, sure," he drawled, opening the passenger door and dumping her onto the seat. "You were sitting in the gutter in the middle of a rainstorm just for the hell of it."

"Well, no," she admitted, flinching under his steady stare. "I...I slipped and turned my ankle. But I could have...could have—"

"What?" he demanded, making no effort to hide his irritation.

Obviously she would have preferred to stay where she was rather than accept his help, and that really annoyed the hell out of him. Granted, he hadn't expected her to look upon him as a knight in shining armor. Not with the kind of reputation he'd fostered for himself around town. But he'd never gone so far as to lead people to believe he was evil incarnate, either.

"I...I don't...know." She lowered her gaze for a moment. Then, shoving her wet hair away from her face, she glanced at him again. "What about my books?" she asked softly. She gestured toward the canvas bag lying on the sidewalk, then crossed her arms over her chest in a seemingly futile attempt to still the shivers shaking her slender body.

Wordlessly he reached over the seat, grabbed the old blanket and bundle of towels he kept on hand for emergencies, and dropped them in her lap.

"Save a couple of towels for me," he instructed, then slammed the door and sprinted down the sidewalk again.

Uttering a choice comment or two about women who looked gift horses in the mouth, Devlin gathered up Laura's books and papers, shoved them into her canvas bag and made what he hoped would be a last mad dash back to the Jeep. He really hated being cold and wet. Almost as much as he hated feeling like a fool.

He should have left the lady sitting in the gutter. And if he hadn't been such a sap, he would have. Unfortunately, it was too late to go back and start over now. But this was definitely the last good deed he was going to do for a long time. A *very* long time.

As he climbed into the Jeep and tossed her bag onto the floor by her feet, Laura offered him a couple of dry towels. Surprised that she'd paid heed to his request, he muttered a word of thanks as he took them from her.

"Actually, I'm the one who should be thanking you, Mr. Gray," she murmured, not quite meeting his gaze. "Now that I've thought about it, I doubt I could have made it home on my own. I'm...I'm very grateful that you stopped to help."

"*De nada,* Ms. Burke," he replied, tossing off the Spanish phrase for "it's nothing" in a nonchalant tone of voice.

While her gratitude was far from overwhelming, at least she'd made an effort to let him know she appreciated what he'd done. Feeling slightly mollified, he started the engine and switched on the heater. Then, as he shook out one of the towels she'd handed him, he eyed her surreptitiously.

With a sense of relief he saw that she'd wrapped the blanket around her shoulders, just as he'd hoped she would. Although he'd been concentrating on not falling on his face as he'd carried her to the Jeep, he'd have to have been dead not to notice that, thanks to the rain, her simple, white cotton blouse had become virtually transparent. All she'd been wearing under it was a lacy scrap of silk that did more to enhance than hide her luscious—

With a muffled groan Devlin scrubbed the towel over his hair. Then, blotting at the rivulets of water running down his neck and chest, he tipped his head against the back of his seat, closed his eyes and willed away the surge of desire shooting through him.

"Are you . . . are you all right?" she queried softly.

Amazed that she cared enough to ask, he regarded her wordlessly. She met his gaze for several seconds. Then, as if embarrassed by her show of concern, she turned and stared out the side window; her long, dark hair, which hung in thick, wet, yet already curling clumps, shielded her face from his view.

"Yeah, sure," he muttered.

Not exactly an honest answer, but one certain to set her mind at ease. He doubted she'd really been worried about his welfare. At the moment she needed his help, and if he happened to pass out, he certainly wouldn't be of much use to her.

Realizing that his cynicism had reached a new high, Devlin threw his wet towels onto the back seat, then grabbed the gear stick and shifted the Jeep into Drive. He had no reason to judge her so harshly. She hadn't asked him to come to her rescue. And, understandably enough, she'd want some reassurance that he was all right, now that she seemed to be more or less at his mercy.

He had no doubt she'd have hopped out of the Jeep fast enough to make his head spin if she'd been able to manage on her own. Which meant he'd probably been right when he'd assumed she'd hurt herself.

"How's your ankle?" he asked as he accelerated slowly.

Swept along by an occasional gust of wind, the rain pounded down harder than ever, and even with the windshield wipers set on high he couldn't see more than a few feet ahead.

"I think I may have sprained it or—or something. But I'm sure it will be all right once I put some ice on it." Plucking at the old wool blanket, she stared out the window for a moment, then gestured toward the cross street just ahead. "I live on Barrancas Street. Just turn right and—"

"I know," Devlin interrupted without thinking, then mentally cursed his slip of the tongue when she whipped around and stared at him, her pale green eyes once again full of fear.

"You do?"

"Yes."

Had he thought it would reassure her in any way, he'd have added that he knew where all the Americans in San Pedro lived. But, considering the kind of person he was supposed to be, he doubted that would put her mind at ease. Also, though he knew she was safer with him than with just about anyone else in town, there was no way he could convince her of that. So he finished what he'd originally intended to say without offering any explanations or excuses.

"And I'll see that you get there. But first, I'm going to take you to the clinic so Dr. Moreno can X-ray your ankle."

"No, really, that's not necessary," she insisted, looking at him uneasily.

Probably worried *her* reputation would be ruined just by being seen with him, he thought. And considering how the people of San Pedro loved to gossip among themselves, he certainly couldn't blame her. But Dr. Juan Carlos Moreno and his American wife, Annie, were her friends. They'd never spread rumors about her. And as long as the rain kept up, it was a good bet no one else would see the two of them together.

"More than likely, you've got a sprained ankle. But, on the off chance that it's broken, the sooner you find out, the better. And the only way to do that is to have Dr. Moreno X-ray it."

"I suppose you're right." With what sounded like a soft sigh of resignation, she turned to stare out the side window once again.

"With the way it's raining, I doubt anyone else will be there, so it shouldn't take too long," Devlin added, hoping to set her mind at ease.

"Probably not," she agreed, shrugging with seeming indifference.

They drove on in silence for a few minutes. Then, although he knew he'd probably be better off letting well enough alone, Devlin gave in to the little niggle of curiosity that teased at the back of his mind.

"Any special reason why *you* were out in the middle of a storm?" he asked quietly.

"I promised my housekeeper I'd come home as soon as school let out so she could visit her daughter," Laura replied after the slightest hesitation. "When I left, it wasn't raining all that hard. But then, all of a sudden, it started to pour. A gust of wind caught my umbrella as I was stepping off the curb, I lost my balance, slipped on the cobblestones and fell. Guess I should have stayed at school until the weather cleared, but..." She shrugged and shook her head. "Poor Flora. She's probably wondering what happened to me."

"You can call her from the clinic and let her know you're all right."

"Yes, of course," she murmured. Then, when he thought she'd say no more, she surprised him by asking quite candidly, "What about you, Mr. Gray? Why were you out in the storm?"

Spurred by her unexpected interest, Devlin spoke once again without really thinking. "I've been out of town on business the past couple of weeks, so I was on my way home, too."

Feeling oddly companionable, he glanced at her and started to smile, then saw the look of trepidation on her face. Instantly he realized he'd made a big mistake mentioning business. As far as everyone in San Pedro was concerned, his "business" had always been equated with criminal activity. Something he would have remembered if he hadn't allowed himself to be lulled into thinking he and Laura were just a normal couple having a casual conversation.

Feeling like even more of a fool than he had earlier, Devlin pulled to a stop under the wide portico sheltering the front entrance of San Pedro's only emergency medical clinic. He was supposed to be one of the good guys, but in order to do his job, he had to pretend to be one of the bad guys. He'd believed that he had reconciled himself to the incongruity of it all years ago. But now, with Laura Burke eyeing him as if he were an alien from outer space, he found himself growing increasingly frustrated with the absurdity of the situation. And much to his dismay he had an almost overwhelming urge to tell her who and what he really was.

Unfortunately, that kind of revelation could very well end up jeopardizing not only him, but her, in ways he didn't even want to consider. Better to let her think he was the scum of the earth. Which meant he'd better go back to acting like the no-good bastard he was supposed to be.

"But I guess you'd rather not know about that, would you?" he continued in a caustic tone of voice.

"I didn't say that—" she began.

"Hey, I don't blame you, sweetheart," he cut in, gazing at her sardonically. "You're much better off not knowing where I've been or what I've been doing lately." He switched off the engine and pulled the key from the ignition, then caught her arm as she turned away from him and fumbled with the door handle. "Stay put while I get a wheelchair. If that ankle's broken, you'll only make it worse trying to walk on it."

"Whatever you say," she muttered, a blush staining her face as she freed herself from his hold.

Feeling anything but proud of himself, Devlin stepped out of the Jeep and strode toward the entrance to the clinic. He walked through the double doors and glanced around the waiting room. As he'd expected, except for Dr. Moreno and his wife, gazing at him intently from where they stood side by side behind the reception desk, the place appeared to be deserted.

"Mind if I borrow this for a minute?" he asked, nodding toward the wheelchair parked just inside the doorway. "Laura Burke's waiting out in my Jeep. She fell and twisted her ankle."

"Of course not." Setting down the file folder he'd been holding, Dr. Moreno walked around the desk and started toward him, his brow furrowed. "Do you need any help?"

"I can manage."

Wheeling the chair ahead of him, Devlin returned to the Jeep where Laura waited, poised on the edge of the passenger seat. Without a word he slid his arms around her, blanket and all, and shifted her into the wheelchair, noting as he did so that her right ankle was now badly swollen.

"And you wanted me to take you straight home?" he chided softly.

"Only because I didn't want you to go out of your way on my account."

"Believe me, I'm not," he assured her as he grabbed her canvas bag and dropped it in her lap. "If I'd had anything else better to do, you'd still be sitting in that gutter."

"Well, then, I guess I should consider myself lucky, shouldn't I?" she snapped back with astonishing spirit.

"If you say so," he agreed, allowing his gaze to flick over her insultingly.

Once again Laura's face turned a dull shade of red, and once again Devlin was anything but proud of himself. Somewhere deep inside, he wished he could be her hero. But, damn it, that simply wasn't possible. And the sooner he accepted it, the better.

More forcefully than was absolutely necessary, he spun the wheelchair around and rolled her toward the entryway. Just inside the waiting room he stepped back, allowing Dr. Moreno to take over for him. Then he sauntered over to the row of chairs lining the far wall.

"I'll just wait over here," he announced to no one in particular.

"Oh, that won't be necessary," Annie Moreno advised, hovering over her friend protectively. "We'll be more than happy to see that Ms. Burke gets home."

For one long moment Devlin thought about telling the doctor's wife what she could do with that idea. He'd always prided himself on finishing what he started, and seeing Laura Burke to her door seemed as good a way as any to end what he'd so foolishly begun almost twenty minutes ago.

But he'd done what he'd originally set out to do. He'd hauled her out of the gutter and taken her to safety. She was in good hands now. And aside from a ride home, which she obviously didn't need, he had nothing to offer her. Which meant he had no reason to hang around any longer. So, he might as well allow himself to be banished like the undesirable element he'd spent the past three years pretending he was. No matter how much it rankled.

Shoving his hands into his pockets, he shrugged carelessly. "Well, in that case, I guess I'll be on my way." He met Laura's gaze and nodded once. "Ms. Burke."

"Mr. Gray," she acknowledged in a quiet voice. "Thank you for your help."

She hesitated, her eyes holding his questioningly, and for just an instant Devlin thought she'd say more. But then, as if having second thoughts, she ducked her head wordlessly.

Aware that there was nothing more he could say, either, Devlin turned and headed toward the double doors, his wet sneakers squishing on the tile floor. Outside, a gust of wind spattered him with raindrops as he climbed into the Jeep. Beyond the shelter of the portico the storm raged on as furiously as ever.

After the kind of day he'd had, he'd be glad to get home. Yet he made no move to turn the key in the ignition. Instead, he propped his forearms on the steering wheel, bent his head and gave in to a weariness that was not only physical but emotional, as well.

Maybe the time had come to take McConnell up on his offer of a job in D.C. teaching young up-and-comers the tricks of the covert operations trade. Although a lot had changed since the end of the cold war, the U.S. government still needed well-trained eyes and ears to keep it apprised of potential problems around the world. And he'd been those eyes and ears for a long time now. He'd more than earned a move up the "company" ladder.

But he hadn't yet tracked down the cold-blooded killer who'd murdered his wife and child—along with almost a dozen other innocent people—during the attempted assassination of the president of El Norte almost four years ago. And until he did, Devlin wasn't going anywhere.

Drago Espinosa hadn't surfaced in almost a year. But considering the political unrest occurring in several Central and South American countries, sooner or later someone somewhere was going to hire him to do a little dirty work. With any luck at all, Devlin would be waiting for him, ready, willing and able to guarantee the bastard never wreaked havoc in anyone's life again. Then maybe he'd finally feel he'd paid his debt to Carly and Melissa.

Having reminded himself yet again of why he continued to lead the kind of life he did, Devlin started the engine and shifted into gear. What he needed right now was a hot shower followed by some of Mrs. Santos's home cooking. After that, he'd feel more like himself again. Then, surely, he'd be better able to put all thought of Laura Burke out of his mind.

Or so he told himself as he pulled onto the deserted street. There wasn't anyplace for her in his world, and there wasn't going to be. One chance encounter, no matter how soul stirring, wasn't going to change that, especially if he chose not to let it. And that was one choice he knew he had to make. For Laura's sake as well as his own.

Staring at the canvas bag in her lap, Laura listened to the sound of Devlin's Jeep fading into the steady beat of the still-falling rain, feeling not only relief but regret. And that was odd, considering how frightened she'd been when she first realized one of San Pedro's more ignominious residents had caught her in what could only have been called a precarious position. For a few moments there, as she'd glanced up and seen him sprinting toward her, she'd actually found herself wondering if she'd still be alive an hour later.

With his dark, shaggy hair, his cold-as-ice gray eyes and a day or two's growth of beard shadowing the hard edge of his jaw, he'd certainly *looked* unsavory. Yet he hadn't behaved in the beastly way rumor had led her to believe he would. Oh, his manner had been unnerving enough, especially when he'd blithely hauled her into his arms and carried her to his Jeep. But he'd been neither cruel nor malicious. And though he certainly could have done so, he hadn't used her vulnerability to his advantage.

Instead, he'd been surprisingly kind and considerate, making her initial fear and anxiety seem foolish. Sitting beside him in the close confines of his Jeep, wrapped in the blanket he'd given her, she'd begun to think he was actually pretty decent. Why, she'd even gone so far as to consider the possibility that maybe people were wrong about him.

But then he'd mentioned his "business" in answer to what she'd thought was an innocent question, and she'd been reminded that Devlin Gray's lack of respectability stemmed not only from the kind of person he was supposed to be, but also from the nefarious schemes in which he was allegedly involved.

Suddenly, despite his seeming concern for her, Laura hadn't been quite so eager to give him the benefit of the doubt. Not when she recalled how doing just that with another man had turned her life upside down.

She'd been young and naive when she'd met Johnny Buschetti six years ago and allowed him to con her into believing he was a good and upright man. But she was older and wiser now. And she had her son to consider, too. If Giovanni got his hands on Timmy because she'd let down her guard with someone like Devlin Gray—

"Earth to Laura, earth to Laura. Come in, please," Annie teased, her gentle voice laced with amusement.

"Oh, Annie, I'm sorry. What did you say?" Drawn from her reverie, Laura glanced up at her friend, offering her a wry smile.

"I was just wondering what in the world you were doing with Devlin Gray," Annie repeated, her bright blue eyes brimming with curiosity.

"Yes, I'd like to know that, too," Juan Carlos prompted as he wheeled Laura toward the room where the clinic's portable X-ray machine was located.

"Actually, I wasn't *with* him. At least, not by choice."

As concisely as she could, Laura told them how Devlin had come to her rescue after she'd slipped and fallen on the cobblestones.

"I'm glad to hear that's all there was to it," Annie said, helping her onto the examination table.

"Me, too," Juan Carlos agreed. He moved the wheelchair off to one side, then rolled the X-ray machine into position. "Devlin Gray's not exactly high on anyone's list of favorite people around here, and from what I've heard, not without good reason."

"I know," Laura admitted, albeit reluctantly. "But he did stop to help me when he could have just as easily kept right on going. As far as I'm concerned, that counts for something. Especially since I'd probably still be sitting in the gutter if he hadn't."

She had no idea why she was defending the man. Like everyone else in San Pedro, she believed he was a criminal of some sort hiding out south of the U.S. border. Granted, she'd never actually seen his picture on a Wanted poster. But she'd heard the rumors about him. And from what she'd seen of him over the past three years, she had to admit he had all the markings of a man living outside the law, markings she'd long ago learned to recognize all too well.

He certainly didn't seem to want for money, at least not for a thirtysomething man with no apparent source of income. To her knowledge, he hadn't worked at any kind of job since he'd come to San Pedro. Nor did he seem to be pursuing any kind of artistic endeavor.

He'd also made a point of keeping his distance from the other expatriate Americans living in the town. Initial overtures made by the more gregarious members of the group had been so rudely rebuffed that he'd since been left to himself.

Yet Laura doubted he was just a loner. Not when strange men were occasionally seen entering or exiting his house at odd hours of the day or night. She'd noticed one or two herself several times when errands had taken her through that part of the neighborhood. And from the secretive air they'd had about them, she'd simply assumed they were up to no good.

Just as she'd discovered her husband of four short months and *his* associates had been, just before he was gunned down in front of—

"You don't think he had any ulterior motives?" Annie asked, drawing Laura back to the present.

Instinctively she wanted to deny the possibility, but Annie often saw things she tended to miss. And Laura trusted her friend's judgment where other people were concerned.

"Why do you say that?" she asked quietly.

"There was something about the way he looked at you just before he left. You had your head down, so you probably didn't notice."

"What?" Laura demanded uneasily.

"A kind of... longing," Annie replied.

"That sounds a bit fanciful even for you, my love," Juan Carlos chided as he probed Laura's ankle with gentle fingertips.

"You're right," Annie hastened to agree. "I probably just imagined it."

"Probably," Laura murmured, hoping her friend really had been mistaken.

The last thing she wanted was to have attracted Devlin Gray's attention, even inadvertently. Granted, she'd found herself wishing more and more lately that she had a man in her life. But not a man like him.

Despite his rather rough appearance, he *was* appealing, in a tall, dark and undeniably handsome way. And she'd been touched by his caring and concern. But she knew better than to allow herself to be swayed by either good looks or one relatively small act of kindness.

That's how she'd gotten into trouble six years ago, and she wasn't about to make the same mistake twice. No matter how scared and lonely she sometimes felt, she and Timmy were better off on their own. They'd gotten by so far with good friends like Annie and Juan Carlos. And Flora had been a real lifesaver on more than one occasion. Which reminded her...

"Would you mind calling Flora and telling her what happened?" she asked, meeting Annie's gaze once again. "She and Timmy are probably wondering where I am."

"Sure thing." Annie patted her hand reassuringly, then added, "How about if I get you some dry clothes, too?"

"That would be wonderful."

Laura offered the other woman a grateful smile. Then, as Annie hurried out of the room, Laura turned her attention to Juan Carlos.

"Do you think my ankle's broken?"

"Probably not," he replied as he positioned the head of the X-ray unit over her ankle. "But I'd like to take a couple of shots of it just to be sure."

Laura was content to sit quietly while Juan Carlos took first one view, then another of her swollen ankle. Afterward, he elevated it slightly, settled an ice pack over it, then stepped into an adjoining room to develop the film.

Left alone at last, Laura finally began to feel the after-effects of her fall. Despite the old blanket still wrapped around her, she was chilled to the bone. Her wet clothing clung to her body and her hair curled damply around her shoulders. Her ankle throbbed painfully, as did the hip on which she'd landed rather forcefully.

She was going to be stiff and sore for several days to come, and that might very well be the least of it. After sitting in the rain the way she had, she could end up coming down with a bad cold. And if her ankle was broken, she'd have to cope with a cast and crutches.

She'd have been better off sitting there trying to figure out how she'd get through the last few weeks of school rather than wasting time worrying about Devlin Gray. Their paths had rarely crossed prior to that afternoon, and she saw no reason that should change. Not if she made an effort to see that it didn't.

She was grateful to the man for what he'd done, but she'd thanked him for his help already. There was no need for her to show any further appreciation, she decided, ignoring the nudge of conscience that insisted on reminding her if he'd been someone else, someone more respectable, she would have at least invited him to come to dinner.

With another twinge of regret, Laura admitted that she really wouldn't have minded seeing him again, if only—

"Good news," Annie announced, smiling as she bustled into the room, her arms loaded with towels and an odd assortment of dry clothing. "You'll have to take it easy the next few days, but your ankle's not broken, just badly sprained. Juan Carlos will wrap it for you after you change clothes."

"Thank goodness," Laura murmured with a sigh of relief. "I was just beginning to realize how much of a problem a cast would be. Keeping up with a classroom full of ten-year-olds is hard enough on two good legs."

"I also talked to Flora and told her what happened. She and Timmy are just fine. They're going to make a batch of homemade cinnamon cookies for you."

"I guess that means you'll be driving me home," Laura teased, returning her friend's smile.

"You know me too well. I wouldn't miss an opportunity to mooch a few of Flora's fresh-from-the-oven cinnamon cookies for anything. Now, why don't you get out of those wet clothes?"

"Gladly."

"Need any help?"

"I don't think so."

"Well, then, I'll leave you to it." Annie started toward the doorway, then turned and met Laura's gaze once again. "About Devlin Gray... I hope I didn't upset you."

"Of course not," Laura assured her.

"He didn't seem all that bad."

"No, he didn't."

"Still, I don't think it would be wise to...encourage him."

"No, it wouldn't," Laura agreed.

Two years ago she'd told Annie why she'd come to live in San Pedro, so she understood her friend's concern. Laura couldn't afford to associate with just anybody. Not if she wanted to remain safely hidden from her dead husband's father. If Giovanni found her and Timmy—

"I was afraid you might have been charmed by him," Annie ventured quite seriously.

"Not hardly," Laura retorted much too quickly.

"Good."

From the dubious look she spied on Annie's face just before she turned away, Laura had a feeling her friend didn't quite believe her. And that wasn't surprising, considering Laura's own ambivalence toward the man. Because he'd come to her rescue, she found it hard to think the worst of him. Yet she couldn't afford to do otherwise. Not when her son's well-being was at stake.

Keeping that thought in mind, Laura unwrapped the blanket from around her shoulders and set it aside. Then, as the door clicked shut, she wearily began to unbutton her blouse. At the moment she wanted nothing more than to be warm and dry again. And after that she wanted to go home to her son and hold him close.

One way or another she'd managed to keep him safe so far. She certainly wasn't about to do anything to put him in jeopardy now. She was just as determined today as she'd been five years ago to make sure her father-in-law didn't get his hands on her child.

And though she couldn't believe Devlin Gray would do anything to hurt her or her son, she knew she'd be better off keeping as much distance between them as possible.

No matter how she wished she could do otherwise.

Chapter 2

"Having fun?" Laura asked, gazing fondly at her young son as they strolled, hand in hand, through the open-air market a few blocks from their house.

"Oh, yes. The market's my very favorite place." Timmy grinned up at her, his pale green eyes bright with childish delight. Then, as a breeze ruffled his dark, curly hair, he turned and pointed to a stall offering kites of every imaginable size, shape and color for sale. "Can we look at those? Please, can we?"

"Of course," Laura agreed.

She probably wouldn't be able to lure him away without buying one, but she didn't mind. He rarely asked for anything, and when he did, it was never anything extravagant. And for more reasons than one, she was feeling especially good this Thursday morning.

Almost five weeks had passed since she'd fallen and sprained her ankle. Except for an occasional twinge, it wasn't giving her any problems, so she could get around on foot quite easily once again. And, as of yesterday afternoon, school was out for the summer, leaving her free to spend as much time with Timmy as she wanted.

He was growing up so fast. They'd be celebrating his fifth birthday in July, and in September he'd be going to the convent school where she taught. She knew he'd do well. He was basically a bright child, and thanks to all the hours she'd worked with him, he was fluent in both Spanish and English.

She'd tried to give him as normal an upbringing as possible. Or as normal an upbringing as an expatriate American woman could provide for her son on her own in a small, quiet Mexican town, Laura mused, standing off to one side and watching as he thoughtfully considered first one kite, then another.

Actually, San Pedro had a lot to offer. In addition to the convent school, there were two public elementary schools, a high school and a small university located within the city limits. There was also a library and the medical clinic, as well as a wealth of shops, stores and restaurants. And, thanks to the town's well-preserved old colonial buildings, including two impressive churches, and its temperate climate, it also boasted a thriving, year-round tourist industry.

All things considered, Laura doubted she could have chosen a better place to raise her son. But more and more often lately she'd found herself wishing she didn't have to do it alone. Not because she resented being solely responsible for her son. She loved Timmy more than anything and she'd never thought of caring for him as a chore. But a boy needed a special man in his life, someone he could look up to with respect and admiration, especially as he grew older.

About a year or so ago Timmy had realized that, unlike his friends, he didn't have a father. When he'd mentioned it to her, she'd explained as simply as she could that his father had died. She'd also shown him the few pictures she had of Johnny and told him how much she'd loved him. Timmy had seemed to not only understand but accept the situation, as well. At least until recently, when he'd begun to hint that maybe they could try to find someone to take Johnny's place.

Laura wished they could, for Timmy's sake if for nothing else. But entering into a close and loving relationship with a man, the kind of relationship that led to marriage, would entail an awful lot of trust on her part. She couldn't, in good conscience, keep her past a secret from someone she intended to wed. And if she fell in love a second time as unwisely as she had the first, revealing the truth about herself and her son could end up putting them in jeopardy.

As if that's something you really have to worry about, she chided herself. Why, she hadn't even met any likely candidates yet.

As the warm, gentle breeze tugged at the hem of her pale pink sundress, Laura suddenly found herself thinking of Devlin Gray. As she had more times over the past five weeks than she would have liked to admit, she gazed down the street, hoping to catch a glimpse of him among the people milling about. Not surprisingly, he was nowhere to be seen. And that was just as well.

She had no right to be thinking about him at all, much less in the same context as love and marriage. And wishing she would run into him somewhere around town was just plain foolhardy.

If their paths did happen to cross, she wouldn't be able to do anything more than exchange a few words with him before continuing on her way. To allow herself to be seen associating with the man in a more overt manner would be highly imprudent. She couldn't allow people to think she was dallying with a man who, by all accounts, would never make an honest woman of her. Not if she wanted to maintain her respectability. And *that* she had to do in order to continue teaching at the convent school.

Since she certainly couldn't afford to lose her job, putting thoughts of Devlin Gray out of her mind should have been easy. However, much to her dismay, Laura hadn't been very successful at it.

Instead of reminding herself that the man was nothing but trouble, she found herself recalling how he'd gone out of his way to be kind to her. And instead of accepting the fact that he was nothing if not dangerous, she dwelled upon how safe she'd felt with him once she'd gotten over her initial fear and anxiety.

Surely, if he'd been a truly bad man, she'd have sensed it. Then again, considering how easily she'd been duped by Johnny Buschetti, maybe not. Just because Devlin Gray had done one good deed—

"Which one do you like best, Mom?" Timmy asked, returning to her side and slipping his hand into hers.

"Mmm, I'm not sure," Laura murmured. Drawn out of her reverie, she eyed the brightly colored kites, trying to recall which of them Timmy had lingered over longest. "The blue one with the puffy white clouds and the rainbow. Or maybe the green one with the orange-and-yellow parrot. How about you?"

"The one with the parrot," he replied without hesitation, gazing up at her hopefully.

From where she stood, Laura saw that it was reasonably priced. And they'd have such fun flying it in the little meadow in the park near the university.

"Well, then, I guess we'd better get it," she said with a smile.

"Really?"

"Yes, really."

She squeezed his hand reassuringly, her smile widening at his unabashed pleasure. Then she turned to the young woman standing behind the counter and spoke to her in Spanish, asking for the kite with the *loro* on it and a ball of twine to go with it.

Instead of the kite on display, the woman gave Laura a disassembled one tucked into a plastic wrapper along with a simple set of directions showing how to put it together.

After adding the kite and twine to the other packages in her string bag, Laura paid the woman, then offered her a word of thanks.

"Where are we going now?" Timmy asked as they left the stall and turned toward the town square.

"The fabric store across the plaza."

Laura could feel her son begin to drag his feet, and almost laughed out loud. Had they been heading for the five-and-dime, she had no doubt he'd be skipping along quite happily.

"I'm getting kinda tired. And hungry, too," he said, suddenly sounding as if he were on his last legs.

"I promise I won't be long. Dr. Moreno's daughter is getting married in August and I want to buy a tablecloth and napkins to embroider for her."

Laura loved doing needlework, but rarely had time during the school year. Now that summer vacation had begun, she could indulge in her favorite hobby a few hours each afternoon or evening.

"Okay." Timmy sighed with such obvious resignation that Laura finally did laugh.

"It won't take me more than ten minutes. I know exactly what I want. Then we'll go straight home, have some lunch, rest a while, put your kite together and take it to the park for a test run. All right?"

"All right," her son agreed, once again in good spirits.

As good as her word, Laura quickly found the tablecloth and napkins she wanted, selected embroidery thread in shades of rose and blue as Annie had suggested, and paid for her purchase.

With her string bag slung over her shoulder and Timmy beside her, holding her hand, Laura headed back the way they'd come. As they walked down the shady sidewalk she saw a group of people gathering in front of the old cathedral on the corner. Tourists, she thought, noting that many of them were carrying cameras. They were rather well-off, if their dress was any indication. For a fleeting moment she wondered where they were from. Probably the States, although San Pedro drew visitors from all over the world.

"Laura? Laura Buschetti?"

Without thinking, Laura turned to see who was calling her name. The masculine voice had sounded vaguely familiar, but she couldn't quite remember where she'd heard it before. Frowning, she scanned the group of tourists now clustered on the steps of the cathedral, wondering who among them could possibly know—

"Oh, no. Oh, please, *no*," she murmured, realizing at the same moment she saw the middle-aged man and woman breaking away from the group and hurrying toward her that no one in San Pedro knew her as Laura *Buschetti*.

But Vincent Petrano and his wife, Cynthia, certainly did. And although she'd met Giovanni Buschetti's most trusted lieutenant only a few times, and five years had passed since she'd last seen him, he obviously hadn't had any trouble recognizing her.

She'd finally begun to believe she and Timmy were safe, that her father-in-law would never find them. But in the blink of an eye, on a sunny summer afternoon, her past had caught up with her in a truly terrifying way.

For one long moment she could do nothing but stand and stare at the man and woman bearing down on her and Timmy as a wave of despair washed over her. Then, aware of how much she stood to lose if she didn't do *something*, she tore her gaze away from them and turned to her son.

"Mommy, what's wrong?" he asked, his voice quavering as he met her gaze.

"That man...he's...not very nice. I'd rather not talk to him. So, let's hurry home, all right?" Bending, she scooped her son into her arms and added soothingly, "He won't be able to bother us there."

"Laura, *wait*," Petrano ordered, his anger and frustration more than evident in his harsh tone of voice.

"Yeah, sure," she muttered, her heart pounding as she whirled around and raced toward the small park in the center of the square.

Since it was just after noon, people had begun to line up in front of the various food vendors there. Laura slipped easily through the growing crowd, hugging Timmy close.

"I thought we were going home," he ventured softly.

"We are, but we're going the long way."

"So the bad man won't find us?"

"Yes."

When she reached the far side of the plaza Laura risked a quick glance over her shoulder. Petrano and his wife were nowhere to be seen, but that didn't mean they weren't somewhere close behind her.

Knowing she was safest surrounded by other people, she ducked into an arcade full of midday shoppers, wove her way to a side exit and headed up a narrow back street. Nearly out of breath, she turned down an alley, cut through a tiny cantina, then stepped out onto the sidewalk that ran along one of the town's busier thoroughfares.

Unable to go any farther carrying her son, she paused in the arched doorway of the local bank and set him on his feet. He clung to her hand wordlessly as she surveyed the street. Finally, satisfied that she'd lost the Petranos, she started down the sidewalk once again.

"*Now* are we going home?" Timmy asked when they turned onto a quiet residential street not far from their house.

"Yes, *now* we're going home." Gazing down at her son, Laura offered him what she hoped was a reassuring smile.

"Who was that man?"

"Someone I used to know a long time ago."

"Do you think he'll find us?"

"No, sweetie, I don't."

"Me, neither," Timmy agreed. "We twisted and turned all over the place, didn't we?"

"We sure did."

Laura hated having scared her son. But he'd known something was wrong almost at once, and lying to him would only have frightened him more. So she'd been as honest as she could with him. Until she'd told him that she didn't think Vincent Petrano would find them.

Not that she believed the man would be able to track her down right away. Since she'd made a point of keeping to herself, she wasn't particularly well-known around town. And the locals as well as most of the expatriate Americans tended to be leery of strangers asking questions. A stranger like Petrano, one with a loud mouth and lots of money, would be given an especially wide berth. So, if he decided to try to locate her on his own, it would more than likely take him a while. He'd have a hard time finding someone who not only knew her but would also be willing to discuss her whereabouts with him.

However, Laura doubted Petrano would act on his own. Instead, good soldier that he'd always been, he'd contact Giovanni first and tell the old man what he'd seen in San Pedro. Then he'd do whatever her father-in-law told him to do.

Being unfamiliar with the language as well as the local phone system, Petrano probably wouldn't be able to get through to Giovanni immediately. That would give her a little more time to decide what to do. Considering how limited her options were, she was going to have to sit tight and do some serious thinking before she acted in any way. One wrong move on her part and her worst nightmare would come true. Giovanni Buschetti would get his hands on her son and she'd never be able to get him back.

Once again beating back a wave of despair, Laura gave Timmy's hand a gentle squeeze, then quickened her pace as their house came into view. The sooner they were out of sight, the better.

Though she knew the sense of security she felt upon entering the cool, quiet confines of her house was only an illusion, she couldn't help but utter a sigh of relief as she did so. For a little while, at least, they'd be safe there.

With Timmy trailing along behind her, Laura walked into her small, sunlit kitchen and set her string bag on the rectangular wooden table tucked under the window overlooking the back garden. Luckily, she and Timmy would be on their own for the next few days. Flora had left for Leon that morning to visit relatives and wouldn't be back until Sunday.

Much as she appreciated her housekeeper's help, Laura had to admit she was glad the woman was gone. She wasn't sure she could have dealt with Flora's happy chatter. And she certainly wouldn't have wanted to upset the elderly lady by telling her what had happened in front of the cathedral.

"Would you rather have a peanut butter and jelly sandwich or a bowl of Flora's homemade chicken soup?" Laura asked, turning to face her son as she paused by the refrigerator.

"Peanut butter and jelly sandwich, please." He offered her a smile, then climbed onto one of the wooden chairs, pulled her string bag close and began to empty the contents onto the table. "Want me to put the tissues and soap in the bathroom?"

"That would be a real help," she answered.

"I'll put my kite in my room, too."

"Good idea."

Laura watched as he scrambled off the chair and crossed the kitchen, his small arms loaded. When he disappeared down the hallway, she opened the refrigerator and took out the jar of grape jelly, then retrieved the peanut butter and a loaf of bread from the pantry. Doing her best to concentrate on the mundane task of making sandwiches, she willed herself to calm down.

She'd never be able to think rationally if she allowed her fear and confusion to get the better of her. Yet each time she recalled the way Vincent Petrano and his wife had stared at first her, then Timmy, her stomach clenched and her hands shook. Even if they hadn't been sure about her, she'd given herself away by responding when Vincent used her married name. And they had to have realized that they'd stumbled across Giovanni's grandson, as well. The boy looked just like his father.

"Is my sandwich ready?" Timmy asked as he joined her in the kitchen once again.

"It sure is." Forcing herself to smile, Laura carried their plates to the table. "Do you want some chips, too?"

"Just a few."

She opened a fresh bag of tortilla chips and put some on his plate, poured a glass of milk for each of them and sat at the table with him. She wasn't the least bit hungry, but after their experience in the square she knew any change in routine on her part would worry her son. He was a sensitive child, attuned to her moods, and she didn't want to upset him any more than absolutely necessary.

With a concerted effort she nibbled on her sandwich and sipped her milk, making small talk with him in between. As if by mutual consent, they avoided any mention of the man who'd sent them running for cover. But Timmy seemed more subdued than usual, leading Laura to believe that, despite her attempts at normalcy, he was still bothered by what had happened earlier.

She wished she could assure him that everything would be all right. But she didn't know that for sure, and she couldn't bring herself to mislead him. Their quiet life had been disrupted in a terrifying way. Unfortunately, she had no idea what she was going to do about it. Once she did, she'd tell him. But until then...

"All done?" she asked, noting that his plate and glass were empty.

"All done," he agreed.

"More milk?"

"No, thanks."

"Some cookies?"

"Maybe later." He yawned and rubbed his eyes. "I'm kinda tired right now."

"Me, too." Standing, Laura offered him her hand. "Want to rest a while before we decide how to spend the afternoon?"

"Okay." As they walked down the hallway to his room, he glanced up at her, the look in his pale green eyes wise beyond his years. "I won't mind if we don't go to the park to fly my kite."

"Maybe it *would* be better to wait until another day," she said, blinking back the sudden rush of tears to her eyes.

How she had gotten so lucky to have such an understanding son, Laura would never know. If anything happened to him because she acted unwisely...

"Here you go, sweetie." More determined than ever to do everything in her power to keep him safe, Laura turned back the light blanket on his bed and plumped up his pillow. "Kick off your sneakers and hop in."

"Can Phil take a nap, too?" he asked.

"Of course," she replied, tucking his favorite stuffed animal, a brown, floppy-eared rabbit, next to him.

"Are you gonna rest, too, Mom?"

"Maybe for a little while." She adjusted the shade on his window, switched on the ceiling fan, then bent and kissed him on the cheek. "Have a good sleep."

"I will." He smiled up at her, sighed deeply and closed his eyes.

Back in the kitchen once again, Laura cleared the table, then washed their plates and glasses at the sink as she finally allowed herself to weigh her options. Unfortunately, she only had two, and at the moment she found one as frightening as the other. Either she could leave San Pedro as soon as possible and find another place to hide, or she could stay and wait for Giovanni Buschetti to come and take her son away from her.

She still had some of Johnny's money stashed away, but not nearly enough to start over somewhere else. And how safe would she and Timmy really be on the run? Her car was old and in need of repair, so she doubted she'd get far in it. And an American woman and a young boy traveling across Mexico on their own would be all too conspicuous. Since Giovanni would know where to start looking, Laura figured it would be only a matter of time before he found her.

Rather than going up against him in an unfamiliar place, she'd probably be better off staying put in San Pedro. She could conserve her limited resources and prepare as best she could for her inevitable confrontation with her father-in-law or his henchmen on her own ground.

"As if you have a better chance of thwarting him now than you did five years ago," she muttered with an almost overwhelming sense of futility.

No matter where she chose to do it, she knew there wasn't any way she could stand up to Giovanni Buschetti on her own and hope to outmaneuver him. He was too rich and too ruthless. He'd have no qualms about doing whatever was necessary to make sure he was the primary influence in his only grandchild's life. He'd made that clear just after Johnny had been killed. And she could only imagine how his determination had grown after five years of impuissance. Now that he knew where to find her...

As a tremor of fear rippled up her spine, Laura turned away from the sink, walked back down the hallway and into her bedroom. Sitting on the edge of the bed, she barely resisted the urge to bury her face in her hands and have a good cry. As tempting as it was, she simply couldn't afford to indulge in hysterics. Not when her son's well-being was at stake.

She wasn't about to allow Giovanni to get the better of her. But the only way to do that was to fight fire with fire. She'd already concluded that she couldn't do it alone. However, with a little help...

She could go to the local police, but she didn't really think they'd put themselves out on her behalf. As an American living on her own, she wouldn't be afforded a great deal of

sympathy to start with. And she'd learned early on that in
Mexico, women were more often than not treated as sec-
ond-class citizens in their dealings with men.

Also, where Giovanni was concerned, it would be her
word against his. Considering how formidable he could be,
Laura doubted he'd have a hard time winning the local authorities over to his side, especially if he offered them some
sort of remuneration.

But who could she ask to come to her aid? Juan Carlos
and Annie Moreno would gladly go up against her father-in-
law with her, but they were such good, decent people. They
wouldn't be any better prepared than she was to do battle
with someone like Giovanni Buschetti. And the man
wouldn't hesitate to hurt them if that was what it would take
to get hold of his grandson.

She couldn't endanger them any more than she could any
of the other people in San Pedro who'd befriended her. The
nuns at school, Father Hernandez, old Mr. Wiley at the library and Flora and her family would be equally at risk if
she involved them in her "feud" with her father-in-law.

She needed someone more like Giovanni on her side.
Someone who would understand exactly what kind of person he was and know how to deal with him. Someone who
could be just as implacable as he under any circumstances.
Someone like... *Devlin Gray.*

For one long moment, as his name echoed in Laura's
mind, hope surged through her. With Devlin Gray on her
side, she might actually be able to keep Giovanni away from
her son. But then, in the next instant, she decided she must
have a screw loose if she honestly thought the man would
blithely come to her rescue a second time.

She'd already concluded that he was some sort of criminal and, as such, he was more than likely somewhat mer-
cenary. As far as she could see, he'd have absolutely nothing
to gain by crossing swords with her father-in-law. She certainly couldn't pay him to do it. At least, not to the same

extent Giovanni could, and *would,* if Devlin were to go to him and offer his services.

Yet, somewhere in the back of her mind, Laura couldn't quite bring herself to believe that Devlin Gray would knowingly do anything to hurt her son. Only a coldhearted bastard would take a child from his mother and hand him over to the likes of Giovanni Buschetti. After her recent encounter with Devlin, she simply couldn't imagine him being capable of that kind of cruelty. Unless he had your basic Dr. Jekyll and Mr. Hyde personality, she doubted he could treat her with such care and consideration on one occasion, then turn around and aid in the kidnapping of her son on another.

Of course, he *could* very well be psychotic. But the more Laura thought about the way he'd behaved toward her that day when he'd come upon her sitting in the gutter in the middle of a rainstorm, the harder it was for her to accept that possibility. Granted, at the moment she was on the verge of giving in to sheer and utter desperation. And she was judging him on the basis of one random act of kindness while paying little heed to all the ugly rumors she'd heard about him. However...

Sitting there alone in her bedroom, Laura had to admit that, all things considered, she had little to lose by going to him and asking for his assistance. She wasn't going to be able to keep Timmy out of Giovanni's reach on her own. But if Devlin agreed to help her...

He'd know how to handle her father-in-law. And maybe, once Giovanni realized she had someone of his ilk on her side, he'd back off. While he could quash her quite easily, Devlin would be another matter altogether. He didn't strike her as the type to let anyone roll over him, especially anyone like Giovanni Buschetti.

So she'd do the one thing her independent soul rebelled against more than anything. She'd go to him and ask for his help. Just as soon as Timmy awoke from his nap.

Having made a decision, Laura thought she'd feel a little more optimistic. But the prospect of having to approach Devlin Gray as a supplicant didn't do much to raise her spirits.

What if he expected her to pay him for his help? As she'd already determined, she didn't have much money, and she certainly didn't relish the idea of being indebted to him for a long period of time. Still, if a cash payment was all he wanted, she'd consider herself lucky. But what if money wasn't enough? What if he wanted her to... service him, as well?

For just an instant Laura thought of what Annie had said that day at the clinic. If he really had looked at her with longing...

Of course, Annie *had* admitted she'd probably only imagined it. And Devlin certainly hadn't acted as if he were interested in her. Had he wanted to see her again, he could easily have caught up with her around town. Or he could simply have come to her house to reclaim the blanket he'd lent her.

Considering he hadn't pursued her in any way, Laura thought it best not to dwell on the possibility that the proverbial fate worse than death awaited her at his hands. No sense buying more trouble. She had enough to deal with already.

"And all thanks to you," she muttered with not only anger and frustration but affection as she gazed at the framed photograph of Johnny that she kept on the nightstand.

For the past five years Laura had wanted to hate him for turning her life upside down, but she just couldn't do it. She'd loved him too much. And, in a way, she knew she always would—despite the fact that he hadn't been quite the man he'd led her to believe he was at the beginning of their whirlwind courtship.

Of course, if she hadn't been so innocent she probably would have realized that he was more than just the charming owner of the Chicago restaurant where she'd worked part-time while going to graduate school at Northwestern. Had she been a bit more savvy, she'd have realized before she married him that he was being groomed to take over his father's extensive business empire, an empire rumored to have ties to organized crime.

They'd married quickly, in a simple ceremony at the county courthouse. He hadn't wanted a long engagement or a big, traditional wedding. Unfortunately, she'd been too enthralled with him to wonder why. Only afterward did she begin to realize that he hadn't wanted to give her time to question exactly who he really was.

Not that knowing the truth about Johnny Buschetti would have made any difference when it came time for her to say "I do." Having lost her father only a few months earlier, she'd really needed someone then. And Johnny had been so very, very good to her that she would have found it impossible to believe anything bad about him.

Even after he'd finally introduced her to his father, she had found it hard to accept the fact that the man she'd married would one day be the head of the Buschetti "family." Johnny simply hadn't seemed ... maleficent enough. And, in her naiveté, she'd honestly thought that she could make a difference, that because of her and the child she carried, Johnny would choose to live a different kind of life than his father had.

Unfortunately, he hadn't lived long enough to prove her right. He'd been killed in a drive-by shooting outside his restaurant when she was four months pregnant.

To say she'd been devastated would be an understatement. Losing Johnny less than a year after losing her father had been almost more than she could bear. Had it not been for the child she was carrying, she wasn't sure what she would have done. But her baby had given her a reason to go on.

Much to her chagrin, she soon realized that her baby was also of paramount importance to Giovanni. Shortly after Johnny's funeral, her father-in-law had insisted that she give up the small house in the city she'd shared with her husband and move into his mansion in the suburbs.

Knowing that he'd never cared for her because of her influence over his son, and not wanting him to have any influence over *her* child, she'd refused. Determined to have his way, Giovanni had then resorted to thinly veiled threats, questioning not only her ability to raise a child on her own, but also her mental stability.

Aware that he wouldn't hesitate to use his wealth and power against her, Laura faced the fact that it would be only a matter of time before he found a way to take her baby from her. So she'd packed some clothes in a suitcase, added the "emergency" money Johnny had kept in the wall safe, and with a cleverness born of desperation had made her roundabout way to San Pedro.

Since she'd never told Johnny about the summers she'd spent there with her father while he'd taught a summer course in linguistics at the university, she'd felt reasonably safe. Still, she'd kept to herself as much as she could. And she'd told no one but Annie and Juan Carlos the truth about how she'd come to live there.

Eventually, she'd hoped to be able to return to the United States so Timmy could complete his education there. But she'd felt that the longer she could put it off, the better. She'd been fairly sure that after ten or twelve years Giovanni would have given up looking for her. And, of course, she wouldn't have relocated anywhere within a thousand miles of Chicago if she could help it.

Now, simply because she'd been in the wrong place at the wrong time, he was going to know exactly where to find her. And, more than likely, he was going to come after her. With a vengeance.

Once again Laura tried to stave off the growing sense of futility that threatened to overwhelm her. She couldn't allow herself to believe she was fighting a losing battle—not even for a moment—or all would be lost. Nor could she give in to the temptation to pick up and run.

Much as she hated feeling like a sitting duck, her best bet was to stay put for a while longer. And in order to do that, she had to cling as tenaciously as she could to what little hope she had that Devlin Gray would help her without expecting anything too awful in exchange.

Her spirit somewhat renewed, Laura stood and crossed to the closet. She lifted one of the floorboards and took out the fireproof box in which she kept her personal papers and a few photographs, along with the last of Johnny's money. Then she retrieved a small canvas carryall and a couple of suitcases from an upper shelf. Much as she wanted to maintain a positive outlook, she knew she'd be wise to be prepared to take to the road just in case Devlin turned her away.

She transferred the contents of the box into the carryall, added the few pieces of jewelry Johnny had given her, the framed photograph on the nightstand and several other mementos she couldn't bear to leave behind. Choosing carefully, she filled one suitcase with her clothing, then stole quietly into Timmy's room, gathered up as many of his things as she could and quickly filled the other.

After tucking the carryall under the floorboards and returning the suitcases to the shelf, she went to the kitchen and put the rest of the bread, the jar of peanut butter, some chips, cookies and fruit into her string bag. Then she went out to the shed behind the house where she kept her car and checked the air in the tires and the coolant in the radiator. Luckily she'd filled the gas tank just a couple of days ago, so if she had to make a run for it, she wouldn't have to risk leaving a trail by stopping anywhere along the way.

Back in the house, she checked on Timmy and saw that he was still sleeping. She thought about waking him, but knew he'd be in a better mood if she let him rest until he was ready to get up on his own. One way or another, she was going to need his cooperation later, and the more agreeable he was, the less likely he'd be to balk at whatever they ended up having to do.

Yielding to her own weariness, Laura retreated to her bedroom. Though she stretched out on the bed, she didn't really think she'd fall asleep. Not with all she had to worry about. But if she lay down for a while, maybe she'd feel somewhat refreshed. Maybe, too, she'd be better prepared to deal with any additional dilemmas that might arise.

What seemed like only a few minutes later—but was actually more like an hour according to the clock on her nightstand—Timmy woke her from a sound sleep. His plaintive "Mommy" had her sitting up and rubbing her eyes, then smiling rather sheepishly at him.

"Are you done resting yet?" he asked as he scrambled onto the bed and sat beside her.

"Do I have a choice?" she teased, nuzzling his neck as she cuddled him close.

"Uh-uh."

"Well, then, I suppose I am."

"Good." He offered her a mischievous grin as he slipped away from her. "Because I'm ready for some cookies and milk."

"Oh, you are, are you?"

Feeling unaccountably lighthearted, Laura swung her legs over the side of her bed and stood, then hoisted her son into her arms and whirled him in the air a moment before setting him on his feet.

"Yes," he giggled.

"I guess we'd better go out to the kitchen and see what we can rustle up, then."

As she followed her son down the hallway Laura couldn't help but be glad that her outlook had improved. While she couldn't honestly say she was more optimistic about her prospects than she'd been earlier, at least she hadn't backed herself into a corner...yet. She still had a few options open, and now all she could do was work her way through them, starting with the one she thought would be most beneficial to her and her son.

"Have you decided what we're going to do this afternoon?" Timmy asked as she set a plate of Flora's cinnamon cookies on the table and poured him a glass of milk.

"Actually, I have." She hesitated a moment. Then, choosing her words carefully, she continued. "We're going to visit a new friend of mine, a man named Devlin Gray."

"How do you know him?" Her son glanced up at her, his eyes bright with curiosity.

"Remember the day I fell and sprained my ankle?"

"Uh-huh."

"He saw me sitting on the curb and stopped to help me."

"So he's a nice man," Timmy stated approvingly.

"Well, yes," she agreed, though not without a qualm or two.

While Devlin *had* been kind to her that day, he certainly wasn't the candidate for sainthood Timmy seemed inclined to make him out to be. But how could she tell her five-year-old son that Devlin's one good deed wasn't much compared to all the bad deeds he'd more than likely done while leading a life of crime? She'd scare the poor child to death.

"Is he married?" Timmy asked as he reached for another cookie.

"Not that I know of."

Her son's eyes brightened even more. "Does he like little boys?"

"I suppose so."

Laura knew exactly what Timmy had in mind. However, she didn't want to say anything that might discourage him. Unless her son was amenable to the idea of her accepting Devlin's help, she couldn't, in good conscience, enter into any kind of arrangement with him.

Unfortunately, Laura was afraid that it wouldn't take much for Timmy to go from amenable to admiring. And she didn't want her son looking up to a man like Devlin Gray any more than she'd wanted him looking up to a man like Giovanni Buschetti.

Talk about being caught between a rock and a hard place....

She'd have to make sure Timmy spent as little time as possible in Devlin's presence, and hope that her "relationship" with the man would be only temporary.

While Timmy finished his snack, Laura slipped into the bathroom, washed her face and hands, freshened her makeup and pinned up her hair. She doubted Devlin would be swayed by her appearance, but looking the best she could made *her* feel better. Considering she was about to throw herself on the mercy of a man who could turn out to be Satan's favorite son, she deemed it wise to bolster her confidence any way she could.

Aware that she'd put off the inevitable as long as possible, she rejoined Timmy in the kitchen and helped him wash his hands at the sink. Then, together, they headed for Devlin's house.

Though it was late afternoon, most people were still enjoying their siestas, so the narrow streets were fairly quiet. To her relief, Laura didn't see anyone suspicious hanging around anywhere along the way. However, spurred on by the memory of the look she'd seen on Vincent Petrano's face, she kept a tight hold of Timmy's hand and walked as fast as she could, with him trotting happily along beside her.

The sooner they got off the street, the safer they'd be. Or so she wanted to believe. More than anything.

Chapter 3

Pausing in front of the arched doorway of the two-story, white stucco house tucked among several similarly styled homes on Avenida Zacateros, Laura sent up a silent prayer that she wasn't making a terrible mistake. Then, taking a deep breath, she reached out, grasped the brass knocker in her hand and rapped it sharply against the heavy wooden door.

After a moment she heard the muffled woof of a dog followed by a snuffling, scrabbling sound just beyond the door. She shifted nervously from one foot to the other, wondering how she could ever have been so audacious as to believe—

"Maybe he's not home," Timmy ventured softly.

"Maybe not," she agreed, aware that she hadn't really considered *that* possibility until now.

She couldn't very well ask for his help if he happened to be away on one of his "business" trips. And she doubted it would be safe to wait more than a day or two for him to return.

So much for covering all the bases, she thought, her spirits sinking.

"We could come back later," Timmy suggested.

"Yes, I suppose we—"

With surprising suddenness a lock clicked, the door whooshed open, and before Laura realized what was happening, a huge, sleekly coated black-and-tan dog lumbered across the threshold and shoved his cold, wet nose against her hand.

Instinctively she bent, scooped Timmy into her arms and took a quick step back, her gaze riveted on the animal. A rottweiler, she thought. But not a vicious one, she decided gratefully, seeing the mildly curious look in the dog's wide, dark eyes.

"Bitsy, mind your manners."

Bitsy? she mused for a moment. Then, recognizing Devlin's voice, Laura shifted her gaze to the man standing just inside the doorway.

"Mr. Gray," she murmured, then lost her train of thought completely when she realized he was wearing nothing but a pair of baggy white cotton pants cinched well below his narrow waist with a loosely tied cord.

His smooth, tanned, well-muscled chest was bare as were his feet. His dark hair, at least an inch longer than it had been five weeks ago, was tied back at the nape of his neck with a scrap of white cloth. And if she were to judge from the growth of beard shadowing his cheeks and jaw, he hadn't bothered to shave for the past few days.

"Ms. Burke," he acknowledged, his deep voice reserved as he studied her gravely.

Not exactly pleased to see her, she surmised. But at least he hadn't shut the door in her face... yet.

"I... I was wondering if I could talk to you," she said, refusing to give up on him until he gave her no other choice.

"What about?" he asked, his icy gray eyes narrowing suspiciously.

"A bad man scared my mom at the market this morning," Timmy interjected, his voice quavering.

"Is that so?"

Devlin's gaze shifted to her son, and for just an instant his expression seemed to soften. But then he looked at her again and Laura realized she must have been mistaken. There was nothing yielding about him at all as he stood in front of her, barring his doorway.

Admitting that she was wasting precious time on what was proving to be a lost cause, she took another step back, then another.

"I'm sorry to have bothered you," she muttered as she lowered her gaze and started to turn away.

"You didn't answer my question," he said, reaching out and catching her by the arm, his grip firm yet gentle.

"It's not important. Really." She met his gaze again uncertainly.

"I asked what you wanted to talk about."

"Actually, it's . . . it's kind of . . . involved."

"Why am I not surprised?"

Though stung by his sarcasm, Laura held her ground, staring at him steadily, willing him to at least give her a chance to state her case. She'd been ready to go quietly, but since he'd stopped her, she'd begun to think that maybe—

"All right," he muttered none too graciously. "Come in and tell me what's upset you."

She wished she had the courage to wrench her arm free and tell him to go to hell, but beggars couldn't be choosers. And she could endure a lot more than a little wounded pride if that was what it took to keep her son safe.

"Thank you, Mr. Gray."

Still holding her arm, he drew her into the cool, dim interior of the house, called to the dog to follow them, then quietly closed the door. As he turned and headed down the narrow hallway, he finally released her. Trying hard to still the sudden pounding of her heart, Laura trailed after him, carrying her son in her arms.

"Is he really your friend, Mommy?" Timmy whispered, clinging to her like a little monkey.

"Yes," she reassured him, although she'd begun to have her doubts.

"But he's not very happy to see us."

Laura certainly couldn't deny that. But her son seemed to be on the verge of tears, and she didn't want to upset him any more than he already was.

"Not right at the moment. But then, we probably woke him from his siesta." Hugging Timmy close, she brushed her lips against his cheek, then added quietly, "Now, hush, okay? Everything's going to be all right."

"Okay, Mommy."

At what proved to be the kitchen doorway, Devlin waited for her to join him. Pausing beside him, Laura saw that the spacious, sunny room was neat and tidy. Pots of herbs sat on the windowsill and a huge bouquet of yellow roses filled a glass bowl on the wooden table, their scent mingling with that of freshly baked bread.

From where she stood at the far counter, an elderly woman with snowy white hair and dark, inquisitive eyes glanced over her shoulder and offered them a warm, welcoming smile.

"You have guests, Señor Gray?" she asked in a lilting voice.

"Mrs. Santos, my...friend, Ms. Laura Burke and her son..."

When he hesitated, eyeing her questioningly, Laura realized he was waiting for her to supply a name.

"Timmy," she said. "My son, Timmy."

"Ms. Burke and I have something to discuss. I thought maybe Timmy might prefer to stay here with you."

"Ah, *sí,* that would be very nice." The woman's smile widened. "You can help me with the bread, *niño.*"

Obviously none too eager to be separated from her, Timmy clung to Laura, burying his face against her shoulder.

"We'll be out in the garden just beyond the door there," Devlin said in a surprisingly gentle tone of voice.

"And you can come out and join us whenever you want," Laura added.

Though she had no doubt Mrs. Santos would take good care of Timmy, she'd have preferred to keep him with her. Yet she didn't want him to hear what she had to say to Devlin. The boy was disconcerted enough as it was.

"What about the dog?" Timmy asked.

Bitsy had padded into the kitchen while they'd been talking, curled up contentedly under the table, and already seemed to be half asleep.

"He won't hurt you," Devlin assured the boy. "But we'll take him outside with us if you want."

"Okay," Timmy agreed.

"Come, then," Mrs. Santos urged. Having wiped the flour from her hands, she crossed the kitchen and held out her arms to him. "We'll put the bread in the oven, then we'll watch the television in the *sala.*"

"You have a television?" Timmy's eyes brightened as he went to her.

"Ah, *sí.* A *color* television," Mrs. Santos replied. "But first—"

"The bread," Timmy said, then giggled happily.

Aware that her son had found a friend, Laura offered Mrs. Santos a word of thanks as Devlin called to the dog. Then, at his direction, she followed him to the door that led out to the back garden.

As she had been when she'd first seen the kitchen, Laura was pleasantly surprised. While not all that large, the garden was well tended. A narrow brick walkway separated several flower beds filled with a wide variety of roses. A round white wrought-iron table and four chairs had been tucked into a shady spot near the kitchen doorway. At the opposite end of the garden a couple of matching benches stood on either side of a burbling fountain.

As he had in the kitchen, Bitsy curled up under the table. Devlin retrieved a white cotton shirt from the back of one of the chairs and slipped into it. Then, not bothering to do up the buttons, he leaned a hip against the table and crossed his arms over his chest.

"So, Ms. Burke, tell me why you're here," he growled, eyeing her narrowly.

More uncertain than ever of how to begin, Laura shrugged wordlessly and turned away. As she wandered aimlessly from one flower bed to another, she realized that she was going to have only one chance to convince him of how much she needed his help. And in order to do that, she was going to have to tell him who she really was.

Had he not been quite so cool and aloof, she might have found it easier. Unfortunately, his attitude toward her was anything but encouraging.

What if she told him her deepest, darkest secrets only to have him dismiss her?

As she stood near the fountain, staring at a cluster of cream-and-pink roses, a wave of desolation washed over her. And suddenly, much to her dismay, her eyes filled with tears.

"What's the matter, Laura? Cat got your tongue?" Devlin asked softly, startling her with his nearness as he rested his hands on her shoulders.

Still hoping for a glimpse of the kind, considerate, caring man who'd come to her rescue five weeks ago, she looked up at him. But his gaze was just as steely as it had been a few moments earlier.

With a devastating sense of defeat, Laura turned away again. She'd been a fool to think that just because Devlin Gray had come to her rescue once, he'd do so again. But, oh, how she'd wanted to believe—

"Tell me what's wrong," he demanded, his grip on her shoulders tightening imperceptibly.

She opened her mouth to speak, then shook her head as a lone tear trickled down her cheek. She took a deep, tremulous breath, willing herself not to weep until she could put some distance between them. Yet she couldn't seem to make herself move away from him.

The splash of water against stones, the muted buzz of the bees skimming from flower to flower, the spicy sweetness of the roses mingling with Devlin's musky scent—they conspired against her, along with the weight of his hands on her shoulders and the tickle of his breath against her neck, to hold her prisoner in the lovely little garden.

Surrendering at last to the sense of utter desolation she'd fought against all afternoon, Laura buried her face in her hands and began to cry.

"Aw, hell," Devlin muttered, turning her toward him.

She tried to resist, but he refused to let her go, and after a moment or two she rested her head against his chest, letting him hold her as she sobbed her heart out.

"Don't cry, Laura. Please don't cry," Devlin whispered against her hair.

He doubted anything he could say or do would soothe her at the moment, yet he gathered her into his arms and tried to comfort her as best he could.

Had he treated her more kindly, she probably wouldn't have gone to pieces. But Laura Burke had been the last person on earth he'd expected to find standing on his front doorstep.

She'd looked damned appealing in her pale pink dress, with wisps of her long, dark hair curling around her face. However, he'd been anything but pleased to see her.

Though he'd been haunted by thoughts of her day and night for the past five weeks, he'd stayed as far away from her as he possibly could. And finally he'd begun to accept the fact that there was no way he could make a place for her in his life. Not as long as Drago Espinosa was on the loose.

Since that hadn't changed, he should have sent her away. But unfortunately, he hadn't been able to bring himself to do that, any more than he'd been able to leave her sitting in a gutter in the middle of a rainstorm. Not after hearing what

Timmy had had to say about a "bad man" frightening her at the market.

Still, Devlin had deemed it wise to maintain some distance between them, physically as well as emotionally. He was willing to do whatever he could to help her. But he didn't want her to get the idea that he was going to make a habit of lending her a hand whenever she got herself into trouble. He wanted as little to do with her as possible, and the sooner she understood that, the better it would be for both of them.

However, he hadn't intended to add to her distress. And he certainly hadn't meant to make her cry. He'd simply wanted her to tell him why she'd come to him. Then, if possible, he'd have helped her deal with her problem and been done with her... again.

But his attempt at remaining cool and aloof had backfired on him. Rather than making it easier for Laura to tell him what she wanted, he'd succeeded only in upsetting her more. And instead of keeping her at arm's length, he'd ended up holding her close, savoring the tantalizingly sweet scent of her as she wept unabashedly, her tears hot and wet against his bare chest.

Never any good at dealing with a weeping woman, Devlin patted Laura's back awkwardly as he murmured a word or two of commiseration. After what seemed like a very long time, but in reality couldn't have been more than a few minutes, she seemed to regain control of her emotions. Drawing away from him, she took a tissue from her pocket and dabbed at her eyes.

"I'm sorry," she said, her voice laced with embarrassment. "I *never* cry."

Recalling how stoic she'd been when she'd found herself at his mercy after falling and spraining her ankle, Devlin tended to believe her. She'd proven then that she wasn't easily flustered. And he'd treated her with no more detachment today than he had when he'd come to her rescue five weeks ago. Which meant he should be warier than ever about getting involved with her again.

From the look of desperation he'd seen in her eyes just before she'd begun to cry, he knew her problem wasn't going to be easily solved. Something, or more likely *someone*, had scared her half to death. But he was already in way too deep where she was concerned to turn his back on her now.

"Why don't we sit down over here?" he suggested, taking her by the arm and leading her over to one of the wrought-iron benches.

Though she avoided meeting his gaze, she went along willingly. When he sat next to her, she glanced at him apprehensively, then once again lowered her gaze as she twisted the tissue she still held in her hands.

"Now, tell me what's wrong," he urged in what he hoped was a more encouraging tone of voice. When she didn't answer immediately, he prompted gently, "Timmy said something about your being frightened by a man at the market, didn't he?"

"Actually, he was at the cathedral. The man ... Vincent Petrano."

Saying the man's name seemed to be all that was necessary to get her started. Taking a deep breath, she offered to begin at the beginning. Then, with admirable composure, she told him about Johnny Buschetti and how her involvement with him had eventually led her to San Pedro.

Much to his amazement, Devlin experienced an unexpected stab of envy as she recounted the details of her whirlwind courtship. She'd obviously loved her husband in a way he doubted she'd ever be able to love anyone again. He wasn't sure why that bothered him. However, he was relieved when his jealousy turned to anger as she told him about the threats her father-in-law had made after Johnny's funeral.

Having dealt with men like Giovanni Buschetti, Devlin could understand why Laura had decided to disappear rather than stay and try to fight him. With his wealth and power, he'd have had no trouble finding "experts" willing to testify that she was incapable of caring for her son if she refused to do as he said. Nor did Devlin have any doubt that her run-in with Vincent Petrano would prove dangerous for her.

What he couldn't quite figure out was why she'd come to *him*. She'd have been better off packing up and getting out of town. Or would she?

"You're sure Petrano recognized you?" he asked, frowning as he stood and paced to the fountain.

"Oh, yes. He called me by my married name and I . . . I responded without even thinking," Laura admitted ruefully. "If only I'd realized. But I wasn't paying any attention at all."

Glancing over his shoulder at her, Devlin saw that she was staring at the tissue she'd shredded as if she was unsure of how she happened to have it in her hands.

"What do you think he'll do about it?" he prodded.

"Contact Giovanni and tell him he's found me. Then Giovanni will come here and try to take Timmy away from me," she stated with remarkable calm.

"You sound as if you're fairly sure Giovanni's still alive."

She thought for a few moments, then nodded. "Oh, yes, he's still alive. Otherwise, I doubt Vincent Petrano would have been so anxious to stop me."

Though he didn't say as much, Devlin had to agree. And that made him wonder all the more why she'd come to him instead of hitting the road.

"Somehow, I can't believe you're just going to stay here and let him take your son," he said at last.

"I don't have much choice about staying here. I can't afford to start over somewhere else, and even if I could, Timmy and I would be too conspicuous traveling across Mexico on our own. But I'm not going to let him get his hands on my son."

Hearing the vehemence in her voice, Devlin turned to face her again. As if aware of him watching her, she raised her head and met his gaze.

"I'm willing to do whatever's necessary to make sure my father-in-law doesn't take Timmy away from me. But I can't fight him on my own." She hesitated, then continued quietly, "But maybe with your help..."

"*My* help, Ms. Burke?" he asked, making no effort to hide his astonishment. Surely there were others in town she'd trust more than him to come to her aid.

"I don't know anyone else here who'd know how to deal with him. I thought of going to Annie and Juan Carlos, but they're such good, decent people," she admitted seemingly without thinking, then quickly lowered her gaze as a blush crept up her cheeks.

"Ah, I see," he murmured.

Not sure whether he was amused or angry that Laura had assumed he had more in common with Giovanni Buschetti than Juan Carlos Moreno, Devlin turned back to the fountain. Obviously she'd chosen to believe the rumors about him, and he couldn't say he blamed her. He'd gone to a lot of trouble to make sure he had a bad reputation, and her opinion of him proved just how successful he'd been.

Yet somewhere in the back of his mind he'd hoped that she thought better of him. He *had* come to her rescue and he'd done so in a kindly way. But he'd been a fool to think that one good deed would be enough to convince her that he could be a decent kind of guy.

"I didn't mean—" she began after several moments of silence.

"I know exactly what you meant, Ms. Burke," he interrupted in a gruff tone of voice. "And you're right. I know a hell of a lot more about how to deal with men like your father-in-law than Dr. Moreno does." Wondering how she'd react to what he had to say next, Devlin faced her again. "So, what would you like me to do? Kill him?"

"Oh, no," she cried, making no effort to hide her alarm as she met his gaze. *"No!"*

"Then what, Ms. Burke?" he demanded, relieved that she wasn't as merciless as he'd feared.

"I thought maybe you could just... hamper any attempt he might make to take Timmy away from me," she replied quite earnestly.

And how was he supposed to do *that?* Devlin wondered.

She'd have to be within shouting distance twenty-four hours a day, seven days a week.

Turning on his heel, he paced across the garden, staring at the bricks beneath his bare feet as his mind spun. He couldn't have her underfoot and hang on to his sanity at the same time. He found her too damned attractive. And *she* found *him* downright repugnant.

He'd be better off giving her a wad of money—which he just happened to have available compliments of Uncle Sam—then sending her on her way. He could repay the government from his own savings and she could start over just about anywhere she wanted.

Only it wasn't that simple. She'd still have her father-in-law hot on her trail.

The thought of her and her son trying to evade a man like Giovanni Buschetti made Devlin's blood run cold. While she might have a chance on her own, he knew the odds were against her with Timmy in tow, especially if Giovanni was as determined to get his hands on the boy as she seemed to believe. And once he caught up with them...

From what Laura had told him, Devlin doubted the man would have any qualms at all about eliminating her if she caused him any trouble.

If anything happened to her or her son because he'd taken the easy way out, he wouldn't be able to live with himself. He'd underestimated the seriousness of a situation once because it had suited his purposes, and as a result his wife and child had been killed.

Much as he wanted to believe that Laura would be better off on her own somewhere else, he knew just the opposite was true. She wouldn't have a snowball's chance in hell of besting Giovanni Buschetti. Regardless of how far she ran, he'd find her, and when he did, he'd destroy her, one way or another.

However, if she stayed in San Pedro where *he* could protect her...

Unfortunately, he couldn't guarantee her safety or her son's unless she agreed to move into his house. Which brought him back to where he'd started five minutes ago.

Granted, having her living in his house wouldn't be easy, but he'd been in more implausible situations in his thirty-seven years and come out none the worse for wear.

He could tolerate having Laura Burke around on a regular basis for a few weeks if that's what it took to make sure Giovanni didn't get his hands on her son. And, under the circumstances, he imagined she could tolerate his company, as well.

Yet Devlin didn't rush to offer her an invitation to move in with him. Not because he was still concerned about how it would affect his peace of mind, but because he was concerned about the long-term effects such an arrangement would have on her.

No matter how innocent their relationship remained, if she lived with him without the benefit of marriage, her reputation would be ruined. Of course, *his* reputation wasn't the best. But he enjoyed a certain amount of respect thanks to the aura of money and power he'd cultivated for himself. And, the culture being what it was, Laura would be afforded that same respect—if she was his wife rather than his mistress.

Not that he thought Laura would mind being treated with disdain if that was the only way she could protect her son. But he minded *for* her. He wasn't about to ask her to do anything that would destroy her good name. In fact, putting her in any kind of position that would ultimately cause her hurt and unhappiness was simply beyond him.

In addition, he had to consider how the local police would respond if Giovanni chose to involve them in any way. He doubted she'd get a fair shake if she had to go up against them on her own. And only as her husband would Devlin have the kind of authority necessary to deal with them on her behalf.

All things considered, marrying Laura seemed the wisest thing to do, he thought, risking a quick look at her as he paced back to the fountain.

Still sitting on the bench, she eyed him warily, her hands clasped together in her lap.

She wasn't going to like what he was about to suggest. Not one bit. But then, he wasn't exactly thrilled with the idea of marriage, either. However, at the moment it seemed like the only viable solution to her problem.

"I can't guarantee Timmy's safety unless you live here with me," he stated baldly, halting a few feet away from her.

"Live here with you?" She glanced up at him in astonishment, then quickly lowered her gaze.

"That's the only way I can make sure Giovanni doesn't get close enough to you to get his hands on your son."

"I . . . I understand." Her face bright red, she tipped her chin up defensively as if readying herself for the worst. "So…what kind of…arrangement do you have in mind?"

He'd been right about her. She'd willingly debase herself if she thought that was what it would take to keep her son safe. He had to admire her courage. Yet, at the same time, he wanted to grab her and shake her.

She was so damned determined to think the worst of him. Apparently she assumed he'd have no compunction at all about putting her in an untenable position. And, for reasons he dared not consider too closely, that supposition on her part cut him to the quick.

"Under the circumstances, I thought marriage might be the best arrangement," he said.

"Marriage?" For one long moment she stared at him, her eyes filled with horror. Then, the color draining from her face, she slumped against the back of the bench. "Marriage," she repeated softly, her aversion to the idea of being tied to him in such a way more than evident in her voice.

Devlin wasn't sure exactly what kind of response he'd expected from her. But he certainly hadn't thought she'd be quite so repulsed. He'd meant only to offer her a means of maintaining her good name while they dealt with whatever threat Giovanni might pose to her and her son. He hadn't intended to exercise his husbandly rights and *take* her as his wife. He had never forced himself on a woman, and he never would.

Of course, he'd just admitted she had a penchant for thinking the worst of him, so he shouldn't have been surprised that she found his idea so detestable. Actually, given his current situation, he should have been glad. He couldn't afford to involve himself emotionally in a real marriage. Not as long as Drago Espinosa was still on the loose. Until he avenged the deaths of his wife and child, there wasn't going to be any happily ever after for him. And, had Laura any fondness for him at all, she might have ended up wanting wedded ... bliss.

As it was, Devlin doubted there was any chance of *that* happening. But just to make sure there weren't any misunderstandings down the line, he'd better make his intentions clear.

Sauntering over to the bench, he sat beside her. Without looking at her, he stretched his legs out in front of him and crossed his arms over his chest.

"Don't look so shocked, Ms. Burke," he drawled. "I'm not proposing we marry in the true sense of the word. What I had in mind was more a marriage of convenience. Unless you'd prefer to have everyone in San Pedro think you're my whore."

From the corner of his eye Devlin saw her flinch, and mentally cursed himself for speaking so harshly. But he knew of no other way to make her understand how limited her choices were.

"I doubt the nuns at the convent school would welcome you back with open arms come September," he continued when she didn't reply. "And if Giovanni chose to involve the local authorities, you probably wouldn't get a hell of a lot of sympathy from them. However, if you find marriage to me completely out of the question..." Still staring straight ahead, he shrugged as if he couldn't have cared less.

"Oh, no," she cried. "I don't want *that*. But, surely, there has to be another alternative to... to..."

"If you can come up with one, I'll be more than willing to give it a try. But as I see it, there's no way I'm going to be able to look after you and your son without ruining your good name unless you're my wife." Turning toward her, Devlin looped an arm around the back of the bench. "What about you, Ms. Burke?" he prodded gently. "Any ideas?"

After what seemed like a very long time, she murmured, "None at all."

As if unable to meet his gaze for more than a moment, she looked away. Her expression was so woebegone that Devlin found himself wanting nothing more than to pull her into his arms and hold her close. However, knowing she wouldn't be comforted by such a gesture on his part, he made no move to touch her.

She'd made sure he understood that she wanted as little to do with him as possible, and he was gentleman enough to accede to her wishes. She needed his help, and he'd give it. But he wouldn't invade her space. At least, not without an invitation.

As if one would ever be forthcoming, he thought. Talk about a cold day in hell. Or rather, a hot night in heaven, he amended, his gaze lingering on the curve of her neck, then lowering to the gentle swell of her breasts.

Suddenly realizing he'd wandered into dangerous territory, Devlin gave himself a firm mental shake. *If* Laura accepted his "proposal," she'd do so out of desperation, and the more often he reminded himself of that fact, the better off he'd be. Allowing himself to think of their "relationship" as anything but a business arrangement would be a big mistake. One he simply couldn't afford to make.

He'd never really expected to marry again, so he shouldn't find it that difficult to remain pragmatic. Especially since she wouldn't be offering him any encouragement to the contrary.

Still, it would have been nice if—

Once again Devlin reined in his wandering thoughts and, ignoring the odd ache in his heart, rested his hand on Laura's shoulder. Startled, she glanced up at him.

"Mr. Gray?"

"We seem to have no recourse, Ms. Burke." He offered her a wry smile. Then, on a more serious note, he added, "So, will you accept my proposal, or not?"

Chapter 4

Laura stared at Devlin wordlessly, her heart pounding. She'd come to him knowing that she desperately needed his help and while she hadn't been so naive as to think he'd want nothing in return, she had imagined they'd simply strike some sort of bargain, then she and Timmy would go home again. Never in her wildest dreams had she imagined he'd end up asking her to marry him!

But then, she hadn't really considered the logistics involved if he was going to have any chance at all of helping her keep her son safe. On their own in her little house, she and Timmy would be much too vulnerable. Like most people in San Pedro, she didn't even have locks on her doors, and she couldn't possibly stand guard twenty-four hours a day. She'd have to sleep sometime. When she did, it would be all too easy for someone to sneak in and snatch her son.

Timmy would definitely be much harder to get at here. From the little she'd seen of it, Devlin's house seemed to be quite secure. There were bolt locks on the front door, the windows facing the street were tightly shuttered and the garden was enclosed by what had to be an eight- or ten-foot-high adobe wall. Entering uninvited would be almost impossible.

In addition, should anyone actually manage to break in, they certainly wouldn't get very far. Bitsy would see to that. Stretched out under the table, snoring softly, the dog appeared to be rather benign. But Laura was fairly sure he functioned as more than just a pet. Should his territory be invaded, he probably wouldn't hesitate to bring down the intruder.

And if, by some chance, someone managed to get past Bitsy, they'd still have Devlin to contend with.

No doubt about it. She and Timmy would be better off living here with him. But, as he had so rudely pointed out, doing so as anything except his wife would cost her dearly.

She couldn't risk losing her teaching job. Finding another would be almost impossible, and she depended on her salary to make ends meet. If Sister Estrelita heard that she'd become Devlin's mistress, she wouldn't think twice about letting her go. As for the local authorities, they *would* be more apt to support her if she was the wife of someone capable of commanding their respect, however grudgingly it might be given.

Under the circumstances, Devlin's solution to her problem did seem to be the best one possible. Still, she wasn't about to blithely agree to what he was proposing.

As far as she could see, taking her as his lawfully wedded wife wasn't going to benefit him in any way. So why had he suggested it? Was it possible that, despite everything she'd heard about him, he was the kind of person who would come to her rescue not once, but twice, without expecting anything in return?

Laura wanted to hope so. Yet she'd learned the hard way how foolhardy it could be to accept at face value the word of a man she didn't really know.

Devlin had said their marriage wouldn't be a *real* one, but what had he actually meant by that?

His definition of the word probably wouldn't affect her final decision one way or another. Not when she already knew that marrying him would be in Timmy's best interest regardless of the conditions he imposed upon her. Still, before they went any further, she figured she had a right to know if his idea of a marriage of convenience meshed with hers.

Granted, he could say whatever he thought she wanted to hear, then change his mind once she was legally tied to him. But somehow she didn't think he'd do that. Because he'd been kind to her once, she couldn't help but feel there was something rather altruistic about him. And that, in turn, made her believe he was a man of his word.

Up till now he'd been fairly understanding. Surely he wouldn't object to answering a few questions. But she'd better get on with it or his patience was going to start wearing thin. He'd not only offered to help her, but had offered to do so in a way that would be more to her advantage than to his. And so far, all she'd done was sit and stare at him uncertainly.

Turning to look out across the garden, now steeped in early evening shadows, Laura took a deep, steadying breath.

"How long would we have to stay married?"

Shifting beside her on the bench, Devlin moved his hand from her shoulder, and with a quiet sigh once again crossed his arms over his chest.

"That's up to you," he said after a moment.

"Up to me?" She glanced at him out of the corner of her eye, but he'd turned his face away, so she couldn't read his expression.

"When you feel Giovanni no longer poses a threat to you or your son, you can have the marriage annulled. I won't offer any opposition. On the contrary, I promise I'll do whatever I can to help expedite the process."

She should have been reassured by his words, and to a certain extent she was. Yet, to her astonishment, she was also slightly miffed. She had no idea why. Feeling the way she did about the situation, she ought to be relieved that he preferred not to be tied to her any longer than absolutely necessary.

But did he have to make it quite so clear that in the meantime he'd be thinking of her as an albatross hung around his neck?

She'd already admitted that she was going to have to accept his proposal. But how would he behave toward her while they were actually husband and wife? Though he certainly seemed averse to having her around, she didn't think he'd treat her badly. But would he expect her to service him sexually? He didn't have to love her, or even *like* her, to use her to satisfy his needs.

Better to find out now exactly what he had in mind. She didn't like surprises. If he intended to bed her, she wanted to be prepared. He was an attractive man and she'd been alone a very long time. And, much to her dismay, she'd savored those few minutes when he'd held her in his arms more than she had any right to.

But she'd felt so safe, so incredibly secure.

Unless she had time to build up her defenses, she could easily end up falling under whatever sensual spell he might choose to cast upon her. And that was the last thing she could allow herself to do. When the time came for them to go their separate ways, she didn't want to have any regrets. At least, not where her personal relationship with Devlin Gray was concerned.

"What about having . . . having . . . sex?" she stammered, wincing at the way her voice wavered.

Beside her, Devlin shifted again, cocking his arm over the back of the bench as he turned to face her. Glancing up at him, Laura saw him watching her, his eyes narrowed, his mouth set in a grim line.

Feeling as if she'd somehow overstepped the bounds of propriety, she swiftly looked away, her face flaming with embarrassment. She should have left well enough alone. He'd said they wouldn't have a *real* marriage.

Yet she'd chosen to make an issue of it, and she had a good idea why. She'd had sex on her mind since she'd first decided to ask Devlin for his help. Now, much to her dismay, she found herself wondering if she was secretly hoping he'd coerce her into an intimate relationship so she could assuage her own prurient desire without remorse.

But no, she'd *never*—

"I don't *have sex,* Ms. Burke," he growled, making no effort to hide his anger. "I make love, and only with a willing partner, so your virtue's safe with me."

Well, she'd certainly gotten the response she wanted, hadn't she? He'd let her know, in no uncertain terms, that he wasn't going to hold her to her wedding vows in any way. She should be grateful. Instead, she was more frustrated than ever. And that, in turn, annoyed the heck out of her.

"Then *why* marry me?" she demanded, giving in to her exasperation as she finally met his gaze. "What, exactly, do you expect to get out of our—our arrangement?"

"Where you're concerned, Ms. Burke, I don't have any expectations at all," he cut in, a surprising hint of sadness in his voice. Then he added quietly, "Any other questions?"

"No," she muttered, looking away once more.

He was doing her a great favor, yet she hadn't shown him any appreciation at all. Instead, she'd acted as if it were her just due. No wonder he wanted as little to do with her as possible.

"Well, then, I think it's time you made up your mind one way or another. There's going to be a lot to do if we want to get this show on the road within the next day or two. So, will you marry me—yes or no?"

At least she hadn't driven him to withdraw his proposal. But the next day or two?

Of course, the sooner she became his wife, the better. More than likely, Giovanni already had someone searching for her. And it wouldn't take long for word to get around that she was staying here with Devlin.

Aware that she had no reason to delay any longer, Laura gave him the only answer she could.

"Yes, I'll marry you," she stated softly, forcing herself to meet his gaze.

Devlin nodded once, his rather stern expression assuring her that he wasn't taking their venture any more lightheartedly than she.

They'd agreed to become husband and wife, but not for the usual reasons. Laura knew people did it all the time. Yet, when she thought of how happy she'd been the day Johnny proposed to her, she felt oddly bereft.

Of course, they'd been madly in love, and unfortunately that wasn't the case with her and Devlin. Had they met under other circumstances and gotten to know each other, maybe they would have fallen in love, too. But as it was, they were just two people trying to make the best of a bad situation. And though that struck her as rather inauspicious, she couldn't afford to wallow in self-pity. Instead, she had to look at the bright side.

She might not be overjoyed at the prospect of marrying Devlin Gray, but from the moment she'd agreed to be his wife, she *had* begun to feel as if a great burden had been lifted from her shoulders.

She'd chosen to trust that he'd protect her and her son as well as keep his word about their marriage. And unless he gave her reason to believe he'd lied to her, she'd continue to put her faith in him.

From what she knew of the man, limited though it was, she didn't think he was intrinsically bad. However, she had no illusions about him, either. For reasons that would probably remain forever unknown to her, he seemed to have chosen to live outside the law. At least she knew that at the outset, and could distance herself from him accordingly.

And, of course, the very fact that he was a renegade made him just the kind of person she needed on her side right now.

But that was all she could allow him to be to her—an ally. As she'd already admitted more than once that day, she was drawn to him in a way she'd rather not consider too closely. And in all honesty, the more she thought about it, the less ambivalent she was about being his wife.

Having someone to watch over her and Timmy, even for a little while, would actually be kind of nice. In fact, with the right attitude, she might be able to make their time together tolerable.

As long as she kept her distance, both physically and emotionally, she shouldn't be tempted to do anything that would deepen their relationship in a way she'd regret. And while anything approaching friendship would probably be best avoided, she could see no reason that they couldn't be civil to each other. Then, when the time came, they could go their separate ways, and neither one of them would be any the worse for... for...

For what? she wondered, suddenly losing her train of thought as she realized that since she'd accepted Devlin's proposal, the steely look in his eyes had begun to soften.

Once again she felt the weight of his hand on her shoulder, then the gentle brush of his fingertips against the bare skin at the base of her neck. Though she knew she should move away, she sat where she was as an odd warmth stole through her. And crazy though it seemed, for just a moment she thought that he might—

"So, kiss the lady, Dev. Or shall I do the honors?"

Startled, Laura spun around. A man stood near the fountain, barely discernible among the shadows. She had no idea how he'd gotten there. But she didn't think it would be all that farfetched to believe he'd simply materialized.

With his finely chiseled features and golden blond curls he certainly didn't look like a mere mortal. Yet something about the sardonic gleam in his eyes and the mocking twist of his lips assured her he was no apparition from above, either.

Shivering slightly, she glanced at Devlin. Though he, too, had turned to look at the stranger, he'd done so much more laconically than she. And though she'd expected him to be angry at the other man's intrusion, he actually seemed amused.

Obviously they knew each other, she thought as she turned to stare at the stranger again. He certainly seemed welcome if Bitsy's response to him was any indication. Having wandered over to the man, the dog was now snuffling happily at his outstretched hand.

As he took a step toward them, she studied him more closely. He was about the same height as Devlin, but more lithely built. And now that he was standing in a patch of sunlight, she realized that he wasn't quite as old as she'd first thought. Dressed as he was in khaki shorts, a pale pink polo shirt and leather deck shoes, he looked more like a wealthy college boy than anything else. He even carried a backpack slung over one shoulder.

But then she met his gaze again and knew instinctively that there was nothing naive or innocent about him. Nor had there been in a very long time. Whatever he'd been through in his young life, she doubted it had been pleasant. And associating with a man like Devlin had probably only added to the unsavory experiences he'd already endured.

"So, rumors of your early demise were greatly exaggerated," Devlin said at last, his deep voice laced with affection.

Again Laura glanced at him, wondering what kind of relationship he had with the man.

"I was down for a while, but as you can see, not out."

He moved a little closer, and as he did, Laura noticed that he was favoring his right leg. A moment later she understood why when she saw the ugly scars crisscrossing his kneecap and slicing down his shin.

"I've been expecting you the past couple of days. I'm glad you finally made it," Devlin continued.

"Oh, yeah? If I were you, I'd be the last one I'd want hanging around," the stranger drawled, his gaze roving over Laura assessingly. "Getting married, are you?"

To Laura's surprise Devlin slid his arm around her shoulders. Before she could really think about what she was doing, she leaned against him gratefully, then hoped her discomfort wasn't as apparent to the stranger as it obviously was to him.

"Yes, we are. I'll fill you in on the details later. But for now, let me introduce you to my fiancée, Laura Burke. And, Laura, this is one of my... associates, Alexander Payton."

"Mr. Payton."

She regarded him even more warily, wondering how long he'd been standing in the shadows and how much he'd overheard of her conversation with Devlin.

"Ms. Burke," he acknowledged, nodding his head, a cynical smile tugging at the corners of his mouth. Then, as if he, too, could read her mind, he added, "And that's *trusted* associate. Right, Dev?"

"Yeah, right," Devlin agreed with obvious reluctance.

"Please consider me at your service." As he continued to study her, Alexander Payton's smile widened lasciviously. "Although I doubt you'll have need of *me*. I have a feeling Dev will be taking very good care of you himself."

"There's a young man in the kitchen with Mrs. Santos. Laura's son, Timmy. Try not to scare the wits out of him when you go in, Alex," Devlin said, all trace of affection now gone from his voice.

"I'm going in?" Alex asked, gazing at Devlin innocuously.

"The sooner, the better. Your room's ready. Stow your gear, then keep Mrs. Santos and Timmy company until Laura and I get back."

Something about Devlin's tone led Laura to believe that Alexander Payton would be doing much more than keeping them company. He'd be standing guard until she and Devlin returned from wherever they were going. And though his manner toward her had bordered on insulting, she knew her son would be safe with him. The man obviously owed Devlin his allegiance, and that was good enough for her.

"We have to pick up a few things at Laura's house on Barrancas Street. Shouldn't take us more than thirty or forty-five minutes," Devlin continued by way of explanation. "Tell Mrs. Santos that Laura and Timmy will be joining us for dinner, then spending the night."

"Anything else, boss?"

"I'm not expecting any other...visitors."

"Gotcha. You taking Bitsy?"

"Yeah."

With a smart salute that made Laura wonder if he'd been in the military, Alex Payton turned and limped slowly, albeit silently, to the door leading into the kitchen.

Once again alone with Devlin, Laura sat quietly for several seconds, wondering how she'd ever managed to get herself into such a strange situation. Then, realizing she was still leaning against Devlin, she quickly straightened and slid away from him.

"He...he works for you?" she asked, smoothing her palms over the skirt of her sundress.

"Sometimes." Devlin stood, crossed to the wrought-iron table and slipped into a pair of worn leather sandals. "Since you'll be staying, I thought you might want to go by your house and get a few things together for yourself and your son," he continued, deftly changing the subject.

"Yes, I would." Reminding herself that she'd really rather not know exactly how Alexander Payton and Devlin Gray had come to be associated, Laura stood, too. "Do you mind if I check on Timmy before we leave?"

"Not at all," Devlin replied, reaching for the set of keys lying on the table. "But I'd rather he stayed here."

Laura nodded her agreement, then turned and entered the house. Though she'd prefer not to be separated from her son, she knew he'd be safer here, especially if someone happened to be waiting for them at her house.

He and Mrs. Santos were no longer in the kitchen, but she had no trouble finding them. She simply followed the sound of Timmy's laughter down the hallway and into the *sala*, where they sat together on the sofa, watching a cartoon show. Across the room Alex Payton lounged in a chair, seemingly engrossed in a legal thriller.

"Mr. Gray's invited us to spend the night here," she said, perching on one arm of the sofa. Tomorrow morning she'd fill him in on the details. For now, however, she felt it best to keep things as simple as possible. "He's offered to take me home so I can get some clothes and stuff. Since we won't be gone long, I thought you might as well stay here."

"That's what Alex told me," Timmy replied.

"Mr. Payton," she corrected automatically.

"He told me I could call him Alex."

Resisting the urge to waste time arguing, Laura asked instead, "Do you want me to pack anything special for you?"

"Phil," he said, naming his favorite stuffed animal as he finally spared her a glance. "And my new kite, too." His gaze shifted to Alex and he smiled admiringly, adding, "Alex promised to help me put it together."

"Sounds like you two have become pretty good friends," she muttered, not exactly thrilled with the idea.

"When he first walked into the kitchen, he kinda scared me. But then Mrs. Santos gave him a big hug and told him how happy she was to see him again. After that, I knew he wasn't a bad person," Timmy stated matter-of-factly.

"Oh, really?"

Glancing at Alex, Laura found him watching her, his expression as acidulous as ever. Yet when he spoke, he did so with such sincerity that he caught her completely off guard.

"I'm afraid I was a bit of a bore earlier. For that I apologize."

"There was no harm done," she murmured.

Though he still made her uncomfortable, she appreciated his attempt to make amends. She was entrusting him with her son's care, after all, and for Timmy's sake she'd prefer not to have any animosity between them.

As if reading her mind, he added, "I'll make sure no harm comes to your son."

"Yes, of course."

Not sure what else she could say to the man, Laura offered him a slight smile. But he only stared at her wordlessly for several seconds before turning back to his book.

Feeling as if she'd been summarily dismissed, Laura once again thanked Mrs. Santos for looking after Timmy, then rose and headed back to the kitchen.

Out in the garden once more, she saw Devlin standing by the fountain. When he motioned for her to join him, she hurried down the walkway, glad that he, and not Alex Payton, held her fate in his hands. While she couldn't deny the two men were cast from the same mold, compared to Alex, Devlin was a real sweetheart. Of course, that wasn't saying much. But she *had* vowed to think positively, hadn't she?

"How's Timmy doing?" he asked as she paused beside him.

"So far, so good," she admitted, not only surprised but gratified by his obvious concern. "He was watching a cartoon show with Mrs. Santos."

"Was Alex with them?"

"Oh, yes," she hastened to assure him. "He was sitting across the room reading a book."

"Good."

Seemingly satisfied that all would be well while they were away, Devlin called to Bitsy. Then, taking Laura by the arm, he ushered her toward a narrow wooden door in the garden wall that was barely visible behind a screen of foliage.

As she watched in amazement, he pressed a series of buttons on a small metal panel set in the adobe. The door slid open soundlessly, revealing a small carport where his Jeep was parked, as well as an enclosed shed. They stepped across the threshold, Bitsy at their heels. Then, using another series of buttons on an identical outside panel, Devlin closed the door again.

So *that* was how Alex had managed to "appear" in the garden, Laura thought, following Devlin to the Jeep and allowing him to help her onto the passenger seat. Talk about state-of-the-art gadgetry. Must have cost a pretty penny. But then, maybe crime *did* pay, after all.

Having been reminded yet again that Devlin was basically an unscrupulous man, Laura twisted her hands together in her lap and gazed out the window sadly.

"Having second thoughts?" Devlin asked.

After letting Bitsy onto the back seat, he'd climbed behind the steering wheel and was now eyeing her quizzically.

What a stupid question. Of course she was having second thoughts. She'd agreed to marry a man she believed to be a common criminal. But admitting she had doubts about the wisdom of what she'd done certainly wouldn't do her any good. She had to at least *appear* sure of herself or she'd end up even more at his mercy than she already was.

"Not at all," she responded quietly, not quite meeting his gaze.

"Well, in that case, I guess we ought to make some wedding plans on the way over to your house." Starting the engine, he shifted into gear and calmly backed out of the carport.

Laura couldn't think of anything she'd rather do less, but there was no going back now. She'd accepted Devlin's proposal, for better or worse. The next logical step would be tying the knot.

Shuddering inwardly at that particular analogy, she glanced at Devlin again. Much to her relief, he seemed intent on watching the road.

"What did you have in mind?" she asked.

"Something simple, yet elegant," he replied. "An exchange of vows at St. Rita's, followed by a small dinner party at the house for our nearest and dearest friends."

Taken off guard as much by the grave tone of his voice as by the words he spoke, Laura turned and stared at him in amazement. He couldn't possibly be serious. Could he?

Meeting her gaze, Devlin arched an eyebrow and smiled slightly as he added, "Of course, I'm open to suggestions. What would *you* like to do?"

Wake up and realize I've been having a terrible nightmare.

Aware that she was wishing for the moon, Laura gazed out the window again.

"I'd rather just go to one of the local judges and have him marry us," she admitted at last.

For some reason she'd always considered a religious ceremony much more binding than a civil one, and since their marriage was only going to be one of convenience—

"We'll have to do that, too, but it will take a couple of weeks to make the arrangements," he advised as he turned onto her street.

"Well, we can't just walk into St. Rita's and demand to be married, either," she argued. "Father Hernandez counsels couples for months before he even allows them to set a wedding date."

"I know," Devlin agreed, pulling to a stop in front of her house. "But I shouldn't have too much trouble talking the old guy into giving us a special dispensation. We both attend services there on a fairly regular basis, so we're not exactly strangers to him. And once he's been apprised of the situation, I think he'll understand our need for haste."

Facing Devlin once more, Laura gazed at him with surprise. She couldn't remember ever seeing him at the little church on the edge of town, and she did go to mass there most Sunday mornings. But then, she and Timmy always arrived early and sat in one of the front pews. If Devlin stayed toward the back, then slipped out as soon as the service was over, she wouldn't have known he'd been there.

Still, she found it hard to believe that a man like Devlin Gray would actually make a habit of going to—

"Don't look so astonished, Ms. Burke," he chided. Then, as if he'd read her mind, he added quietly, "You're not the only one who needs a little solace on occasion."

"No, of course not," she murmured, feeling oddly ill at ease.

Less than thirty minutes ago Laura had been sure she knew enough about Devlin Gray to accept his proposal. However, the more time she spent with him, the more of an enigma he seemed to become.

He had most people in San Pedro—including her—convinced he was a common criminal. Yet he'd just admitted he sometimes sought comfort the same way she did, sitting through a Sunday service at St. Rita's.

She imagined she should be pleased that he seemed to be a better man than she'd originally believed him to be. Instead, she was more confused than ever.

Who was Devlin Gray? Who was he, *really?*

Laura doubted she'd ever find out, but that was probably just as well. Though she'd already learned that what she didn't know *could* hurt her, she'd rather remain as blissfully ignorant as possible where he was concerned. Then she wouldn't be tempted to grow any more attached to him than absolutely necessary.

No matter who or what he was, she needed him desperately right now. And if he turned out to be as decent as he seemed, she'd count herself lucky. But as soon as she felt she and Timmy would be safe living on their own again, she wanted to be able to walk away from him without any second thoughts.

As Devlin switched off the engine Laura glanced at him again. He met her gaze for a moment, a distant look in his eyes, then shifted slightly so that he could survey the area around her house.

"Notice anything out of the ordinary?" he asked.

"Not really."

Except for a small group of children half a block away playing with a soccer ball, the street was quiet, and to Laura, that was normal.

"Me, neither. But I'd rather you stay here while I take a look in the house."

"All right," she agreed, then looked at him questioningly when he stayed where he was.

"Your key," he prodded.

"There aren't any locks on the doors, so you don't need one."

"You've got to be kidding," he retorted, gazing at her in disbelief.

"I've never had any problems," she assured him, tipping her chin up defensively.

Muttering something about her being damn lucky, Devlin opened the car door, stepped onto the street and called to Bitsy. The dog jumped over the seat and out the door, then the two of them headed up her walkway.

Aware that curtains had begun to twitch at the windows of several of the surrounding houses, Laura willed Devlin to hurry. She didn't want to answer any questions, but she'd have no choice if one of her nosier neighbors came out and confronted her.

A couple of minutes later Devlin signaled for her to join him. Slipping out of the Jeep, Laura hurried into the cool, quiet house with a sense of relief.

"Gather up whatever you think you'll need for the next day or so," Devlin advised. "We'll come back and get the rest when we have more time."

"I've already packed a couple of suitcases," she replied, brushing past him on her way to the bedroom. "Just in case we had to leave San Pedro after all."

"Smart lady," he murmured as he trailed after her. "Now let's hope nobody stole them while you were gone."

Refusing to let him get to her, Laura opened the closet door and pointed to the suitcases still sitting on the floor where she'd left them.

"Satisfied?"

"Not by a long shot," he growled as he took them from her, then added, "Anything else?"

"Just my canvas carryall and a couple of toys for Timmy. Oh, and my string bag. It's on the kitchen table."

"You bring your carryall and Timmy's toys, and I'll get your string bag," he instructed as he headed back down the hallway.

Laura quickly pulled up the floorboards and retrieved her carryall, then hesitated as her gaze fell upon the garment bag hanging in the back of the closet. When she'd thought that she and Timmy might end up on the run, she'd packed only her sturdiest, most serviceable clothing. She hadn't thought she'd have any use for the cream-colored satin-and-lace dress she'd bought almost a year ago and had been saving for a special occasion. Since then, however, she'd agreed to marry Devlin Gray.

She didn't want to make a big deal of her marriage. Not at all. But he had sounded so serious when he'd said he wanted a "simple yet elegant" wedding. Considering all he was doing for her, it would be rather shabby of her to treat their exchange of vows as an everyday occurrence. Especially when she could just as easily go along with his wishes by wearing her best dress. The gesture would cost her nothing. And if he was pleased by it . . .

Then *what?* she wondered as she slung the garment bag over her arm.

She had no intention of going out of her way to make him happy. But she could see no reason that she couldn't do her part toward peaceful coexistence. At least as long as he seemed inclined to do the same.

She glanced around her bedroom one last time, wondering how long it would be until she could sleep safely in her own bed again. Then, squaring her shoulders determinedly, she crossed to Timmy's room, where she gathered up his kite, the ball of string and good old Phil. Had she had more time, she'd have grabbed a few of his other toys, as well. But she'd already taken longer than she'd intended.

Not wanting to keep Devlin waiting, she whirled around, started toward the doorway, head down, and ran straight into him.

"Whoa, take it easy," he chided teasingly, catching her by the shoulders to steady her.

Startled by his unexpected presence, she gazed up at him wordlessly. Then, aware of just how alone they were in her house, she took a step back, trying to shrug free of his hold on her. For one long moment he eyed her reproachfully, then released her.

"Have you got everything?" he asked, his voice suddenly businesslike.

"Yes," she replied, feeling like a fool.

Devlin had gone out of his way to make sure she understood he wouldn't do anything to harm her. Yet she'd responded to his nearness with such trepidation that she'd obviously, albeit inadvertently, offended him—again.

"I'm sorry. I didn't mean to...to..." she stammered, aware that she owed him an apology but not quite sure how to word it.

"Act as if I have the plague?" he supplied, arching an eyebrow inquisitively.

Unable to meet his gaze, she nodded ruefully.

"Don't worry, sweetheart. You're not the first, and I doubt you'll be the last."

He took the kite and Phil from her, then turned and headed back down the hallway, leaving her to follow on her own.

They made the drive back to Devlin's house in silence, which was just fine with Laura. After the kind of day she'd had, she was no longer up to watching what she said. And she certainly didn't want to risk insulting him any more than she already had. She'd chosen to accept his help, knowing exactly who and what he was. So she didn't really have any right to treat him with contempt, even unintentionally.

With a quiet sigh she stared out the window, wishing she could focus on something other than her dilemma, at least for a little while. But her mind whirled a mile a minute with thoughts of all she'd have to do the next day.

First thing in the morning she'd have to explain the situation to Timmy as simply as she could. She had no idea how he'd react when he found out she was marrying Devlin. But considering how much he seemed to want a father, she had a feeling he'd be happy. Which meant she'd also have to try to make him understand that Devlin wasn't going to be around permanently. Otherwise the poor child would be deeply upset when they eventually went their separate ways.

She'd also have to call Flora, tell her what had happened, then ask her not to come back to San Pedro just yet. Until they'd dealt with Giovanni, she didn't want the elderly woman staying alone in her house. And as long as she offered to continue paying her salary, Laura didn't think Flora would have any problem extending her visit with her relatives.

She'd have to talk to Annie, too. But not until after the wedding, she thought. Knowing her friend, she'd try to convince her not to marry Devlin, and Laura was just ambivalent enough to foolishly allow herself to be swayed. Better to present Annie with a fait accompli than accept her help and risk endangering her, too.

"I imagine Mrs. Santos has dinner just about ready," Devlin said, his tone still matter-of-fact as he pulled in to the carport behind his house. "Why don't you see if she needs any help in the kitchen while I take your things up to your room?"

Drawn from her reverie, Laura readily agreed. Hopping out of the Jeep, she followed Devlin to the door, waited while he punched in the code, then slipped into the garden.

Both Timmy and Mrs. Santos greeted her cheerfully as she walked into the kitchen, and her mood lightened considerably. But then she caught sight of Alex Payton sitting by the counter. He regarded her dispassionately for several seconds, got up and limped out to the garden.

Probably going to have a word with Devlin, she thought, trying not to let his rudeness get to her as she hugged her son, then offered Mrs. Santos her services.

Waving to a tray of dishes, glasses, cutlery and linen napkins on the sideboard, the housekeeper indicated she and Timmy could set the table in the dining alcove at the far end of the kitchen.

As she arranged knives, forks and spoons around the plates Timmy set on the table, Laura realized the last thing she felt like doing was eating. Even the wonderful aromas wafting from the oven couldn't seem to stir her appetite. However, she wasn't about to say so. Devlin was treating her much more hospitably than she deserved. The least she could do to show her appreciation was share a meal with him.

By the time she and Timmy finished with the table, Mrs. Santos seemed just about ready to serve. Excusing herself, Laura went in search of a bathroom, found one in the hallway, spent a few minutes freshening up, then returned to the kitchen. Devlin and Alex were also there, one looking as cool and aloof as the other as they studied her from across the room.

Discomfited by their silent scrutiny, she took Timmy by the hand and, at Mrs. Santos's urging, gladly led the way to the table.

Thanks to her son, dining with her nemeses wasn't nearly as unbearable as she'd thought it would be. Encouraged by Devlin's friendly questions, Timmy chattered happily about how he'd spent the afternoon watching television with Mrs. Santos and playing cards with Alex.

Laura pushed her food around on her plate and said little, concentrating instead on willing away the weary, weepy feeling that had come upon her almost as soon as she'd sat down. More than anything, she wanted to bury her face in her hands and cry. But she'd fallen apart once already in front of Devlin. She simply couldn't humiliate herself that way again.

"Aren't you feeling good, Mommy?" Timmy asked after a while, a hint of worry in his voice.

"I feel fine." Forcing herself to smile, she met his gaze, then glanced at Devlin and Alex, hoping to fool them, too. When they looked at her disbelievingly, she added hastily, "But I am a little tired."

"Me, too," Timmy admitted, pushing his empty plate away.

"Well, then, if you're finished, why don't I show you to your room?" Devlin suggested.

"I think that would be a good idea," Laura agreed, aware that she'd just about reached the end of her rope.

With Timmy clinging to her hand, she followed Devlin out of the kitchen and up the stairs to the second floor. At the end of the hall he paused in front of an open door, the only open door she'd seen along the way, and gestured for them to enter.

"I hope the two of you will be comfortable in here."

"I'm sure we will," Laura replied without hesitation.

Though sparsely furnished, the spacious room contained all they could possibly need—twin beds with a nightstand between them, a dresser and mirror, and an upholstered chair by the window, as well as a couple of lamps that provided more than enough light to ward off the growing darkness.

"The bathroom's through that doorway," Devlin added, nodding toward the far side of the room. "Mrs. Santos put out fresh towels and toiletries for you, but if you need anything else, let me know. I'll be right across the hall." He indicated the closed door opposite them, then met her gaze again.

"Thank you," she murmured, meaning it from the bottom of her heart.

"*De nada.*"

She wanted to refute his casual dismissal of the kindness he was showing her, but once again she felt as if she were on the verge of tears.

"I . . . I guess I'll see you tomorrow, then."

"Yes, tomorrow." He hesitated, then reached out and gently touched her cheek. "Don't worry, Laura. Everything's going to be all right."

Moved by his concern, she nodded wordlessly, wanting to believe him.

"Get some sleep, okay?"

"Okay."

"You, too," he added, smiling down at her son.

"Yes, sir," Timmy replied.

After another moment or two, Devlin finally turned away. But he did so with such obvious reluctance that Laura almost called him back. She ought to at least try to reassure him that she wasn't going to break into a thousand tiny pieces. But since she wasn't quite convinced of that herself, she let him go.

Somehow she managed to get Timmy bathed, changed into his pajamas and tucked into bed along with Phil. The familiarity of their nightly routine went a long way toward soothing her jumbled emotions, and by the time she finished her own ablutions she had regained some of her equanimity.

Though she'd put herself and her son at the mercy of a man who could possibly be as villainous as her father-in-law, she knew they were safe for the time being. And that was all that mattered, she thought, smoothing a hand over her son's dark, curly hair.

Knowing she'd never make it through the next day if she didn't get some rest, Laura crossed to her bed, crawled under the blankets and switched off the lamp. With all she had on her mind, she was sure she'd end up tossing and turning for hours. However, not five minutes later, lulled by the night noises filtering through the open window from the garden below, she drifted off to sleep.

Chapter 5

"What I'd like to know is why she thought she could come to you in the first place," Alex muttered as he prowled around the back room Devlin used as his communication center. "Aren't you supposed to have a rather unsavory reputation around here?"

"I came to her rescue after she fell and sprained her ankle during a rainstorm. Hauled her out of the gutter, then took her to the local clinic," Devlin admitted, rocking back in his desk chair.

Had Alex been merely a "business associate" passing through San Pedro, Devlin wouldn't have bothered to elaborate on his relationship with Laura. But he counted the younger man among his few close, personal friends, and thus felt he owed him more than the cursory explanation he'd already offered.

"And here I thought you had more sense than to play the Good Samaritan," Alex chided.

"Yeah, well, so did I." Eyeing the information scrolling

up on the computer screen in front of him, Devlin shrugged dismissively. "Guess I'll know better next time."

"I hate to be the one to break it to you, but I think you're already knee-deep in 'next time.' Why didn't you just take her to Mexico City and put her on a plane? I doubt she'd have had that much trouble getting lost in the crowd somewhere like New York or Los Angeles."

"Believe me, I considered it. But if Giovanni's as determined to get his hands on her son as she thinks he is, he'd have tracked her down sooner or later. And I honestly didn't like the idea of her having to go up against him on her own in a strange place."

"Seems to me the operative word here is *if*. For all you know, Buschetti could be whiling away his days in a nursing home, too old and infirm to remember he has a grandson. Or he could already be planted six feet under."

"About thirty minutes ago I contacted a couple of our men in the Chicago area and asked them to put together a dossier on him. Depending on what they send back, I should be able to determine whether or not he actually poses a threat to her."

"Then what?" Alex prodded.

"Then we'll either go through with the wedding or we won't," Devlin stated pragmatically.

He'd never intended to marry Laura unless he was sure there was no other way to guarantee her son's safety, but he'd preferred not to say as much to her. Knowing how she felt about the situation, he hadn't wanted to get her hopes up only to have to dash them again. Nor had he wanted to tell her how he could come by reliable information on her father-in-law so quickly and easily.

"As simple as that, huh?" Gazing at him skeptically, Alex retraced his steps, his limp more noticeable than it had been earlier.

"Yeah, as simple as that. I'll be just as happy as she'll be if we can go our separate ways tomorrow morning."

"Of course you will."

"Come on, Alex, give me a break," Devlin retorted, unable to hide his annoyance. "You think I *want* to be saddled with Laura Burke and her problems?"

"You certainly haven't seemed all that averse to taking her as your lawfully wedded wife. In fact, I'd say you're actually looking forward to it. Not that I blame you. She comes across as kinda shy and quiet, but I bet she's really one hot little—"

"You want to shut up or do you want me to shut you up?" Devlin cut in, his voice deceptively soft.

"Ah, touched a nerve, did I? Sorry," Alex replied without any hint of contrition.

He had, but Devlin wasn't about to admit it. If he'd found the thought of marrying Laura truly unpalatable, he'd never have suggested it. He wasn't *that* beneficent, not by any stretch of the imagination.

Yet, contrary to what Alex had insinuated, he didn't have any ulterior motives where she was concerned, either. He'd promised her a marriage of convenience and that was what they'd have. Unless she decided otherwise.

"I just thought maybe you'd hoped to get more out of your, uh, marriage than the satisfaction of doing a good deed for a damsel in distress," Alex persisted.

"Well, obviously you thought wrong," Devlin advised him curtly.

"Obviously." With a slight smile Alex leaned a hip against the edge of Devlin's desk, then veered off on another tangent. "When are you going to tell her what you're really doing in San Pedro?"

"I'm not."

"You don't think she'll have a right to know once she's your wife?"

"We're going to be married only a few weeks, maybe a month or two at most. Might as well let her believe the worst of me for that short amount of time rather than risk blowing my cover."

"Oh, yeah, right. She could decide to go on national television and tell everyone all about you," Alex retorted. "Come on, Dev, give the lady a break. She's almost as scared of you as she is of her father-in-law. What could it hurt to tell her you're one of the good guys?"

Devlin knew Alex was right. He could put Laura's mind at ease by telling her the truth about himself. But maintaining his villainous persona was crucial if he wanted to keep some distance between them.

Once Laura realized he wasn't the rogue she was so intent on believing him to be, she might begin to look upon him in a more favorable way. Already he sensed that she'd begun to trust him despite her better judgment. As he'd determined earlier, any additional softening toward him on her part would be all too hard for him to resist. He wanted her in the most intimate way a man could want a woman. But having her truly be a part of his life would mean he'd once again have something, *someone,* to lose.

Laura had been in his thoughts more than she should have been before she'd come to him to ask for his help. He couldn't afford to allow his attention to be diverted to a greater degree. Not as long as he still had to deal with Drago Espinosa.

Of course, he saw no reason to explain all that to Alex. How he handled his relationship with Laura was *his* business. Obviously his young friend had forgotten that, but Devlin was more than willing to offer him a reminder.

"By now you ought to be aware that I operate on a need-to-know basis, and as far as I'm concerned, at this time Ms. Burke has no real need to know anything about me other than what she already does," he advised as he held Alex's gaze. "Understood?"

"Yes, sir. Anything you say, *sir,*" Alex replied, snapping off a smart salute, then continuing rather caustically. "What about McConnell? Have you told him about your impending marriage to Ms. Burke?"

"Now, there's a switch. *You* worrying about *me* keeping our boss informed."

"So, you're keeping him in the dark," Alex gloated. "Wise move, Dev. The old man would blow a gasket if he had any idea what you were planning to do. Then, thanks to that new department policy regarding married agents, he'd haul your butt out of San Pedro so fast your head would spin, and you'd never be able to put Drago out of commission."

Everything Alex had said was true, but Devlin had worked for McConnell long enough to know just how far out of bounds he could step without seriously jeopardizing his job. To a certain extent, so did Alex. But he'd really pushed the envelope on his way to San Pedro.

Recalling that fact, Devlin gladly changed the subject. "Speaking of McConnell blowing a gasket," he began, then continued almost indifferently, "what did you do to those poor fools he assigned to accompany you here?"

Because of his reputation as something of a loose cannon, Alex had been sent to San Pedro under escort to recuperate from injuries he'd sustained while on assignment in the Middle East. However, somewhere between D.C. and Devlin's house he'd dumped the two seasoned marines and continued on his own.

"Tied them to the beds in the motel room, then told the manager they didn't want to be disturbed for at least twenty-four hours," Alex stated proudly.

"That was three days ago in Houston, Texas. What took you so long to get here? Make any side trips along the way?"

"Maybe."

"Thought you were going to stay away from her."

"I did."

"Why don't you just *talk* to her, tell her you're sorry?"

"I'm sorry, all right," Alex sneered. "One sorry son of—"

For a moment his eyes glittered with anger and pain. Then, his expression shuttered once again, he shoved away from the desk and headed toward the door, now all but dragging his injured leg.

"Will you need me for anything in the morning?" he asked, his voice deceptively calm.

"Just to be here in case anyone comes snooping around while I'm out making arrangements for the wedding."

"Right, then. If I'm not up when you're ready to leave, drag me out of bed."

"Whatever you say," Devlin replied, though he doubted that would be necessary since Alex rarely slept more than a few hours at a time.

Wishing he hadn't pushed the younger man quite so hard, Devlin watched him disappear down the hallway. Then he turned back to his desk and sifted through the faxes he'd received earlier, searching for any information on Drago.

He was halfway through the stack when the machine came to life again. After crossing to the credenza, he picked up the first sheet it spewed out and began to read.

Ten minutes later, having been advised by his contact in Chicago that Giovanni Buschetti was not only alive and well but just as rich and powerful as Laura had indicated, Devlin accepted the fact that they'd have to go through with the wedding.

Though he couldn't say he was overjoyed at the prospect, he wasn't upset, either. They were both adults capable of dealing with the situation in a mature way. When all was said and done, neither one of them should end up with any regrets.

Or so he hoped as he returned to his desk and resumed his hunt for the ruthless killer who'd already taken the lives of too many innocent people.

"You look really pretty, Mom."

Dressed in his Sunday best—navy blue shorts, a white, short-sleeved shirt, white socks and navy blue sandals—Timmy sat on the edge of the bathtub, keeping Laura company while she put the finishing touches on her makeup.

"Why, thank you, sweetheart." Turning away from the mirror, she offered him an appreciative smile.

She'd been wondering if she was a bit overdressed for what was really only a marriage of convenience. But her son's admiring gaze was all the encouragement she needed to wear the satin-and-lace dress instead of changing into something simpler. Now, if only she could decide what to do with her hair.

Curling loosely around her shoulders, it looked much too wild, but pinning it into a coil at the nape of her neck would be too severe. If she'd thought to buy a hat to match her dress, she could have tucked the whole mess up under it. But she hadn't. However, she did have a rather pretty gold hair clip studded with pearls that would add just the right touch of elegance while complementing quite nicely the gold-and-pearl drop earrings she already wore.

Eyeing her reflection once again, she swept her hair off her neck, then secured the tumble of long, dark curls with the clip. Only the faint trembling of her hands revealed her growing anxiety. Very soon now they'd be leaving for the church, and within an hour she'd be married to Devlin Gray.

For most of the day she'd managed to avoid thinking too closely about what she was getting herself into. Still, more than once she'd had to beat back a wave of panic as she caught herself considering the possibility that she might actually be jumping from the frying pan into the fire. Then she would look at Timmy and be reminded of exactly what she stood to lose if she tried to go up against Giovanni on her own. Having reassured herself that she had made the right decision, she would calm down. Until she'd allow her mind to wander once again.

At least the day hadn't dragged by, as she'd fully expected it to do. Instead, much to her relief, time had passed rather quickly.

She'd awakened feeling remarkably rested to find Timmy sitting at the foot of her bed, looking at her quizzically. Knowing that the time had come to explain the situation to him, she'd motioned for him to join her. They'd snuggled under the covers for a few minutes as they did most mornings. Then she'd told him as simply as she could that there was a chance the man they'd run into at the cathedral would try to harm them if they went back to their house. As Timmy had gazed at her, wide-eyed, she'd quickly added that Devlin would keep them safe as long as they stayed with him, but only if she married him.

Her son had nodded as if he understood. Then, bless his good little soul, he'd asked about Flora, wanting to be sure she'd be safe, too. Laura had told him the housekeeper would be staying with her family in Leon until the danger had passed. He'd also wanted to know if they could go back to their house to get the rest of his toys. Laura had assured him they would sometime within the next few days. Finally he'd asked the question she'd dreaded most, in such a hopeful tone of voice that she hadn't had the heart to discourage him too much.

"Is Mr. Gray going to be my dad now?"

"In a way he will. At least, as long as we live here with him," she'd admitted. Then she'd added lightly, "But once it's safe, we'll be going back to our own home. Then he'll just be our friend again."

"I wish he could be my dad for always."

"I know. But Mr. Gray and I aren't really...in love with each other," she'd said gently. "He's only marrying me because we really need his help. And it wouldn't be very nice of us to take advantage of his kindness any longer than absolutely necessary, would it?"

"No," he'd murmured in such a grudging tone of voice Laura had wished she could tell him what he wanted to hear.

However, she'd known that misleading him then would only mean he'd end up being hurt worse somewhere down the road. So, hoping to divert his attention, she'd taken the coward's way out, tickling his tummy until she'd had him giggling with childish glee.

They'd finally dressed and gone down to the kitchen, where they'd found Mrs. Santos stirring one of several pots already simmering on the stove while Alex sat at the table, chopping vegetables with a nasty-looking knife he wielded with more skill than Laura thought any normal man should have.

As she and Timmy had helped themselves to homemade cinnamon rolls and glasses of milk, he'd favored her with a cool glance, then ever so politely advised that the marriage ceremony had been scheduled for six o'clock that evening. Beaming with happy anticipation, Mrs. Santos had added that she'd already begun preparing a very special wedding supper for them.

Devlin had been nowhere to be seen. Out for the day, according to Alex, to which Mrs. Santos had nodded in agreement. And, as far as Laura knew, he had stayed out until late that afternoon.

Not that she'd minded in the least. After she'd finished breakfast and phoned Flora, she'd had more than enough to occupy her time helping Mrs. Santos and entertaining Timmy. She certainly hadn't wanted or needed to have Devlin around to keep her company. In fact, she'd been glad not to have to worry about running into him in the close confines of his house. She'd been keyed up enough as it was, and though she knew he wouldn't intentionally do anything to hurt her, she still found him rather daunting.

By the time he'd come home, she and Timmy had returned to their room. Having finally gotten her son down for a much-needed nap, she'd been about to indulge in a long, leisurely soak in the huge tile bathtub when she'd heard Devlin's voice out in the hallway. She'd gathered he was talking to Alex, but she hadn't been able to make out what he was saying. It hadn't mattered. She'd been relieved just to hear the sound of his voice. At least he hadn't abandoned her as she'd half feared somewhere in the back of her mind most of the day.

Still staring at her reflection in the mirror, Laura realized just how confused her feelings for Devlin Gray were. On the one hand she hadn't wanted him around, yet her anxiety had been allayed the moment he'd returned. Talk about not having her head screwed on straight.

The rap of knuckles against her bedroom door followed by Alex Payton's curt "Are you ready, Ms. Burke?" startled her out of her reverie.

"As ready as I'll ever be," she muttered to herself. Then, smiling at her son and holding out her hand to him, she pitched her voice a little louder and replied with all the confidence she could muster, "Yes, of course. Be right there."

She crossed the bedroom and opened the door, then hesitated, holding her breath, as Alex boldly surveyed her up and down. When he finally met her gaze, a glimmer of approval in his eyes, she couldn't help but sigh with relief.

"Very nice," he commented dryly.

"Thank you." She tipped her chin up and looked back at him unwaveringly. "You're not too shabby yourself."

"Some of us clean up better than others," he replied, then offered her his arm. "Shall we?"

She hesitated again, wondering why he was there instead of Devlin. As if reading her mind, he added, "The groom asked me to escort you to the church."

"I thought he was here earlier," she ventured as she took Timmy by the hand and started down the hallway.

"For about an hour. Then he took off again. Probably didn't want to jinx your chances of marital bliss by seeing you before the wedding."

Laura thought he must be kidding. But when she glanced at him, he met her gaze without the slightest hint of amusement. Wondering what Devlin had told Alex about their arrangement, she walked slowly down the staircase.

Since the two men seemed to be friends as well as business associates, she'd assumed Devlin had apprised him of the situation. Surely he'd also advised Alex that their marriage was one of convenience only, and thus would *not* be consummated, blissfully or otherwise, if Devlin kept his word.

"I doubt that," she answered as they reached the downstairs hallway, determined to set him straight just in case Devlin hadn't. "He's only marrying me so he can help me keep my father-in-law from getting his hands on my son."

"Whatever you say," Alex drawled as they reached the downstairs hallway.

His cynicism was so obvious that Laura was tempted to argue with him. But what good would that do? She knew Devlin didn't have any ulterior motives where she was concerned. She also trusted him to keep his word about their physical relationship, or lack thereof. And *she* was the one who mattered here.

Maybe Devlin had purposely misled Alex for reasons of his own. Having to admit there wasn't going to be any "marital bliss" would be a blow to most men's pride. And while Devlin hadn't struck her as the kind of man who'd find it necessary to brag about his sexual conquests, he might want to maintain a certain image among his subordinates. She could understand that and, for his sake, go along with it, at least up to a point.

Mrs. Santos, wearing a lavender silk dress and matching lace mantilla, waited for them in the kitchen. As Alex had done, she eyed Laura with approval, then offered her a warm, kindly smile. Glad that she'd made an effort to look her best, Laura smiled, too.

She'd realized early on that despite Devlin's reputation around town, he had somehow managed to earn not only Mrs. Santos's loyalty but her affection, as well. And Laura was inordinately pleased that she also seemed to be in the elderly woman's good graces. Why, she wasn't really sure. But she liked Mrs. Santos, and because of that, the housekeeper's opinion mattered. In an odd way, Laura also found it reassuring to know that someone of her stature thought well of the man she was about to marry.

Bustling across the kitchen, Mrs. Santos opened the refrigerator door, took out a small bouquet of flowers and handed it to Laura. Arranged in a paper doily were half a dozen of the cream-and-pink roses she'd admired in the garden yesterday along with bits of greenery and several stems of baby's breath.

"Oh, Mrs. Santos, how lovely," Laura murmured, inhaling the spicy scent of the roses. "Thank you."

"Don't thank me, *señora*. Thank Señor Gray. He chose the very finest of his flowers for you."

"Señor Gray?" Laura gazed at the housekeeper in bewilderment.

She'd never have given Devlin credit for the well-tended roses in his garden. Which only proved she knew even less about him than she'd thought.

"A man of many talents, your Devlin," Alex purred. Then, not waiting for her to respond, he gestured toward the door. "We'd better go or we'll be late, Ms. Burke."

Thrown off balance yet again, Laura gripped Timmy's hand a little tighter and led the way out to the garden, Alex's words whirling in her mind.

A man of many talents, your Devlin. Your Devlin...

She could only wonder what Alex had meant by "many talents" because she was afraid he'd answer in detail if she came right out and asked. She didn't mind knowing that he had a green thumb. But she had a feeling his other skills were much more nefarious. As for the "your Devlin," she wasn't naive enough to believe he'd ever be anything but his own man even if he were to care for her. Which he wouldn't.

With Alex at the wheel of Devlin's Jeep, they drove the short distance to St. Rita's in silence. Laura sat in the passenger seat, holding her bouquet in her lap and staring out the window.

As they slowly traversed one street, then another, the scent of the roses wafted around her, reminding her of the time she'd spent with Devlin in his garden the day before.

And, unaccountably, her anxiety eased as she recalled how considerate he'd been to her then.

His kindness had also carried over into today. Though she was sure he'd had things to do, she doubted he'd really had reason to stay out all day. Somehow he'd seemed to know that she needed a little time, a little space, to come to terms with the decision she'd made. Probably because he'd had to do the same, she realized.

Until now she hadn't given much thought to how *he* must feel about the way she'd made herself at home in his house. Nor had she considered the possibility that unless he was more hard-hearted than she'd assumed, he couldn't have found it all that easy to accept the fact that she was using him.

And that was exactly what she was doing, she realized with genuine dismay. Using him quite blatantly for her own benefit. Feeling ashamed of herself, she stared at the flowers she held. She'd never thought much of people who exploited others for whatever reason. Yet here she was, imposing upon Devlin Gray in a truly self-serving way.

Granted, he might not be the best of men, but that didn't give her the right to take advantage of him. Not when he'd treated her with such kindness. Why, he'd even allowed her to dictate the terms of their agreement, all of which had been in her favor. And in return she'd intended to spend the next few weeks doing everything in her power to avoid him.

Now Laura had to admit that didn't seem like much of a way to repay Devlin for all he'd offered to do for her. She didn't want to force herself on him any more than she already had. But neither did she want to drive him out of his own home with her standoffishness, as she was afraid she'd done today.

She'd have to find some sort of happy medium, she decided. And the best way to do that was to start thinking of him as a person rather than merely a means to an end. She'd told him almost everything there was to know about her, but she hadn't shown any real interest in him beyond how he could help her. She had no idea what kind of life he'd lived before he came to San Pedro, simply because she hadn't bothered to ask.

Not that he would have appreciated her prodding into his background. But it wouldn't have hurt her to exhibit at least a modicum of concern toward him. And she would, she vowed as they pulled to a stop in front of the church. Even a wife in name only owed her husband some regard.

"Having second thoughts, Ms. Burke?" Alex asked as he set the parking brake and switched off the engine.

"Not the kind you mean." She smiled ruefully as she met his gaze.

He studied her intently, then nodded once as if he not only understood what she meant, but approved, as well. Once again she was heartened by his support, though she had no idea why. Garnering the approbation of someone she assumed had a criminal bent wasn't something she'd ever aspired to do. However, under the circumstances, the more people she had on her side, the better. And, as she'd concluded yesterday, beggars couldn't be choosers.

Keeping that thought in mind, Laura reached for the door handle as Mrs. Santos and Timmy clambered out of the back seat.

As she stepped onto the sidewalk, she gazed up at the old church, bathed in the golden glow of late-afternoon sunlight. The wooden doors stood open, welcoming any and all who chose to enter the cool, dim interior, but only a few elderly women dressed in black shuffled across the threshold.

With Mrs. Santos and Timmy leading the way and Alex's hand on her arm, Laura walked up the stone steps, clutching her bouquet. She'd thought Devlin would be waiting for her at the door, but she didn't see him there.

"Do you think he's here yet?" she asked softly as they stepped into the vestibule and paused for a moment, allowing their eyes to adjust to the comparative darkness of the church.

"He's standing by the side altar with Father Hernandez," Alex advised.

With his back to them, Devlin seemed to be studying the statue of Mary set amidst a bank of votive candles above the altar. But then, as if sensing their presence, he turned toward them, causing Laura's breath to catch in her throat.

He was wearing a pale gray suit, white shirt and patterned tie, with his face clean shaven and his dark hair tied back at the nape of his neck. He looked almost...civilized. Almost.

No matter how smartly dressed he was, he couldn't quite hide his rugged masculinity. The hard line of his jaw and the square set of his shoulders as well as the hint of defiance in his stance left no doubt of his virility. And though she knew giving in to the longing that had settled deep in her soul would only cause her more heartache, Laura found herself drawn to him as if she were a lovesick schoolgirl without any sense at all.

Suddenly, aware that he was staring at her and she was staring right back, Laura looked away. As she did so, she noticed that several people sat in the pews nearest the side altar. Several people she knew personally.

Annie and Juan Carlos Moreno, Sister Estrelita and Sister Raphaela and old Mr. Wiley gazed at her, their expressions full of surprise and confusion.

Obviously, unbeknownst to her, Devlin had invited her few friends to the wedding. But why? she wondered with dismay. She'd just as soon have married him as privately as possible.

But then, what better way could there have been to have their union sanctioned than by asking those closest to her to witness their marriage ceremony? Now there would be no question as to whether she was really Devlin's wife.

Meeting his gaze once again, Laura saw that he was still watching her, watching and waiting, his pale eyes glinting with desire. Even at a distance she could sense the wanting in him, a wanting to which she responded with a wistfulness she couldn't quite understand.

"Are you coming, Mommy?" Timmy asked, his voice hushed.

"Yes, of course," she assured him, though she couldn't seem to take that first step down the aisle.

"Why don't you go on ahead with Mrs. Santos," Alex suggested. "We'll be right behind you."

"Okay," he agreed.

As Mrs. Santos and Timmy walked down the narrow aisle, Alex took her hand and looped it over his arm.

"Don't look so scared," he muttered.

"Easy for you to say," she retorted, her voice quavering shamefully.

"He's not going to eat you, you know. At least, not here in front of God and everybody," he teased softly. "Of course, later..."

Wondering if he'd meant what she thought, Laura glanced up at him. His lascivious grin was all the confirmation she needed. Her face flaming, she turned away, trying unsuccessfully to block out the wholly inappropriate yet not altogether unpleasant images of intimacy his comment had conjured in her mind.

She gave Alex a warning glance as they started down the aisle. Then, clinging to Alex's arm, Laura met Devlin's gaze again. To her surprise he smiled encouragingly, and she found herself smiling back. He wasn't going to do her any harm, there or anywhere. He was going to help her keep her son safe the best way he knew how. And, as far as she was concerned, nothing else mattered at the moment.

She'd have time enough in the days ahead to deal with the repercussions of what she'd chosen to do. Time enough, too, to answer the questions she knew her friends would be asking just as soon as they had a chance. And there would be many of them, she thought as she passed the pew where Annie sat and caught a glimpse of her friend's face.

Not only did she look shocked, but hurt, as well. Laura didn't blame her. They'd been so close the past few years, sharing their hopes and fears. She had to be wondering why Laura hadn't told her about her decision to marry Devlin. But if she had, Annie would have tried to talk her out of it, and Laura simply couldn't have allowed herself to be swayed that way.

Hoping her friend would give her a chance to explain, Laura continued down the aisle. Automatically her attention focused on Devlin once more. Her husband-to-be, she thought, with unintended and totally unreasonable anticipation.

As they joined Devlin at the foot of the altar, Alex handed her over to him with a gentlemanly bow and quietly backed away. Drawing her close to his side, Devlin offered her another reassuring smile, then turned to face Father Hernandez.

Grateful for his solid, steadying embrace, Laura leaned against him as she, too, met the elderly priest's beneficent gaze. Whatever qualms he might have had about their hasty marriage, Devlin had apparently managed to assuage them.

With an almost enervating sense of unreality, Laura listened as Father Hernandez began the marriage ceremony, but his softly spoken words seemed to hold no substance for her.

The scent of candle wax and incense mingled with the scent of the roses she held, reminding her that she was, indeed, in the midst of a church wedding. And, as if on autopilot, she responded in the right way at the right times, reciting her vows in a voice that wavered only slightly. However, it wasn't until Devlin produced two wide gold wedding bands for the priest to bless that she stopped feeling as if she was a mere onlooker.

Considering how carefully Devlin had orchestrated everything else to do with their wedding, she shouldn't have been surprised to see that he intended them to exchange rings. Yet she was.

There was something undeniably binding about wearing a gold band on the third finger of your left hand, she thought as Devlin slid her ring into place, then she did the same with his. Something that connected you in a way words alone never could.

Finally, after a few last words, Father Hernandez declared them husband and wife, joyfully adding that Devlin could now kiss his bride.

Expecting a chaste peck on the cheek, Laura tipped her face up, meeting his gaze for the first time since the ceremony had begun. As she had earlier, she saw a glimmer of desire in his eyes, now also edged with pride and—could it be—possessiveness, and felt herself responding with an instinctive yearning all her own.

Murmuring her name, he put his hands on her shoulders and drew her close, then bent his head and brushed his lips over hers. With a soft sigh she closed her eyes and leaned against him, resting one hand on his chest.

For just an instant she thought he was going to ease away from her. But then, as if sensing her unspoken need, he pulled her hard against him and deepened their kiss, nudging her mouth open with masterful skill.

One kiss, she thought, knotting her fingers in the fabric of his suit coat. Just one kiss...

Chapter 6

One *real* kiss, Devlin told himself, savoring the sweet taste of her as his tongue swirled over hers, teasing, tempting until she sighed again, relaxed in his arms and responded in kind.

Had Father Hernandez not cleared his throat so reprovingly, Devlin wasn't sure he'd ever have let her go. But the elderly priest's gentle reminder that now was not the time, nor the sanctuary of St. Rita's the place to lose control was all he needed to come to his senses and ease away from her.

With a vague sense of dismay he realized that he'd gone so far out of his way to make sure everyone would accept their marriage as the real thing that for a few moments, he'd gotten more caught up in the charade than he should have. Although there hadn't been any pretense at all in the way he'd kissed her.

No matter how he wished he could deny it, that primitive claiming had come from the heart.

For all intents and purposes, Laura Burke Buschetti was his wife now. And while he'd willingly given up his right to bed her, some dark, secret part of him hadn't been able to resist letting all those present know that she belonged to him, and him alone.

She was staring up at him, her lips still slightly parted, her eyes filled with surprise and confusion. He reached out and touched her cheek. Then, as he'd done several times since she'd first walked into the church, he offered her what he hoped was a reassuring smile. He had no intention of taking advantage of what he assumed had been nothing more than a momentary aberration on her part, and he wanted her to know it.

"Don't worry, Mrs. Gray," he murmured, pitching his voice for her ears only. "That's as physical as we're going to get."

For one long moment she stared at him with what might have been regret. But then she lowered her gaze and stepped away from him, and he thought perhaps he'd misread her expression, after all. Obviously she had no more desire to lie down with him than she had yesterday, and for that he should be grateful. Should be, but wasn't, he acknowledged as he offered her his arm.

"I believe we're supposed to lead the way out now," he said when she glanced at him questioningly.

"Oh, yes, of course."

Keeping her eyes averted, she looped her arm through his and started up the aisle at his side. As they came to the pew where Timmy sat with Mrs. Santos, Devlin paused a moment and gestured for the boy to join them. Grinning happily, the child sidled close to his mother, clinging to her hand.

His family, Devlin thought with inordinate pride as the three of them continued on to the back of the church, their guests falling in behind them. Only for a few weeks, of course, but that didn't mean he couldn't make the most of it while he had the chance.

Or so he thought until he caught a glimpse of the all-too-knowing look on Alex's face and realized he was skirting dangerous territory. As he seemed to keep forgetting, he had no right to expend any more time or energy on Laura and her son than was absolutely necessary. Not as long as Drago Espinosa was still on the loose.

He'd already taken off all day today. There was no telling what vital information might have come in while he'd been busy conning Father Hernandez into marrying them, then coercing Laura's few friends into attending the ceremony as well as the small dinner party he'd organized for them afterward. Information he wouldn't be able to process until later that night, by which point a delay could prove costly.

He couldn't afford that kind of inattention to duty on a regular basis. But then, he would have no reason to be quite so preoccupied with Laura and her son now that there could be no doubt he had the right to legally act on her behalf.

Establishing himself as her husband had been of paramount importance. Now that he'd done so—with flying colors—he could go about his business, as unaffected by the presence of her and her son as he chose to be.

Determined to regain some of the impassiveness he'd acquired over the past four years, Devlin paused in a patch of shade just outside the church, then made the mistake of glancing at Laura. Gritting his teeth, he quickly turned away again, unable to remain totally indifferent to her unconscious allure.

In the early-evening light she looked even more lovely than she had when he'd first caught sight of her standing in the vestibule. Her cream silk dress clung to her trim figure in an enticingly modest way, while her long, dark curls, swept up in seemingly artless disarray, added just a touch of wantonness to her otherwise ladylike appearance.

For one agonizingly erotic instant he thought of how wondrous it would be if he could scoop her into his arms, carry her home, throw her on his bed and . . . ravish her.

Oh, yeah, he wasn't going to have any trouble at all keeping his distance in the days to come, he scoffed silently, thoroughly disgusted with himself and the turn his thoughts had taken.

Giving himself a firm mental shake, he let go of Laura's arm and stepped away from her, ignoring her questioning gaze as he accepted first Father Hernandez's congratulations, then those of Laura's friends.

Beside him, smiling gamely, Laura murmured her own thanks, though Devlin noticed she avoided meeting anyone's gaze. He had no doubt she was embarrassed by her hasty marriage to a man of such ill repute. Even as thick-skinned as he was, he hadn't been completely impervious to the shock and distaste with which his announcement of their impending marriage had been met by her friends.

Empathizing with her, he reached out and drew her close to his side once again. She came willingly, her swift glance full of gratitude. Whether he liked it or not, they were in this together, and no matter how her nearness tested his self-control, the least he could do was stand by her when she needed him, as she so obviously did at that moment.

As he had when he'd first approached them earlier in the day, Devlin once again invited the Morenos, the nuns, Father Hernandez and Mr. Wiley to join them for a celebratory dinner at his house. Reluctantly everyone accepted, and for Laura's sake he was glad.

While he realized he couldn't allay her anxiety altogether, he'd wanted their wedding to be as pleasant an experience as possible for her. And though he sensed that she was somewhat overwhelmed by the reality of what she'd done, she seemed to be holding up rather well under the circumstances.

All too aware of how her quiet life had been turned upside down in the past twenty-four hours, he couldn't help but admire her tenacity. She was the kind of woman any man would be proud to have by his side. Just as he was now.

Unfortunately, despite Alex's urging, he'd given her no reason to feel the same way about him. But then, that was the way he wanted it to be, wasn't it? No matter how much he cared for her—and he did, to an alarming degree, he realized with something akin to despair—eventually Giovanni Buschetti would no longer be a threat to her, and she'd leave him. The sooner he learned to live with that fact, the better off he'd be.

It was decided that Sister Estrelita and Sister Raphaela would ride to Devlin's house with Juan Carlos and Annie Moreno, while Father Hernandez and Mr. Wiley would walk the short distance together. With Alex, Mrs. Santos and Timmy in the back seat of the Jeep and Laura sitting beside him, Devlin drove on ahead.

Not surprisingly, no one said much, but at least the general mood wasn't as dour as it could have been. Alex was his usual laconic self, but Timmy bounced excitedly on the seat and Mrs. Santos smiled serenely. As for Laura, she alternately stared out the window and gazed surreptitiously at the gold wedding band she now wore, a bemused expression on her face.

Devlin had thought long and hard about buying the rings. They hadn't been absolutely necessary. But the fact that they would signify his union with Laura as husband and wife in an irrefutable way had finally decided him.

That and his own foolish desire to have her wear his ring, if only for a short time.

They arrived at the house a few minutes before their guests, and as they were crossing the garden Devlin had the most ridiculous urge to sweep Laura into his arms and carry her across his threshold.

Talk about crazy, he thought. He'd already done more than enough to make their marriage look like the real thing. And he doubted Laura would appreciate the gesture.

But once the idea had taken hold, he couldn't seem to stop himself.

"Wait," he murmured, catching her by the hand as Alex, Mrs. Santos and Timmy preceded them through the doorway.

"What?" She gazed up at him, her eyes questioning.

"I just wanted to welcome you home," he said as he scooped her up, strode into the house, then set her on her feet again. "Mrs. Gray."

"Thank you," she stammered, blushing prettily as Timmy giggled gleefully, Mrs. Santos nodded her approval and Alex shook his head disgustedly.

Feeling rather pleased with himself, Devlin grabbed Bitsy by the collar before the dog had a chance to slobber on Laura's dress.

"I'd better get the mutt out of here before our guests arrive," he said, hauling the dog across the kitchen.

While Devlin banished Bitsy to his office, then returned to the kitchen and opened the champagne he'd had chilling in the refrigerator, Mrs. Santos donned her apron and put the finishing touches on the meal she'd been preparing most of the day.

Laura leaned against the counter, looking slightly shell-shocked, but as soon as her friends joined them, she seemed to pull herself together. Plastering a bright smile on her face, she accepted the glass of sparkling wine Devlin offered her, then stood beside him, holding her head high, as Juan Carlos proposed a toast to the bride and groom.

Devlin had expected her to spend the time before dinner huddling with Annie and the others, but she stayed close to him, looping her arm through his as if she not only needed but wanted his support, as well. He was more than happy to oblige her, showing off the talent for trading inanities he'd honed while on assignment at the embassy in El Norte.

From the glaring looks Annie Moreno shot his way, he knew the woman wanted more than anything to get Laura alone. But as long as Laura seemed disinclined to leave his side, he wasn't about to take the hint. He'd vowed to protect her, and if that meant from her well-meaning friends as well as her enemies, then so be it.

Luckily Timmy did his part, as well, albeit unintentionally, as he went from one guest to another, drawing their attention away from his mother with his happy chatter.

Dinner was served buffet-style, and as Devlin and Laura waited for the others to help themselves, Mrs. Santos took him aside for a moment.

"Is everything all right, Señor Gray?" she asked, her cheeks rosy from the heat of the oven, her dark eyes sparkling mischievously.

"Everything is perfect," he assured her, grateful as always for the elderly woman's loyalty and devotion.

He wasn't sure how he'd earned it. Nor was he sure why she chose not to believe the worst of him as almost everyone in San Pedro did. But her staunch support meant a lot to him.

"Then, with your permission, I will slip away for a short while and move the *señora*'s things into your bedroom."

Taken aback, Devlin stared at the woman wordlessly. He'd been so sure he'd thought of everything, but he hadn't considered how their sleeping arrangements would change, *should* change, once he and Laura were husband and wife.

Glancing at Laura, he was grateful to see that she was busy helping Timmy fill a plate with food and apparently hadn't overheard Mrs. Santos's remark. Not that her knowing would make any difference as to whether or not he accepted the housekeeper's offer. The way he saw it, he had no real choice. Still, he'd rather explain the situation to Laura in private.

Even Mrs. Santos, loyal soul that she was, would find it odd if he and his bride didn't share the same bedroom. And though she was normally closemouthed, he knew she'd have a hard time keeping such information to herself.

Devlin could think of nothing he'd rather do less than spend night after night for weeks, maybe even months, lying beside Laura, unable to take her in his arms, to hold her, kiss her, caress her. Talk about sheer torture.

But if he had any hope at all of staving off an attempt by Giovanni to get his hands on Timmy, Devlin knew he'd have to be damn sure there could be no question that he was Laura's husband... in every way.

Forcing himself to smile appreciatively, he nodded to the housekeeper.

"Thank you, Mrs. Santos. That's very kind of you."

The meal progressed smoothly with everyone seated around the dining room table. Mrs. Santos returned to the kitchen as they were finishing and served the richly decorated cake she'd baked herself. Soon afterward, Timmy began to yawn and the housekeeper offered to put him to bed. Then Father Hernandez, Mr. Wiley and the good sisters announced that they were ready to take their leave.

Though they didn't have far to go, Devlin offered to have Alex drive them home. However, as it was still relatively early, they decided to make the most of the lovely evening and walk, instead.

Returning to the dining room after seeing them out, Devlin found it empty. No one was in the living room or the kitchen, either. For a moment he wondered if Juan Carlos and Annie had somehow managed to whisk Laura away while he was otherwise occupied. Then, hearing voices coming from the garden, he shook his head at his foolishness.

He started toward the door, intending to join them, only to pause uncertainly as Annie Moreno's voice drifted into the kitchen.

"But why didn't you come to us? We could have helped you. Why did you have to marry *him?*"

"Giovanni is a dangerous man, and Devlin knows better than you do how to deal with his type," Laura replied, her voice matter-of-fact. "And I didn't *have* to marry Devlin, Annie. He asked and I accepted."

"Even knowing he's a—a criminal?"

"All I really know about Devlin Gray is that he's been good to me and my son. He's also promised to keep us safe, and I believe he will."

"I just wish you hadn't acted so hastily," Annie said. "If you'd at least told us yourself—"

"I'm sorry, I couldn't," Laura cut in. "But thanks for coming to the wedding on such short notice. You don't know how much your being there meant to me. And I hope you'll find it in your heart to accept Devlin as my husband. Otherwise...otherwise I think it would be best if we...went our separate ways."

He'd thought the moment Laura was alone with her friends she'd seek their commiseration. Yet she was not only defending him but placing herself firmly in his camp.

Somehow Devlin hadn't expected that kind of loyalty from her. That she was giving it, willingly, filled him with unwonted pleasure.

"So, the lady's more than a little fond of you after all," Alex murmured, causing him to miss Annie's response to Laura's ultimatum. "Congratulations, pal."

Startled half out of his wits, Devlin whirled and glared at the younger man.

"One of these days, Payton, you're going to sneak up on me and I'm going to punch your lights out," he muttered angrily.

"I'll be looking forward to your trying," Alex retorted, then nodded toward the doorway. "But right now I'd move away from the door if I were you. Looks like they're coming back inside again."

As Alex disappeared down the hallway, Devlin crossed to the counter and busied himself pouring brandy into a snifter. He had no real desire for the heady liquor, but he didn't want Laura and her friends to know he'd been spying on them, either.

Glancing his way as she led the Morenos into the kitchen, Laura smiled hesitantly.

"I...I was showing Annie and Juan Carlos the garden," she explained with a cheerfulness that did nothing to belie the weariness Devlin saw in her eyes.

"Your roses are lovely," Annie offered in a grudging tone, her gaze no warmer than it had been earlier.

"Very lovely," Juan Carlos agreed, not exactly overly affable himself.

Sighing inwardly, Devlin raised his glass. "Can I offer you a brandy, or perhaps another cup of coffee?"

He knew better than to think they'd be easily won over, even with Laura standing up for him. Not with the reputation he'd made for himself over the past few years. But at least they weren't quite as openly hostile anymore.

"Thank you, no," Juan Carlos replied. "I think we'd best be going." He took his wife by the arm and nodded graciously. "We appreciate your hospitality, Mr. Gray." Turning to Laura, he smiled affectionately as he added, "All the best to you, my dear."

"Yes, all the best," Annie said in a conciliatory tone.

"Thank you," Laura murmured.

The two women exchanged a quick hug, then stepped apart self-consciously.

Setting his brandy aside, Devlin took Laura by the hand and together they led their guests to the front door. After saying a final goodbye, Devlin closed and locked the door, then walked back to the kitchen with Laura.

Having tucked Timmy into bed, Mrs. Santos had returned to the kitchen, too, and had begun to put away the leftovers. When Laura offered to help, the woman shook her head reproachfully.

"Oh, no, señora, not on your wedding night. I will take care of everything down here. You go upstairs with your husband."

Her face bright red, Laura lowered her gaze.

"Of course," she muttered as she turned and headed toward the hallway.

As she passed him, Devlin caught her hand and squeezed it reassuringly.

"I'll be up in a minute. I have to let Bitsy out."

She stared at him uncertainly, then continued on her way.

"I would have seen to the dog, *señor,*" Mrs. Santos chided.

"I know, but he's been cooped up all evening. He's probably feeling a little miffed."

"Ah, don't tell me you're nervous," she teased.

"Not at all," he growled, ignoring her laughter.

Bitsy greeted him lazily, none the worse for having spent the past few hours sleeping on the old sofa in Devlin's office. Stalling shamelessly, Devlin roughhoused with the dog for a few minutes. Finally, aware that he couldn't wait any longer if he wanted to talk to Laura privately about the change in their sleeping arrangements, he sent Bitsy off to the kitchen.

Then, recalling how Laura had come to his defense out in the garden, he crossed his fingers and hoped for the best as he started up the staircase.

She was standing in the dimly lit hallway, her back against the wall just outside the doorway of the room she'd shared with her son the night before. As he walked toward her, she gazed at him, her eyes filled with confusion.

"Is Timmy all right?" he asked

"He's sound asleep." A smile flickered across her lips. "He didn't even stir when I kissed him good-night. But..." As her voice trailed away, she ducked her head with obvious anxiety.

"What?" he prodded as if he didn't already know.

"My things." She paused and glanced at him, then looked away again. "They're gone."

Wordlessly Devlin took her gently by the arm. He led her across the hallway, opened his bedroom door and, sensing her sudden hesitation, drew her inside, then quickly shut the door again.

In the warm, golden glow of the small bedside lamp, Devlin saw that Mrs. Santos had outdone herself preparing the wedding chamber. Vases of roses sat atop the dresser and chest, while Laura's bouquet lay on the nightstand. The brass bed, freshly polished and made up with lace-edged white linen sheets and pillowcases and a navy-and-white-pin-striped satin comforter, gleamed invitingly. As a final touch,

Mrs. Santos had draped a pale pink cotton nightgown—Laura's, he presumed—over the armchair near the window.

He didn't need this. Did *not* need this at all.

"You, you said...you wouldn't—we wouldn't," Laura stammered, her voice barely above a whisper as she shrank away from him.

"And I meant it," he said, shrugging off the hurt he felt at her all-too-apparent aversion to him. "Believe me, this wasn't *my* idea."

"Then, why...?" She gestured toward the bed as if at a loss for words.

"Mrs. Santos assumed that as my wife you'd naturally share my bed."

"But we agreed—"

"I know. Unfortunately, I didn't consider how it would look to someone like Mrs. Santos if we didn't sleep together. She's a fairly trustworthy old soul. But I doubt she'd be able to resist telling her friends we were sleeping in separate rooms. And you know as well as I do that we have to make sure no one can question whether we're really husband and wife, especially until I can arrange for the civil ceremony."

Without a word Laura crossed the bedroom, seeming to want to put as much distance between them as possible. She paused by one of the windows and stood with her back to him, her dejection evident in the sudden slump of her shoulders.

"I'm not any happier about this than you are," he continued, pulling off his jacket and tossing it on the bed, then working loose the knot in his tie. "But for the time being we're going to have to make the best of the situation." He hung his tie over the brass footboard, unbuttoned his shirt halfway down his chest and rolled up his sleeves. "Whether we like it or not, you're going to have to sleep in here with me."

Still, she stayed by the window, staring silently into the darkness.

"Listen, I've got some work to do down in my office. I won't be finished until well past midnight, and I won't... disturb you when I come back."

She glanced over her shoulder at him then, but standing in the shadows as she was, her pale eyes were unreadable. He wished she'd say something, *anything*, but after no more than a moment or two, she turned away again.

Fighting the urge to go to her, to put his hands on her, to make her look at him—really *look*—and listen to what he wanted, more than anything, to tell her, Devlin spun on his heel, strode across the room and walked out, quietly closing the door after him.

He walked down the stairs as swiftly and silently as he could, glad that Mrs. Santos was still busy in the kitchen. Unlocking the door to his office, he stepped inside, then shut and locked it again.

After taking the day off, he had more than enough to keep him busy well into the night. By the time he returned to his "bride" she should be fast asleep. And he should have his raging hormones under control again.

With a flip of a switch he turned on his computer, then typed in the first of the many codes that would eventually connect him to the "home office." But as he stared at the screen, all he could see was his bed, covered in linen and lace, and Laura, standing by the window, willing him to be gone.

With only the soft hum of the computer cutting through the silence surrounding him, Devlin tried to focus on the past. But his heart ached with loneliness, and longing stirred in his soul, rendering him unable to think of anything, or anyone, but his wife.

Long after Devlin left her, Laura stood by the bedroom window, staring out into the darkness as the cool, fragrant air of late evening wafted over her. Once again she'd chased him away, and once again she knew it was for the best. Yet she couldn't help feeling that she'd wounded him in some way by her silence.

But considering the tack their conversation had taken, what could she have said to him? That she didn't mind sharing his bed? Not after he'd insisted it hadn't been his idea. And, anyway, she would have been lying. Wouldn't she?

Twisting the gold band she now wore on the third finger of her left hand, Laura thought of the way he'd kissed her at the church and the way she'd kissed him back, and she knew, deep in her foolish heart, that she would have actually been telling the sad truth.

Oh, she'd been honestly shocked, even momentarily appalled, when she'd first realized she was going to have to sleep in the same bed with him. But not because she'd found the prospect distasteful. She simply hadn't been prepared for the possibility of having to do so even though she could understand now why it was necessary.

Since they'd agreed their relationship wouldn't include sex, she'd assumed she'd just go on sharing the room across the hall with her son. Finding out that wasn't to be the case had been a surprise, but one from which she'd recovered quickly enough.

And suddenly, as she'd gazed at the brass bed made up with white linen, lace and elegantly striped satin, she'd found herself thinking of what it would be like to have Devlin make love to her there.

Everything he'd said and done since she'd joined him at the altar at St. Rita's had made her feel as if they really were husband and wife. He'd been kind to her, even oddly affectionate, and he'd seemed so proud to have her by his side.

She'd been increasingly drawn to him, physically as well as emotionally, until, standing there in his bedroom, she'd thought for one long, nonsensical moment that surely it *couldn't* hurt to give in to her inordinate yearning.

But then, Devlin had made it clear that he was anything but enthusiastic about the situation.

I'm not any happier about this than you are.

His words came back to her, making her cringe all over again. He'd probably meant to reassure her, but instead, she'd felt as if she'd been firmly put in her place. Though he'd put on a good show for her friends, he'd let her know that he was only doing what he must to help her keep her son safe.

Afraid that her overwhelming sense of regret would be all too apparent, she'd crossed to the window and turned her back on him. He was only abiding by the ground rules she'd insisted upon at the outset, she'd reminded herself. By mutual agreement their marriage was intended to be only a sham, and obviously, one kiss hadn't changed that for Devlin.

Just as she wouldn't allow it to change anything for her, she'd silently vowed as he'd made his excuses, then left her alone at last.

Yet there she was, feeling as if she'd somehow hurt *his* feelings.

Surely she'd only imagined the anguished look in his eyes when she'd glanced at him just before he'd gone. He'd been so adamant about his own dismay at having to share a bed with her that he couldn't possibly have minded that she'd given the impression—as she sincerely hoped she had—that she felt the same way, too.

But what if he had minded?

Then he should have said something. She wasn't a mind reader, after all. She'd sworn she was going to be more considerate of him, and she'd assumed she was doing just that by keeping her innermost wants and needs to herself. She was taking enough advantage of him. She had no right to use him to assuage her vague, unaccountable and, almost certainly, fleeting desire to be held and kissed and caressed.

More weary and confused than she ever thought she'd be, Laura finally moved away from the window. She'd had two long, emotionally tumultuous days. She couldn't expect herself to still be thinking straight, much less acting rationally. The last thing she needed was another confrontation with him tonight. And if he came back to the room and caught her moping about...

Better to be "safely" tucked into bed, sound asleep, or at least pretending to be, before he returned. Otherwise, she might end up making a real fool of herself.

Wishing she had something more substantial to sleep in, something like flannel pajamas, she grabbed her pale pink cotton nightgown off the chair and crossed to the bathroom.

Mrs. Santos's indulgent touch was evident there, too. On the counter a crystal bud vase held a single red rose, while candles of varying sizes and shapes had been strategically placed around the deep, old-fashioned, square tile bathtub. A selection of bath oils and lotions had been set out, as well, along with piles of fresh, fluffy towels.

For one long moment Laura thought of Devlin again, thought of joining him in the bathtub, the candles burning and warm water lapping over their bodies as they touched—

Aware that she'd allowed herself to be drawn into the sensual spell the housekeeper had tried so valiantly to cast, Laura gave herself a firm mental shake. There would be no long, leisurely bath, nor any mad, passionate lovemaking with Devlin Gray tonight—or any night—she reminded herself as she kicked off her pumps and stripped out of her dress, hose and underwear.

She stepped into the bathtub and stood under the shower spray just long enough to cool her heated skin. Then she put on her gown, washed her face, brushed her teeth and returned to the bedroom. She hung her dress in the closet that held the rest of her clothes, then hung the coat and tie Devlin had left on the bed in the other one.

Finally she walked back to the bed. Hesitating a moment, she tried to decide which side she should sleep on. Then, with a slight shrug, she pulled back the top sheet and satin coverlet and sat on "her" side. If Devlin wanted to trade tomorrow night, he could say so, she thought as she pulled the pearl clip from her hair, tossing it on the nightstand along with her earrings. She ran her fingers through her hair, massaging her scalp, willing herself to relax.

When she could put if off no longer, she reached up and switched off the lamp. Turning her back to the bedroom door, she scooted as close to the edge of the double bed as she could and snuggled into her pillow. The linen sheets and pillowcase, smelling of lemon soap and sunshine, felt incredibly soft and cool against her skin. And the moonlight filtering through the windows, casting odd yet amicable shadows around the room, combined with the familiar night noises she was used to hearing at home to fill her with a sense of well-being.

With a soft sigh of what could almost have been contentment, she closed her eyes and gradually began to relax. As she had the night before, she knew she needed to sleep. Then she'd be ready to face whatever awaited her tomorrow....

The sound of the bedroom door opening and closing, no more than a gentle click followed by a quiet whoosh, then another click, startled her out of what must have been a light sleep. According to the clock on the nightstand, over an hour had passed since she'd turned off the lamp. It was after midnight, and if the sounds of splashing water coming from behind the bathroom door were any indication, Devlin was getting ready to come to bed.

Lying as still as she could, hardly daring to breath, Laura heard him return to the bedroom, his footfall barely noticeable against the tile floor. He tossed something onto the chair by the window—probably his shirt and slacks, from the rustling sound she heard—and continued on to the bed, where he eased back the top sheet and coverlet on his side, obviously trying not to disturb her.

As she had, he lay down as close to his edge of the mattress as he could, leaving what seemed like a huge, gaping space between them even though they were sharing a relatively small double bed. However, she sensed that rather than turning his back to her, he'd stretched out facing her, so that she could almost feel him watching her as she stared into the moonlit darkness.

Why? she wondered, forcing herself to breathe slowly, evenly, though every nerve ending in her body tingled with awareness. Did he know she was awake? And if so, did it make any difference to him? Surely not. He couldn't possibly want to *talk* to her at this late hour. As for anything else . . .

He'd sworn he wouldn't touch her without an invitation which she certainly wasn't about to offer. So why didn't he just roll over and go to sleep so she could do the same? Why was he so intent on studying her silently as the shadows shifted around them?

Despite the tension thrumming through her, she gradually grew attuned to the rhythm of his breathing, taking a breath, then letting it out along with him, almost as if they were one. And though he continued to keep his distance, she couldn't help but feel the warmth radiating from his body against her back.

Strangely soothed by his seemingly benign presence, she began to feel herself relax once more. Her eyelids drifted closed and she uttered a soft sigh, then shivered slightly as a wisp of cool breeze drifted over her bare shoulders.

A moment later her eyes flew open and she tensed again as Devlin gently drew the lace-edged sheet up over her. For an instant his hand smoothed over her tangled curls, his touch light and undemanding. Then, finally, with the barest hint of a groan, he rolled away from her, leaving her with an odd, inexplicable sense of desolation.

For the space of a heartbeat or two, she'd almost hoped—

Silly fool, she chided herself mercilessly. He was just being considerate. Stupid to make something out of nothing more than a kind gesture. Especially when the "something" she found herself wanting would only cause her grief in the long run.

Wondering if she'd ever learn from her mistakes, Laura closed her eyes again. She hadn't reminded herself once all day of what she'd gotten herself into by falling in love with Johnny Buschetti. Maybe if she had, she wouldn't have been drawn to Devlin quite so easily.

However, it certainly wasn't too late to start now. In fact, this seemed like the perfect time to dwell on just how worrisome life could be when your husband chose to live outside the law. Especially when you had more than your own well-being to consider.

Turning her face into her pillow, she willed away the hot sting of hopeless tears in her eyes. She'd cried in front of Devlin Gray once. She wouldn't do it again, even here in the dark. Especially here in the dark.

Instead, she'd think of the future when she and Timmy would be on their own again, free to do as they pleased once Giovanni was no longer a threat. They could go to the market, walk in the park, fly his kite, just the two of them. As for Devlin Gray, he'd be only a memory.

A memory she could live with, as long as it wasn't painful. But only she could guarantee it wouldn't be.

Devlin knew the instant Laura finally drifted off to sleep, just as he'd known by her unnatural stillness and her short, shallow breaths that she'd been awake when he'd first lain down beside her.

She'd probably been afraid he'd renege on his promise. And the way he'd been feeling, he would have if he'd been born without a conscience. Then he'd have been able to have his way with her without regret.

Unfortunately...

With a weary sigh he eased onto his back and stared at the ceiling. Aside from ascertaining that Drago Espinosa hadn't surfaced anywhere in the past twenty-four hours, he'd gotten very little work done after he'd left Laura alone in their bedroom. And now it looked as if he wasn't going to get any rest, either.

While suffering through two more or less sleepless nights in a row wasn't all that unusual for him, insomnia coupled with his current state of arousal was going to leave him feeling just a mite irritable come morning. He'd probably do something obnoxious like snarl at poor Mrs. Santos. Then the elderly woman would realize his wedding night hadn't been a success, and this charade would end up being all for nothing.

But he didn't dare get up and go back to the bathroom for the cold shower and sleeping pills that would help him get the rest he needed for fear of disturbing Laura. At least as long as she was asleep.

Beside him she murmured softly, unintelligibly, then shifted onto her right side, facing him, all without waking. Hardly daring to breathe, Devlin turned toward her, as if drawn by a magnet, and studied her face in the moonlight.

She was lovely, so very lovely with her fair skin and thick, dark tangle of curls. Ever so gently he traced the line of one finely arched brow with the tip of his finger, then brushed a wisp of hair away from her face, his gaze lingering on the curve of her lips, then lowering slowly to the swell of her breast, rose tipped beneath the fabric of her—

She murmured again, and he swiftly pulled his hand away, aware that he was not only increasing his torment but also running the risk of scaring her half to death. If she awoke and found him fondling her, she'd more than likely scream bloody murder.

Again Laura shifted beside him, this time closing the distance between them. Suddenly she was curled close to him, one hand resting on his chest, one leg brushing against his thigh, her head tucked under his chin.

For what seemed like an eternity he lay perfectly still, sure that she would realize what she'd done and move away from him again. Instead, she seemed to settle in contentedly, turning her face so that her lips grazed the bare skin at the base of his throat.

His body fairly humming with desire, he finally put his arms around her.

"Devlin?" she whispered, her voice slurred.

"Right here, sweetheart," he soothed, stroking her back.

As if his simple statement had reassured her, she quieted, her breathing once again slow and deep.

Feeling as if he'd been given a wondrous gift, Devlin tightened his hold on her imperceptibly. In the clear light of day she'd more than likely come to her senses. But for tonight...

Tonight she belonged to him.

Chapter 7

It was the twitter and chirp of birds greeting the new day that first lured Laura out of the deep, restful sleep that had taken her through the night. But it was the sudden realization that she was not only lying in Devlin's bed but in his arms that startled her into complete wakefulness.

How on earth had she ended up pressed against him, one arm thrown across his narrow waist just above the waistband of his briefs, a leg drawn up over his, her head against his bare, bronzed chest? If she wasn't mistaken, she'd started out on the other side of the mattress, her back turned to him. For the life of her, she couldn't remember moving, but obviously she must have.

Maybe the temperature had dropped lower than normal during the night and she'd unconsciously sought out the heat of his body. Yes, that had to be it.

But she wasn't cold now. Quite the contrary, in fact.

As she lay close to him, breathing in the clean, slightly musky, wholly masculine scent of him, his warmth seemed to envelop her. She hadn't felt quite so safe, so secure, so at peace since Johnny had been killed.

Nor had she felt so aroused, she realized as she gradually became aware of how her breast nudged Devlin's chest through the thin fabric of her nightgown, how the softness of her belly molded around his hip, how, by shifting ever so slightly, she could rub—

"So, you *are* awake," Devlin murmured, his deep, husky voice rumbling through her.

Her pulse racing, her face flushing with embarrassment, Laura tried to pull away from him.

What in the world had come over her? Bad enough that she'd invaded his space unknowingly sometime during the night. Especially when he hadn't wanted her in his bed in the first place. But to linger there once she was awake, luxuriating in lascivious thoughts...

She ought to be ashamed of herself for not moving away from him immediately. She *was* ashamed of herself.

"I'm—I'm sorry. I didn't mean to..."

Her voice trailed away as she realized he wasn't letting her go. Instead, he'd tightened his hold on her, not painfully but just enough so that she couldn't easily slip out of his arms.

"No problem," he said, dismissing her apology, his breath whispering against the wisps of hair curling around her face.

Beneath her cheek she could feel the slow, steady beat of his heart.

"But I shouldn't..." she protested, tipping her face up and meeting his gaze.

Though his long, dark hair was tousled and the line of his jaw once again bewhiskered, he looked as if he'd been awake for quite some time. And though she wasn't sure why, just the thought of that made her extremely nervous.

"Shouldn't what?" He regarded her steadily, his expression rather grave, seemingly in no hurry to release her.

Shouldn't be anywhere near you if I want to keep my wits about me.

She ducked her head in confusion. Why was he torment-ing her? He had to know how uncomfortable she was. And since he didn't want—

Or did he?

Had she unwittingly started something he now expected her to finish? There was no denying *she* had sought him out during the night. They were clearly lying as close to *his* side of the bed as they possibly could.

But surely he must realize she hadn't been cognizant of what she'd done. She'd been sound asleep, for goodness' sake.

And only a real cad would take such an obviously unin-tentional indiscretion as an invitation.

"Shouldn't have imposed on you this way," she stated primly. "I must have caught a chill during the night or—or something."

"Or something." He slid a finger under her chin and tilted her face up, forcing her to look at him. "You're not impos-ing on me, Laura. Not at all."

Before she could offer any further protest, he bent his head and kissed her, teasing her lips apart with a tender in-sistence that left her powerless to resist. And, as she had in the church, she clung to him and kissed him back.

With a low groan Devlin shifted slightly, leaning over her, pressing her against the mattress, his fingertips trailing down the side of her neck, then grazing over the swell of her breast to tease at her nipple.

Feeling as if she were on fire, Laura arched against him, running her hands down his bare back, wanting, *needing*, so much more.

Groaning again, Devlin tore his mouth from hers.

"Take your gown off, Laura," he urged, nipping at her neck as he ran his hand down the length of her body, then up under the soft cotton fabric.

At the touch of his callused palm against the bare skin of her belly, Laura suddenly came to her senses. She had to stop him—stop *herself*—now.

"You promised," she whispered, unable to keep the panic welling through her from reverberating in her voice. "You promised we wouldn't..."

If she let him make love to her, or worse, made love *with* him—as she more than likely would—she'd be lost.

"I thought maybe you'd changed your mind," he muttered. "But I guess not, huh?"

"No," she said, trying desperately to deny the wave of longing that washed over her, then pooled deep in the core of her femininity, as she turned her face away.

When he didn't release her immediately, she risked another glance at him. He met her gaze, his eyes filled with regret, then finally rolled away from her.

"Sorry, I seem to have misunderstood," he said as he swung his legs over the side of the bed and stood.

Pulling the edge of the sheet up over her shoulders, Laura scooted away from him, aware as she did so of how ridiculously she was behaving. One minute she was all but begging him to make love to her, and the next she was acting like a prudish old maid.

"I'm the one who should apologize. I didn't intend to lead you on."

Gathering her courage, she looked up at him; then, her mouth going dry, sincerely wished she hadn't.

Naked except for a pair of black cotton briefs, against which the evidence of his masculine desire thrust boldly, he gave new meaning to the term *male animal*. She had found him attractive before, but now...

Staring at his sun-bronzed, sleekly muscled body, Laura trembled not with fear, but anticipation. He hadn't acted like a man who didn't want her in his bed. Oh, he'd acceded to her wishes...for now. But if the gleam in his eyes was any indication, he wasn't finished with her yet. Not by a long shot.

As for her, she could deny her desire all she wanted. But her first night with him, she'd instinctively sought him out in her sleep. And when he'd literally welcomed her with open arms, what little resistance she'd finally mustered had been token at best.

She knew she was fighting a losing battle, but what else could she do? Once she gave herself to him, heart and soul, walking away from him would be impossible. Yet, how could she tie herself to a man like Devlin Gray? What kind of future would Timmy have if she knowingly threw in her lot with a common criminal?

"You didn't lead me on," Devlin said, his tone amazingly nonchalant as he drew her from her reverie.

She'd assumed he'd be angry or upset, or maybe even hurt, but from the look on his face he seemed not to mind at all that he'd been so rudely rebuffed. In fact, if she hadn't seen for herself how sexually aroused he'd been, she'd have been tempted to believe that he'd only been toying with her.

"Maybe we could put a pillow between us tonight," she suggested, lowering her gaze again.

"Whatever you want," he readily agreed, then added as he turned away, "I'll be out of here in fifteen minutes max. Then you can have the room to yourself again."

Leaning back against her pillow, Laura watched as Devlin opened first one dresser drawer then another, pulling out clean underwear, a gray T-shirt and a pair of faded cutoffs.

She doubted she'd go back to sleep, especially since Timmy would probably be awake soon. But once they were up and dressed, she had no idea what Devlin expected them to do with themselves. She imagined he'd appreciate it if they stayed out of his way, and she'd be more than happy to oblige. But first, she had to have an idea of how best to go about it.

"Do you...do you have any plans for today?" she asked, hesitant to pry into what he might not feel was her business.

"Not really." He glanced over his shoulder at her. "Why? Is there something special you'd like to do?"

Encouraged by his solicitous tone of voice, Laura told him about Timmy's desire to go back to their house and get a few more of his things.

"We can drive over after breakfast if that's agreeable to you," Devlin offered.

"Oh, yes," Laura assured him gratefully.

"Anything else?"

"Not that I can think of."

"Well, just let me know if you do. I'll take you wherever you want to go."

"Oh, you don't have to do that," she protested, not wanting to impose on him any more than was absolutely necessary.

"For the time being, I don't think it would be a good idea for you and your son to go out alone," he observed pragmatically.

Aware that he was right, Laura murmured a quiet, "Yes, of course."

With a curt nod Devlin strode into the bathroom and closed the door.

Feeling as if she'd been dismissed, Laura plumped up her pillow and turned onto her side. Too bad she couldn't put him out of her mind so easily, she thought, watching the pale beams of sunlight play across the tile floor. But the sound of the shower made that impossible. Squeezing her eyes shut, she tried to will away the tantalizing image of steamy water sluicing over his naked body.

Unfortunately, it wasn't until he walked out the bedroom door, presumably groomed and dressed, that she finally felt some of her tension dissolve.

Unless she found an acceptable way to deal with her attraction to Devlin, she was afraid she was going to end up in a truly sorry state of mind. And she certainly wouldn't be of any use to her son then.

She was married to the man temporarily. She had to sleep in his bed, also temporarily. But she was strong enough to resist his incredibly potent allure despite their forced intimacy. She had to be.

Otherwise, she'd have to resign herself to living with the consequences, no matter how deplorable they turned out to be.

Her resolve reinforced once again, Laura climbed out of bed and crossed to the window. Leaning on the sill, she inhaled a breath of cool morning air as she gazed down at the quiet street below, then off toward the mountains rising into the clear blue sky beyond the northern edge of town.

Until Thursday, when Vincent Petrano had called her name, she'd always felt safe in San Pedro. And, to a certain extent, she still did. She had no doubt that Devlin would protect her and her son from Giovanni. But only she could guard against the danger Devlin posed to her. Could and would, once she had some idea how to go about it.

Turning away from the window, she looked around the bedroom with sudden interest. Last night she'd been too distracted to notice much about her surroundings beyond the lovely, antique brass bed. Now she saw that the other furnishings were of good quality, as well. The richly polished dark wood of the dresser, oval mirror, chest of drawers and matching nightstands contrasted nicely with the white stucco walls, adding warmth to the room.

At least he had good taste, she mused. However, after three years she'd have thought the place would have a more lived-in look about it. But aside from her bouquet, hair clip and earrings, the room seemed oddly impersonal to her.

There were no photographs, no books or papers, no mementos of any kind atop the dresser or chest. Nothing at all that marked the room as Devlin's. Had she not known better, she'd have thought she was in a hotel room rather than someone's private sleeping quarters.

Of course, he could have had Mrs. Santos put everything away, but Laura doubted it. Devlin might live in this house and sleep in this bedroom, but from all she'd seen so far, this wasn't his *home*. This was merely the place where he'd chosen to stay until...

He was forced to move on?

He didn't act like a man on the run. But from the look of his bedroom, he didn't appear to have put down roots here, either, even after three years.

As she had more often than she'd liked to admit over the past few weeks, Laura wondered what Devlin Gray was really doing in San Pedro. Maybe he wasn't some sort of criminal, after all, she thought with a surge of hope that thoroughly disconcerted her.

But if he was something other than what he'd gone to such great lengths to lead everyone in town to think he was, wouldn't he have told her Thursday night? Surely he wouldn't have allowed her to believe he was capable of dealing with someone like Giovanni Buschetti if he really wasn't.

Not that he had to be in the same league as her father-in-law to be just as ruthless.

Maybe he was actually a high-powered business executive, a corporate CEO, on some kind of sabbatical, and Alex Payton was a member of his upper-level management team, come to report on how the company was faring in his absence.

Talk about wishful thinking, Laura chided herself, shaking her head at her foolishness. Still...

Her curiosity piqued, she crossed to the dresser. She hesitated a moment; then, telling herself she wasn't really snooping through Devlin's things but rather searching for her own clothes, she opened one of the top drawers.

Ten minutes later she finished hanging up the shirt and trousers Devlin had left on the chair by the window, closed the closet door and stood staring into space. Having pawed through all the drawers in the dresser, chest and nightstands and having searched both closets carefully, she knew hardly anything more about her husband than she had when she started.

He favored cotton briefs and unadorned T-shirts in white and a variety of dark colors. He owned several pairs of jeans, ranging from almost new to old and faded, some sweatpants, shorts and cutoffs. He also had two suits, both well tailored, and a total of three dress shirts, maybe half a dozen silk ties, a pair of Italian loafers, two pairs of sneakers and some sandals. Except for a pair of gold cuff links, a matching tiepin and a relatively inexpensive watch, she hadn't come across any jewelry. Nor had she found any photographs or personal papers.

She wasn't sure what she'd expected, but she was honestly amazed at how modest his tastes seemed to be. And as for his seeming lack of photographs and personal papers, now that she thought about it, she had a feeling he'd moved those into the locked room at the end of the downstairs hallway that Mrs. Santos had told her was his office, so that if she got nosy and poked around among his possessions— as she had, she admitted with a twinge of guilt—she wouldn't happen upon anything incriminating.

Oh, well, she had to at least *try* to find out all she could about him, especially now that she'd thrown in her lot with him, she justified. Although she wouldn't go so far as to attempt to search his office. No, she definitely wouldn't do that.

Of course, simply asking him what she wanted to know might be the simplest way to get some answers. But the mere thought of confronting him face-to-face sent a shiver of apprehension up her spine. While there were some things she'd like to be certain of where Devlin was concerned, she was sure there were also quite a few things she'd rather not know about him.

Since she couldn't choose to listen to only what she wanted to hear, Laura figured she'd be better off letting well enough alone. The more she knew about him, the more of a threat he could perceive her to be. And since she could only hope that he realized she'd never betray him after all he was doing for her, she'd rather not be privy to any of his deepest, darkest secrets if she could possibly help it.

Returning to the dresser, Laura took out fresh underwear for herself, crossed to the closet to retrieve a kelly green, short-sleeved knit dress and sandals, and headed for the bathroom. After she'd washed and dressed, she straightened the bed covers and plumped up the pillows, then walked across the hallway to check on her son.

His room was empty, his bed unmade, but her initial anxiety faded quickly as the sound of his laughter drifted up the staircase.

She found him in the kitchen, sitting on the floor with Devlin, giggling delightedly as Bitsy licked his face, while Mrs. Santos looked on fondly from where she stood by the stove.

"See, I told you he likes little boys," Devlin said to Timmy.

"But he looks kinda scary," her son replied.

"Yeah, well, sometimes looks can be deceiving."

Though Devlin spoke to Timmy, he glanced at Laura as she paused by the counter, leaving no doubt in her mind that his words had been meant for her, as well. And not necessarily in relation to the dog.

"What are you doing?" she asked, turning her attention back to her son as she filled a mug with coffee.

"Making friends with Bitsy," Timmy replied. "I was kinda scared of him when me and Devlin first walked into the kitchen, but I'm not anymore." To prove his point, he rested his cheek against the rottweiler's massive head and gave the dog a hug. "See, Mom? He's really gentle, but only if he likes you." Gazing up at Devlin, he frowned slightly. "What about my mom? Do you think he likes her, too?"

"Oh, I'm sure he does. She's a very likable lady, isn't she?"

Flustered all over again, Laura stared at the mug she held. She had no reason to be so heartened by such an offhand compliment. He was probably just letting her know that he didn't bear any hard feelings toward her despite the way she'd put him off earlier. Yet something about the way he'd looked at her as he spoke made her feel as if she'd been offered more than an idle tribute.

"Breakfast is almost ready, *señor*," Mrs. Santos advised, then added as she turned to Laura, "The men requested *migas, señora*, but if you would prefer something else, I will be happy to prepare it for you."

"Oh, no, *migas* will be fine," she assured the housekeeper.

The dish, made with scrambled eggs, chorizo—a spicy Mexican sausage—and crisp tortillas, was not only one of Timmy's favorites but one of Laura's, too.

"Come on, son," Devlin said, standing easily and helping Timmy to his feet. "Let's wash our hands before we join your mom at the table."

As if he'd been doing it regularly since Timmy was a baby, Devlin boosted the boy up so they could soap their hands at the kitchen sink. Laura's heart warmed toward Devlin considerably as she watched them.

Timmy had obviously taken to him in the short time they'd spent together that morning, and the feeling seemed to be mutual. For that, if nothing else, Laura owed Devlin her deepest gratitude. No matter how difficult the next few weeks might prove to be for her, if her son was not only safe, but secure, as well, she'd manage somehow.

As the three of them sat down at the table in the kitchen alcove, Laura asked about Alex, wondering if they should wait for the younger man to come down.

"He went out very early this morning, *señora*," Mrs. Santos said as she set the dish of steaming *migas* on the table, along with a basket of fresh flour tortillas.

"He's not a very sociable person," Devlin added ruefully. "He also has a bad habit of doing as he pleases regardless of what anyone else expects."

Laura had already assumed as much about him. From the pained look she'd seen on his handsome face on and off yesterday evening, she'd figured he'd been present at the wedding and reception only because Devlin had insisted. Yet, in his own irreverent way, he'd offered her the moral support she'd needed to actually walk down the aisle at St. Rita's and exchange vows with Devlin.

Underneath his cold, hard facade there was something basically decent about him, just as there was about Devlin, and Laura found that reassuring. She'd always believed you could judge a man by the company he kept.

Unfortunately, she hadn't paid much attention to Johnny's friends and associates. She'd been too in love with him to be aware of anyone else. However, she was older and wiser now, and she couldn't help but feel that the more she knew about Alex Payton, the more she would know, albeit indirectly, about Devlin Gray.

"How long will he be staying with . . . us?" she ventured, spooning a generous helping of *migas* onto her plate.

"I'm not sure," Devlin replied, his answer seeming purposely vague. "Does it matter to you?" He frowned thoughtfully, gazing at her from across the table as he rolled a tortilla, then dipped it into a little dish of honey. "He hasn't said or done anything to upset you, has he?"

"No, of course not," she hastened to assure him. "I was just curious."

"I doubt you'll know he's here most of the time, but tell me if he gives you any hassle. He can be rather caustic on occasion."

Talk about the pot calling the kettle black, Laura thought as she lowered her gaze and reached for her mug of coffee. But then, she had an idea that in their line of work, whatever it was, brusque behavior served as a kind of buffer between them and any law-abiding citizens who might otherwise attempt to get in their way.

Granted, Devlin hadn't been quite as boorish as she'd originally expected him to be. But his manner was just aloof enough to let her know that she'd be wise to keep her distance whenever she could.

After breakfast they drove to her house as planned. As Devlin helped her out of the Jeep he dug a set of keys from his pocket and handed them to her.

"What are these for?" she asked.

"The locks on your doors and windows," he stated simply. "I took the liberty of installing them yesterday. Thought it might be a good idea, since you won't be here for a while."

Going to the back of the Jeep, he unloaded the cardboard boxes and two empty suitcases they'd brought with them.

"Thanks." She smiled gratefully as she took the boxes from him, handed one to Timmy and started toward the door.

"*De nada,*" He tossed it off casually, as seemed to be his habit.

Pausing, Laura glanced over her shoulder at him. "Actually, it was very thoughtful of you, Devlin, and I want you to know how much I appreciate it, as well as everything else you've done for us."

"It's been my pleasure, Laura," he replied, holding her gaze in such a way that she had no doubt about his sincerity.

"Are you gonna open the door, Mommy?" Timmy asked.

"Oh, yes."

Feeling slightly disconcerted, Laura fumbled with the set of keys, finally finding the one that fit the front-door lock. She wished Devlin would stop saying things like that to her. When he did, he threw her off balance emotionally, and it seemed to take her longer and longer to recover each time. She was finding it difficult enough to keep her defenses intact. How was she supposed to resist his allure if he continued to beguile her in such a charming way?

While Devlin helped Timmy pack his toys in the boxes, Laura filled the suitcases with the rest of their clothes and a few personal items of her own that she'd originally chosen to leave behind.

Back at his house, they reversed the process, Devlin once again helping Timmy with his toys while Laura unpacked the suitcases. As she carried an armful of shorts and T-shirts into Timmy's room, she overheard her son telling Devlin about his kite.

"My mom bought it for me at the market and Alex helped me put it together. Now I have to see if it will fly. But I don't think my mom wants us to go to the park by ourselves."

"Maybe we could take a picnic lunch and all go together," Devlin suggested, jumping into the opening her son had so guilelessly left him.

"Today?" Timmy pressed.

"Now, Timmy," Laura cautioned. "Remember what we talked about yesterday morning? Devlin may have some work to do this afternoon."

"But, Mom, it's Saturday," he protested.

"Yeah, Mom, it's Saturday, and I don't work on weekends if I can help it. So, unless you have any objections, I say we have a picnic in the park, then do a little kite flying."

Looking from one to the other, Laura figured that if she did oppose the idea, they'd simply go off without her. And it wasn't as if she had any real problem with Devlin's suggestion. She was glad he was making an effort to get along with her son.

Yet she was protective enough of her child not to want them to hit it off *too* well. Timmy both wanted and needed a father figure in his life, but Devlin wasn't exactly the kind of role model from whom an impressionable young boy could benefit. And, of course, she wasn't planning on having him fill the position permanently.

Still, spending an afternoon at the park with Devlin, especially under her watchful eye, shouldn't do her son any serious harm. In fact, after the tumult of the past two days, doing something as simple and mundane as flying a kite would probably do all of them a world of good.

"No objections," she acquiesced at last.

"Then I'll ask Mrs. Santos to pack a lunch for us," Devlin said as Timmy whooped with joy.

Their afternoon turned out to be even more enjoyable than Laura had thought it would be. Though consciously on the lookout for Vincent Petrano or anyone else who might be associated with Giovanni, she managed to relax a little as she sat on the blanket Devlin had spread under a tree along the edge of the meadow, watching him help Timmy launch his kite and keep it aloft.

For a short time, at least, she felt like a normal wife and mother, and while she knew the feeling was dangerously deceptive, she was almost as sorry as her son when twilight began to fall and Devlin announced that it was time for them to go home.

Alex was waiting for them in the garden, stretched out languidly on one of the benches by the fountain, the book he'd been reading open in his lap.

"Ah, the happy family returns," he commented sarcastically, his gaze sweeping over her, then clashing with the warning look she saw in Devlin's eyes. "Did you have a nice time?"

"Oh, yes," Timmy enthused, oblivious to the undercurrents swirling between the two men. "We had a picnic and flew my kite real high, didn't we, Devlin?"

"We did, indeed, Timmy," Devlin replied, tousling the boy's hair affectionately before turning his attention back to Alex. "Were you looking for me for some reason?"

"Not me." He picked up his book, stood and stretched. "Mrs. Santos left something warming in the oven for dinner."

"Have you eaten?"

"About an hour ago."

Limping slowly, his jaw clenched, Alex preceded them into the house. Without pausing in the kitchen, he bid them a curt good-night and disappeared down the hallway.

Frowning, Devlin set the picnic basket on the counter. For a moment Laura thought he'd go after the other man, but he turned to her instead.

"Mrs. Santos has Saturday evening as well as Sunday off. She'll be back first thing Monday morning, but in the meantime, we'll have to fend for ourselves."

"In that case, why don't you help Timmy put his kite away while I set the table?"

Fending for herself, at least around the house, was one thing Laura had been good at since she was twelve and her mother died.

They talked little during dinner, all three of them worn out from their long afternoon out-of-doors. When they finished, Devlin offered to clean up the kitchen while she took Timmy upstairs for a bath. Laura accepted gratefully, and after tucking her son into bed, crossed to their bedroom instead of going back downstairs.

Devlin had probably had enough of her company already, and as she had last night, she'd just as soon be in bed asleep before he joined her. Although, with Mrs. Santos gone for the night, maybe he'd sleep in one of the empty bedrooms down the hall. Then again, maybe not, she thought, eyeing the extra pillow that had been added to the bed sometime during the day.

Maybe we could put a pillow between us.

That had seemed like a reasonable solution to a potential problem, but after showering and slipping into her nightgown then climbing into bed, Laura wasn't all that eager to be the one to put a barrier, however flimsy, between them. Instead, she set the extra pillow atop Devlin's. If he wanted to use it, she'd understand.

Though it was still early, she switched off the lamp, but despite her weariness, she couldn't seem to fall asleep. At least, not until Devlin came to bed a couple of hours later.

Once he'd stretched out beside her, a sense of well-being stole over her, probably due in no small part to the fact that he'd tossed the extra pillow onto the chair. Strange how the presence of someone who filled her with such misgivings could be so comforting, she mused as she uttered a soft sigh and closed her eyes. Very strange, indeed.

As she had Saturday morning, Laura awoke in Devlin's arms again on Sunday without any idea at all how she'd gotten there. But unlike yesterday, her first instinct was to move away from him as swiftly as she could.

She was almost certain he was awake, as well, and she didn't want them starting something she didn't intend to finish. Stopping Devlin the first time had been hard enough. She wasn't sure she had the fortitude to resist his kisses and caresses again.

Yet she stayed where she was, unable to deny herself a few more moments of peace before facing whatever the day held in store for her. Giovanni or his chosen representative could very well show up in San Pedro and demand to see her. Not all that much time had passed since Vincent Petrano had spotted her and Timmy outside the cathedral Thursday morning. But her former father-in-law had never been the type to wait patiently for what he wanted.

As Laura thought of facing him again, a shiver of fear raced up her spine. An instant later she was aware of Devlin stroking her arm, the brush of his fingertips over her skin light and soothing.

Knowing the time had definitely come to put some distance between them, she eased away from him. Wordlessly he let her go, then stood and started toward the bathroom.

She tugged the edge of the sheet up to her chin and lay back against her pillow. Then, feeling as if she'd treated him rather churlishly, she risked a glance at him. At the same moment he looked over his shoulder at her, his gaze almost indifferent.

"I think it would be a good idea if the three of us went to mass at St. Rita's this morning," he said. When she looked at him with surprise, he added, "The more we're seen together, the better."

"Yes, of course," she agreed as she sat up and shoved her hair out of her face.

Somehow she hadn't expected him to be thinking of mass at St. Rita's just then.

"If you can be ready to leave in about an hour, we can make the early service."

"I'll get Timmy up and dressed right away."

"Then I'll see to breakfast so you can dress. Do you and Timmy like French toast?"

"Mmm, yes."

"Good." He smiled slightly, then turned away again. "That's all I know how to make."

As she pulled her lightweight robe from the closet and slipped into it, Laura admitted that Devlin had certainly adjusted to the role of husband and father quite well. At the park he'd been especially good with Timmy. And just now he'd offered to do his share so she wouldn't have to rush.

She was almost tempted to believe that she and Timmy weren't the first wife and child he'd had in his life. But if that was true, then what had happened to them? Had he abandoned them to pursue his criminal activities? Or had he been the one abandoned when the chips were down?

As she had yesterday morning after she'd gone through his things, Laura knew the simplest way to find out was to ask him. But once again, she also realized she might find out a lot more about him than she'd bargained for.

Maybe, as a result of his involvement in a variety of nefarious schemes, Devlin Gray was simply a chameleon of sorts, capable of playing almost any part under almost any circumstances in order to get what he wanted.

Only, he wasn't going to get anything out of helping her and Timmy. Unless she succumbed to the desire that stirred deep inside her whenever he lured her into forgetting their marriage was only a sham.

Quite a few members of the congregation stared at them curiously during the church service, but Laura didn't mind at all. In fact, she took special care to flash her wedding band every chance she got, wanting to be sure as many people as possible spread the word around San Pedro that she was Devlin's wife.

Whatever frowning and tsk-tsking they might do didn't matter to her. Since Devlin's reputation was the one thing that might just give Giovanni Buschetti pause, she could live with a little disapproval from people she didn't really know anyway.

As they left the church after mass, several acquaintances from the expatriate community said hello. Glad to have Devlin's arm around her shoulders, she responded to their greetings, smiling indomitably.

However, when she saw Annie and Juan Carlos standing on the steps, obviously waiting for them, her expression grew more tentative. Annie's friendship meant a lot to her, but Laura wasn't about to let her disparage Devlin no matter how noble her intentions might be.

As the two men shook hands, Annie studied her searchingly, then stepped forward and gave her a quick hug.

"How are you?" she whispered, making no effort to hide her concern.

"I'm fine. Just fine," Laura assured her with a slight laugh. Recalling Alex's comment before the wedding, she added for Annie's ears only, "As you can see, he hasn't eaten me yet."

"Ah, but from the way he looks at you, he'd *like* to," Annie retorted as they moved apart again.

"Like to what?" Devlin asked, putting his arm around Laura's shoulders again in a way she found comforting.

"Uh, invite the three of you to come back to the house and have lunch with us," Annie said, barely missing a beat. "Wouldn't you, Juan Carlos?"

Juan Carlos gazed at his wife quizzically for several moments, then nodded agreeably. "Of course, my dear. Whatever you say."

Laura knew the invitation was spur-of-the-moment at best. She also sensed that Devlin wasn't all that enthusiastic about accepting. And while she'd enjoy visiting with her friends, she now felt that she owed him her first allegiance.

"I'm not sure what Devlin has planned," she said, deferring to him.

"Oh, please, can we?" Timmy begged. "They have swings and monkey bars and a big slide in their garden."

"Now, Timmy—" Laura began.

"We'd enjoy that quite a bit," Devlin cut in graciously, swayed in no small part by her son, she was sure.

Laura wanted to protest that he was doing enough for them already. He shouldn't have to sit through a meal with her friends, too. Especially when they still tended to look at him askance.

But he smiled at her so reassuringly that she could almost have believed there was nothing else he'd rather do. Almost...

They walked the short distance to the Morenos' house. There Devlin and Juan Carlos took Timmy out to the garden while Laura helped Annie put together a light lunch of cold chicken, salad and fresh fruit.

She had no idea what the men would have to discuss, but she trusted Devlin would hold his own with the good doctor. As for her and Annie...

"So, are you having sex with him?" her friend demanded, her voice low, as soon as they were alone.

"Annie, please," Laura begged, frowning discouragingly. "I thought I made it clear that we married only so Devlin could help me keep Johnny's father from getting his hands on Timmy."

"You did. But, Laura, he's tall, dark and dangerously attractive. And you haven't been with anyone for a very long time. You're living in the same house. Of course, if you're not sleeping in the same bedroom..."

Annie's voice trailed away invitingly, but Laura refused to respond as obviously expected. Annie was her closest friend in San Pedro, and they'd talked a lot about their pasts as well as their hopes and dreams for the future. Annie knew why Laura had come to San Pedro. And Laura knew about Annie's flight from her wealthy Texas family, a flight that had ended in a near-fatal automobile accident on a winding mountain road north of town.

Juan Carlos, a recent widower with three young daughters, had saved her life, and despite the twenty-year difference in their ages, Annie had married him and gladly raised his children.

However, that didn't mean Laura had to divulge the details of her physical relationship, or lack thereof, with Devlin.

"Would you like me to slice those carrots?" she asked, avoiding her friend's penetrating gaze.

"You're falling in love with him, aren't you?" Annie murmured, a hint of wonderment in her voice.

"Don't be silly," Laura chided. "I hardly know the man. I'm just grateful to him for helping me keep Timmy safe. Like you were grateful to Juan Carlos after he saved your life."

"I rest my case." Annie smiled triumphantly.

"But Juan Carlos is a doctor. Devlin is...is..." Laura shrugged and shook her head.

What, exactly, was he? She was finding it harder and harder to believe he was a common criminal. Yet what other choice did she have? After watching him spend the past three years acting just like Johnny and his cronies had, she'd be a fool not to see him for what he really was.

"Have you asked him anything about himself? Anything personal?" Annie prodded. "He could be living in San Pedro for some perfectly legitimate reason, you know."

"I've thought that myself, but I haven't had the courage to come right out and ask. I keep hoping he'll tell me on his own. If there's something to tell." Laura glanced at her friend, then lowered her gaze again, unable to bear the sympathy she saw in the other woman's eyes. "I let him know early on that I believed the rumors about him. He didn't say anything to the contrary then, and he hasn't since. Maybe that's because there's nothing to say."

"Talk to him, Laura. For your own peace of mind," Annie urged.

"And if he admits to being a drug runner or an ax murderer, then what?"

"Somehow, I don't think he's either. But if I'm wrong, I suggest you run for your life," Annie said only half-teasingly.

"I tried that once and look where it got me," Laura retorted.

"We'll help you any way we can. You know that, don't you?"

"Yes, I know. Now, do you want me to slice those carrots or not?"

"I'd really rather you tell me if you're having sex with your husband. But since you're not going to, yes, you can slice the carrots."

Much later, as she lay alone in bed waiting for Devlin to join her, Laura thought of her conversation with Annie once again. Her friend had been right about two things. Whether out of simple gratitude or something much more visceral, she *had* begun to care for Devlin quite a bit. And, that being the case, she was going to have to at least try to find out who and what he really was.

But first, she was going to have to be sure she could handle the truth regardless of what it turned out to be. Until they'd dealt with Giovanni, she was going to have to live in Devlin's house and sleep in his bed. And she wasn't sure how she could do that without alienating him completely if she found out he really was the human equivalent of pond scum.

For the time being it seemed wiser to go along as she had been, acknowledging his basic decency and accepting the kindness and consideration he continued to show her and her son while keeping as much distance between them as she could.

"Coward," she muttered, punching her pillow, then going still as the door opened and Devlin walked quietly into the room.

He'd behaved in a reserved yet cordial manner toward her and the Morenos at lunch. When they'd returned home, he'd said he had work to do, then had gone into his office with Alex. She hadn't seen him again until the two men joined her and Timmy for the dinner she'd prepared in Mrs. Santos's absence. And afterward, they'd both gone back to the office again.

Wanting to spend some time alone with her son, Laura hadn't minded Devlin's sudden reclusiveness. But now...

As the mattress shifted under Devlin's weight, she admitted that she was glad to have him near again. In fact, for one long moment she was tempted to turn toward him, to ask him to put his arms around her, to hold her close and chase away her demons.

Yet, how could she, when he might very well prove to be the one she should fear most?

Until she had the guts to find out the truth about him, she couldn't afford to bind herself to him any more deeply than she already had. Bad enough that she sought him out in her sleep. But to do so consciously at this point in their relationship...

Nothing else she could do would be more foolhardy.

Chapter 8

Devlin couldn't count the number of nights he'd sat out in the garden, surrounded by darkness, feeling relatively at peace as he listened to the splash of water in the fountain and savored the spicy scent of his roses. But he did know that tonight wasn't going to be one of them.

Hands shoved in the side pockets of his faded jeans, he paced, barefoot, along the brick walkway, his thoughts in turmoil. He'd known from the first that his marriage to Laura would take a toll on him, and he'd been determined to minimize the damage by maintaining as much distance between them as he could. Unfortunately, he hadn't taken into account how impossible that would be once she was living in his house and sleeping in his bed.

Oh, he could have treated her coldly and avoided her company over the past five days if he'd really put his mind to it. But he hadn't. Instead, he'd gone out of his way to spend as much time as he could with her and Timmy.

He hadn't been obligated to take them to the park or to lunch at the Morenos' as he'd done over the weekend. Nor had it been necessary for him to arrange any of the other outings they'd shared the past couple of days. But then, he couldn't have allowed Laura and Timmy to go to the market or the library or back to the park for another round of kite flying on their own, could he?

Not that those excursions had been their idea. Both Laura and Timmy seemed content to stay at the house. But Devlin hadn't wanted them to grow bored or restless or to feel too confined.

Or so he'd told himself each time he'd come up with another excuse to be with them.

And at night, when Laura sought him out in her sleep, he didn't have to welcome her with open arms. He could have—*should* have—turned his back on her. And he would have if he'd had more fortitude.

However, he was just feckless enough to look forward to that moment with a yearning that was equaled only by his despair when she eased away from his embrace again each morning.

Although she was lingering longer and longer after she awoke.

Muttering a curse, Devlin sat on one of the benches by the fountain, buried his face in his hands and tried to ignore the way his body stirred at the mere thought of having her curled up close beside him, soft and warm, yet obstinately unwilling.

He wanted her so much, and he sensed that she wanted him, too. Still, he couldn't blame her for resisting. Not when she believed the worst of him.

Of course, he could remedy that easily enough. Yet, despite Alex's continued urging, Devlin wasn't quite ready to tell Laura the truth about himself. He knew she'd be angry with him for misleading her, but that wasn't what was holding him back.

Once he decided to be honest with her, he'd also have to tell her what he knew about Giovanni Buschetti, and that could very well start her thinking about an annulment.

According to his sources in the Chicago area, while the old man had been living quietly since the death of his son, he was still a powerful figure in the underworld there. When he wanted something done, it was done, no questions asked.

Yet, although Vincent Petrano and his wife had cut short their vacation to Mexico and returned to Chicago last Friday, to date there had been no indication Giovanni was making plans to either come after Timmy himself or send someone after the boy in his place.

He could be biding his time, getting the lay of the land through contacts Devlin and his associates in the States were unaware of. But Devlin doubted it.

If Giovanni wanted to get his hands on his grandson, Devlin was of the opinion he'd have tried to do so as quickly and quietly as possible once he knew where to find him. That he hadn't could mean any number of things, not necessarily all favorable. But Laura might assume from Giovanni's seeming lack of interest that she no longer had anything to fear from him, and thus no longer had any need of Devlin's help.

While that could be true, Devlin didn't want her rushing off just yet. He knew she didn't like being beholden to him. And he would prefer her to be staying with him because she wanted to. But for the time being—

"Still trying to decide whether or not to come clean with her?" Alex asked, his voice cutting through the quiet of the night.

Looking up, Devlin saw him standing by the fountain. Once again he'd managed to slip through the shadows with startling silence, coming upon Devlin when he'd much rather have been alone.

"I think we've had this conversation before," Devlin replied, his tone deprecating.

"Several times, but obviously to no effect." Alex slumped onto the bench on the other side of the fountain. "The longer you wait to tell her the truth, the angrier she's going to be."

"Yeah, well, you should know," Devlin retorted acidly, hoping his allusion to Alex's unhappy past would shut him up.

"Hey, you want to go through the same hell I have, suit yourself."

"What makes you think I will?"

"You're more than half in love with her, pal. Her and the kid. And you're starting to think happily-ever-after thoughts again," Alex stated simply.

"Why do you say that?" Devlin eyed him narrowly, wondering how he'd come to that conclusion.

"I talked to McConnell this afternoon while you were at the park. He mentioned you'd been asking about that slot opening up in D.C. He wanted to know why."

"What did you tell him?" Devlin demanded.

He hated it when McConnell went behind his back. Luckily he didn't do it often. Only when he was suspicious about something...

"That you were getting tired of beans and tortillas," Alex said. "And, no, I didn't say anything about your change in marital status, even though I was sorely tempted. Best thing he could do is haul your butt out of here. You could take Laura and Timmy with you, start over in the States."

"Not yet."

"Don't you think it's time you let go of the past? Carly wouldn't want you to—"

"I can't. Not until I put Drago out of commission," Devlin snapped.

"Then at least talk to Laura. Tell her what's going on."

"Once I do that, I'll have to tell her what we've found out about Giovanni, too."

"You have a problem with that?" His confusion evident, Alex frowned and shook his head. "She's terrified he's going to appear out of nowhere and snatch the kid. Why not ease her mind?"

"Because then she might decide she doesn't want to stay here anymore," Devlin admitted, none too proud of his reasoning.

"If you believe that, then you *really* haven't been paying attention. She's got it so bad for you wild horses couldn't drag her away from here. But then, I guess you've been so busy being honorable that you haven't noticed how she looks at you whenever you're together. Of course, any man who can sleep in the same bed with a woman like her and not—"

"If I were you, I'd quit while I was ahead," Devlin warned. "What goes on in my bedroom is none of your damn business."

"Oh, my. I seem to have struck a nerve... again. How insensitive of me," Alex drawled.

Cursing himself for taking the bait his friend had dangled so deftly, Devlin stood and started toward the house.

"I wouldn't have expected anything less of you. But I think it would be a good idea if we didn't discuss my relationship with my wife anymore. I'll deal with her in my own way and in my own time."

"Hey, no problem. I just thought maybe one of us could learn from my mistakes. If I'd just talked to Kari..."

Hearing the anguish underlying Alex's blasé tone of voice, Devlin paused and glanced back at him.

"It's not too late, you know."

"For me it's way too late," Alex said abruptly. "But you and Laura still have a chance to make some kind of life together. Forget about Drago Espinosa, tell Laura the truth, then get her and the kid out of here. McConnell owes you that job in D.C., and you owe it to yourself to take it."

Devlin couldn't think of anything he'd rather do more. After having Laura and Timmy around for almost a week, he'd begun to realize just how lonely he'd been the past three years. He didn't want to go back to living that way ever again. In a perfect world, he'd have Laura and Timmy with him from now on, with the kind of safe, secure life they deserved.

But in a perfect world there'd be no Drago Espinosa. If only the bastard would surface somewhere.

"At least think about what I've said," Alex urged, drawing Devlin from his reverie.

"I will."

"So, what's on the agenda tomorrow?"

"I'm taking Laura and Timmy up to the hot springs. Want to come with us? The water would probably do your leg some good."

"Probably, but I'd rather not have to be on my best behavior. And maybe if I'm not around, you'll have a chance to talk to Laura."

"Maybe," Devlin conceded as he started toward the house again. "Are you coming in?"

"Later."

As Devlin crossed the kitchen, walked down the hallway and climbed the staircase, he made no effort to suppress the anticipation welling up inside him. He'd stayed away longer than usual tonight, and now he wanted nothing more than to lie down beside Laura and take her in his arms.

And make her *his* in the most intimate way a man could claim a woman.

Only he didn't have that right yet, and he wouldn't until he'd told her the truth about himself. For him, their pretend marriage was starting to feel way too real—but a real marriage had to start with a foundation of trust. And how would she ever be able to believe in him down the line if he wasn't honest with her now?

He couldn't change the fact that he'd misled her at the outset about his identity. But before they went any further, deepening their relationship in any way, he was going to have to talk to her.

He wasn't looking forward to risking her wrath, or worse, having her choose to walk away from him without a backward glance. Yet after his conversation with Alex he knew he couldn't go on deceiving her, either. Not when that meant he'd also be causing her unnecessary anxiety.

He owed her whatever peace of mind he could give her, no matter what it cost him. And if Alex was right, coming clean with her could very well benefit him, as well.

Once Laura knew he wasn't really in the same league as Johnny Buschetti had been, maybe she'd take another, closer look at him. Maybe...

As he had each night on his way to bed, Devlin stopped in Timmy's room to check on the boy. As usual, Laura's son lay on his back, snoring softly, his light cotton blanket kicked down around his feet.

Smiling to himself, Devlin tucked the blanket around the boy again. He was as bright and sensitive as his mother, and Devlin found his delight in the simple things of life infectious. Within the space of a few days he'd realized that it would give him great pleasure to watch this little boy grow into a young man. And if he could also offer a little guidance along the way, he'd be more than honored to do so.

Shaking his head at the direction of his thoughts, Devlin backed out of the room, turned and opened the door to his bedroom. He hesitated a moment just inside the doorway, gazing across the room at Laura, curled on her side with her back to him, then moved on to the bathroom.

He shucked his jeans and T-shirt, washed his face and brushed his teeth and, as he had done since Friday night, slipped back into the bedroom as quietly as he could.

Even though she'd insisted on pretending to be asleep the past few nights, Devlin had known she was still awake each time he'd joined her in bed. But tonight he realized, as soon as he stretched out beside her, that she'd already fallen asleep.

His own fault, since he'd stayed out in the garden so long, he thought, trying unsuccessfully to suppress his disappointment.

Now that he'd psyched himself into talking to her, he didn't want to wait. And somewhere in the back of his mind he'd kind of hoped he could get it over with now, even though it was almost two o'clock in the morning.

Turning on his side to face her, he willed her to roll over so that he could gather her into his arms. However, after several minutes had ticked past without her moving, he eased across the mattress, closing the distance between them so that his body curved around hers spoon-style.

As if she'd been expecting him, Laura muttered softly, sighed, then snuggled her bottom against him in a deliciously intimate way.

Although he groaned inwardly at the manner in which his body sprang to life, Devlin didn't move away. Instead, he put his arm around her, resting his hand possessively on the faint curve of her belly, and feathered his lips along the side of her neck, inhaling the sweet scent of her skin.

She murmured again, undulating against him provocatively, but still didn't wake up.

Knowing that was just as well, and that he, too, needed to get some rest, Devlin silently ordered himself to settle down. Much as he needed to talk to Laura, he'd rather wait until she was coherent enough to make sense of what he had to say. He didn't want to risk having her misunderstand him or his motives. And there was a possibility that could happen if they weren't both wide awake and at least an arm's length apart when he finally told her what he did for a living.

Though he dozed off and on, Devlin never really fell into a sound sleep. He was too aware of Laura, pressed up against him so intimately that his state of arousal remained painfully constant. In addition, his mind whirled with possible solutions to the problems they'd have to face in the coming weeks should she choose to stay with him once she knew why he was really living in San Pedro.

It might be crazy, but he wanted to make a life for her and Timmy in the States. First, however, he had to deal with Drago. He hoped she'd understand, but if she didn't . . .

He wasn't sure what he'd do. He didn't want to lose Laura. Yet he still felt as if he had a debt of honor to pay before he could really commit himself to her...to anyone.

When the room began to lighten with the first edges of dawn, Devlin decided he might as well get up. Much as he would have liked to start the day with Laura awakening in his arms, he didn't think it would be wise this morning.

He wouldn't have been able to stop himself from making love to her if she'd given him any encouragement at all. And from the way she'd responded to his gentle petting the past couple of days, he didn't think he'd find it all that difficult to breach her defenses.

However, that wasn't how he wanted their first mating to be. He refused to coerce her in even the subtlest of ways. He wanted her to want him without reservation, and he was willing to wait until he was sure that she did.

Still, when he finally eased away from her, he did so regretfully. Then, not wanting to risk waking her, he took fresh clothes from the dresser and went down to the hall bath to shower and dress.

In the kitchen he put on a pot of coffee to tide him over until Mrs. Santos started breakfast at seven. When it was ready, he filled a mug with the steaming brew and, with it and his yard tools in hand, headed out to the garden, Bitsy ambling along behind him. He'd been neglecting his roses lately, and much to his dismay they'd begun to show it.

Over an hour and a half later Devlin sat back on his heels, rolled his shoulders to work out the kinks, then tipped his face up to the first rays of sunlight peeking over the top of the garden wall.

He'd deadheaded the large-flowered hybrids, weeded the beds, then stirred up the soil around the more well-established bushes. As a result, his tension had eased considerably, and along with a renewed sense of accomplishment had come a feeling of personal satisfaction.

He'd never claimed to be a saint. He'd made his fair share of mistakes, some of which had cost him dearly. But he'd also righted a lot of wrongs. And that was exactly what he intended to do with Laura before the day was out.

Aware that the tantalizing aroma of freshly baked cinnamon bread had begun to waft through the garden, mingling in a heady way with the scent of coffee and roses, Devlin gathered up his spade, three-pronged cultivator and pruning shears. As he stood, he heard the back door open. Expecting to see Mrs. Santos or Alex, he glanced over his shoulder, then went still as Laura stepped outside.

He'd grown used to her wearing dresses or skirts with hems falling modestly to midcalf. But this morning, perhaps in anticipation of their planned trip to the hot springs, she'd donned short white shorts and a hot pink sleeveless knit shirt. With her dark, curly hair pulled into a ponytail high at the top of her head, she looked young and lovely as well as heart-stoppingly sexy.

"You must have gotten up early this morning," she said, walking toward him, a mug of coffee in her hands.

Though he couldn't be absolutely sure, Devlin thought he'd heard the barest hint of reproach in her lilting voice. That she'd possibly missed waking in his arms gave him an inordinate amount of pleasure.

However, never one to jump to conclusions, he offered her a slight smile, then shrugged with feigned nonchalance.

"Just before dawn. Guess my conscience was bothering me."

"Oh, really?"

She paused halfway down the walk and regarded him questioningly, a frown furrowing her forehead.

"I haven't been tending my roses the way I should." He gestured toward the newly tidy beds. "But I think I've redeemed myself, don't you?"

She surveyed the garden slowly, then finally nodded. "You most certainly have."

Basking in her approval, he started toward her. Maybe now would be a good time to talk to her. He could get rid of his yard tools, wash his hands, refill his mug and join her out by the fountain. They could—

"Mom... Devlin. Mrs. Santos said to tell you breakfast is almost ready," Timmy announced as he barreled out the door and skidded to a halt beside Laura, his pale green eyes bright with excitement.

Then again, Devlin decided, maybe waiting until tonight, when her son was sound asleep in his bed, would be wiser.

"Well, then, I guess I'd better get cleaned up," he said.

"Right away," Timmy urged, hopping from one foot to the other, obviously anxious for them to eat so they could be on their way.

"You certainly seem to be in a hurry this morning," Laura teased affectionately. "Why is that?"

"Because the sooner we get to the hot springs, the sooner I can learn how to swim. Right, Devlin?"

"Right," Devlin agreed, ruffling a hand through the boy's dark, silky curls. He'd promised to teach him how to swim and was surprised not only at how much Timmy was looking forward to it, but how much *he* was, as well. "So, let's go eat. Okay, Mom?"

"Okay." Laura smiled at Devlin appreciatively, her eyes meeting his in a way that stirred his soul. Then she turned and followed her son into the kitchen.

Filled with a renewed sense of hope, Devlin trailed a few steps behind them. He intended to make today one they'd always remember, a time of togetherness that would strengthen their bond as a family.

Then tonight, with the groundwork laid, he'd put his heart on the line, and finally tell Laura the truth about himself.

Laura had been to the hot springs many years ago during the summers she'd spent with her father in San Pedro, and had enjoyed the place immensely.

Located in the foothills on the dry side of the mountain range north of town, the springs had created an oasis of rich, green, grassy meadows surrounded by groves of mesquite and cottonwood trees in the midst of what was otherwise rocky scrubland.

Several decades ago someone had bought the property from the original owner and built a cluster of tiny villas as well as a huge swimming pool into which the hot springs had been diverted. The villas, which could be rented by the day, week or month, were especially popular among wealthy Mexicans who traveled to the area from Mexico City; the swimming pool was open on a daily basis to anyone able to pay the small admission fee.

When Devlin had suggested the outing yesterday, Laura had been more than happy to agree. She'd hoped that spending an entire day not only out of the house but away from San Pedro would help to dispel some of the restlessness that seemed to be driving her nearer and nearer to climbing the walls with each day that passed.

She'd always hated feeling as if she were waiting for the other shoe to drop. She much preferred to take control of a situation, to make a decision and run with it, literally if necessary. When she'd originally felt threatened by Giovanni, she'd made her roundabout way to San Pedro. And when she'd come to the conclusion that she couldn't run from him again, she'd gone to Devlin for help. But since she'd married him, she seemed to be caught in a kind of limbo.

To her knowledge, Giovanni hadn't made any move at all to come after Timmy, leading her to wonder if she'd misjudged the old man's interest in her child. Maybe he was simply too old or infirm to make an effort to get his hands on the boy.

Maybe. But then again, maybe not.

He could be waiting for what he deemed to be just the right moment to try to take Timmy away from her. In fact, she wouldn't have been surprised to find out that he was

planning to spring some sort of surprise attack on her weeks
or even months from now when she'd grown complacent
once again.

And, unfortunately, as long as she didn't know for sure
what he had up his sleeve, she had to go on pretending to be
Devlin's wife.

Not that doing so had been any great hardship. He'd gone
out of his way to see to her and her son's needs, continuing
to show them both kindness and consideration. Yet Laura
was finding it more and more difficult to live with him as if
she were his wife while not actually being so in every way.
Especially when she knew she could change her status permanently whenever she wanted.

She would have had to have been in a coma not to realize
that Devlin wanted her as much as she'd finally begun to
admit to herself that she wanted him. When he held her, he
made sure she was aware of his arousal. Yet, aside from
stroking her back or her arm or, as he had yesterday morning, the gentle swell of her breast, he'd done nothing to ini-
tiate sex with her.

And since she couldn't quite bring herself to offer the invitation for which he seemed to be ever so patiently waiting, her level of discontent had been mounting steadily.

Now, as she packed away the leftovers from their picnic
lunch while Devlin took Timmy to the rest room, she recalled how the urge to pound her fists into her pillow and
scream bloody murder had all but overtaken her when she'd
awakened alone in bed that morning. She'd wanted to blame
her frustration on raging hormones, but she'd known there
was much more to her disappointment than that.

She'd found herself wondering if he'd come to bed at all,
or if he had finally decided he could sleep alone once again
without jeopardizing his position as her husband. She'd
been astonished at how dismayed she'd been at that possibility. Yet she hadn't had the courage to ask him outright if
that had been the case.

At least he hadn't treated her coldly any time today. Quite the contrary, she admitted, setting aside the picnic basket, then sitting with her back against the trunk of the tree under which they'd spread their blanket, watching as he and Timmy walked toward her, hand in hand.

From the moment she'd come upon him in the garden he'd seemed happy to have her company as well as her son's. On the drive up he'd even made an effort at polite conversation, asking if she'd ever gone to the hot springs. She'd told her about the times she'd been there with her father, and he'd listened with such obvious interest, then asked other questions about the summers they'd spent in San Pedro, that she'd found herself telling him all sorts of things she'd thought she had long since forgotten.

Perhaps as a result, she'd suffered a short bout of melancholy when they'd first arrived at the springs. But thanks to Devlin's gentle teasing, she'd soon been splashing around just as merrily as he and Timmy in the deliciously warm water filling the huge concrete swimming pool.

By lunchtime Devlin had Timmy jumping into the water, coming up for air and paddling gamely back to the side again. Laura had been impressed by how patiently he'd worked with her son, but not really surprised. She'd seen them together enough over the past few days to admit, at least to herself, that she couldn't have asked him to be any kinder to her son than he already was.

Now if she could only find some way to magically transform him into a world-renowned, yet reclusive, horticulturist who was secretly developing a new variety of rosebush—

"Thinking about your father again?" Devlin asked, interrupting her reverie as he and Timmy hunkered down beside her on the blanket.

Realizing that her sudden sadness must have shown on her face, Laura smiled slightly as she nodded. "Among other things. He really loved it here and now I remember why.

Even with all the activity around the pool, it's so peaceful."

"You're right. It is," Devlin agreed.

"How long before I can swim again?" Timmy asked, wriggling around on the blanket impatiently.

"About an hour," Devlin replied for at least the third time since they'd finished eating.

"Still?"

"Still," Laura stated, her tone brooking no argument. "So put your T-shirt on, stretch out and try to rest a while. Then you'll really feel like swimming again."

"But I'm not tired," he protested.

"Well, I am." Yawning mightily, Devlin flopped down on his back, closed his eyes and immediately started to snore softly.

Giggling, Timmy did likewise, and within a matter of minutes was miraculously sound asleep.

"Don't tell me it worked," Devlin said, sitting up again.

"Like a charm."

Laughing quietly, Laura glanced at him, then quickly looked away when she saw him watching her intently. She'd pulled her shorts on over her royal blue tank suit, but hadn't bothered with her knit shirt. Now she suddenly wished that she had.

"You're really good with him," she murmured, hoping to divert his attention.

"He's a nice child, bright and funny and fairly easy to reason with. Melissa was like that, too."

Melissa?

Startled, Laura turned to look at him, but he was gazing off into the distance.

"Your... niece?" she ventured.

"My daughter."

"You have a daughter?"

Though she realized how stupid she must have sounded, Laura hadn't been able to think of anything else to say.

"*Had* a daughter. She and my wife were killed almost four years ago," he replied, his tone matter-of-fact.

"Oh, Devlin, I'm so sorry."

She offered her sympathy with all her heart. Nobody deserved to suffer a double loss like that.

Yet somewhere in the back of her mind Laura couldn't help but wonder why he was telling her about them now. Maybe hearing her talk about her father had stirred up his own memories, and he'd decided to share some of his past with her. But Laura had a feeling there was more to his sudden revelation than that.

As if sensing her concern, Devlin turned to face her. "I'm the one who should be sorry. I didn't mean to upset you."

What he'd told her was distressing, and she couldn't pretend otherwise. Nor could she keep from giving in to her curiosity now that he'd finally chosen to reveal a little bit about himself.

"What—what happened?" she stammered, not quite meeting his gaze.

"They were caught in the cross fire during a terrorist attack at the airport in El Norte," he replied after a moment's hesitation.

"Were you with them?"

"I should have been, but I wasn't. I was…detained at the American embassy."

He turned away from her again, the pained look on his face leaving no doubt in Laura's mind that he blamed himself for their deaths.

"Surely what happened to them wasn't your fault, Devlin," she insisted.

"Not directly." He paused, his jaw clenched, his hands balled into fists, then added, "But if it hadn't been for me, they'd have never been there in the first place."

His simple statement rang with such truth that Laura had no idea what to say. Nor did she have the heart to pry any deeper, though her mind whirled with unasked questions.

What had he been doing in a country where political upheaval had been as much an everyday occurrence four years ago as it was today? And why had his wife and daughter been there with him?

And why, she wondered once again, had he broached such a harrowing subject now? Had losing his wife and daughter somehow been the catalyst for his coming to San Pedro? And, if so, in what way?

Could talking about them be his way of working up to other, perhaps even more anguishing, revelations?

While a part of her shied away from that possibility, another, more primitively feminine part of her longed to help him bear his burden, no matter what it turned out to be.

Yet, as Devlin lay back and closed his eyes again, Laura allowed herself an inner sigh of relief. Coward that she was, she'd just as soon wait a while longer to find out exactly what kind of onus was weighing him down.

Edging closer to him, she reached out and smoothed a shaggy lock of dark hair off his forehead. She had to be crazy sitting here with him like this. She had enough problems of her own to deal with. She didn't need—

Lightning quick, Devlin caught her hand in his. Rolling toward her, he pressed his lips against her palm.

"Laura," he murmured, then leaned over her and trailed a series of hot, wet kisses along the bare skin of her inner thigh.

"Yes, Devlin?" she whispered as a languorous heat pooled deep in her belly.

"I wish…" His voice trailing away, he sat up and met her gaze.

"What?"

He shook his head, as if at a loss for words. Yet the mingling of hope and despair she saw in his eyes spoke volumes. She'd dealt unsuccessfully with those warring emotions herself, so she understood all too well how he felt. But she had no idea how to help him lay to rest the demons that were so obviously tormenting him.

As he started to turn away from her, she knew she should let the moment pass. Yet she couldn't. Murmuring his name, she reached out and touched his face.

Seemingly galvanized by her simple gesture, he turned back to her and pulled her onto his lap, then bent his head and took her mouth with such fierce possessiveness that her breath caught in her throat.

Instinctively she tried to draw away, frightened by his urgency, but he refused to let her go. His hands skimmed over her bare back masterfully while his thumbs slid under the fabric of her swimsuit to tease her breasts, and suddenly she couldn't think of any good reason to resist.

He needed her, and she needed him, and at that moment nothing else mattered.

"Hey, Mom, I thought you said you and Devlin were just friends."

As if they'd been doused with a bucket of cold water, Laura and Devlin jerked apart, then turned to stare at her son. Lying on his tummy, elbows cocked so that his chin rested in his hands, he gazed at them with unabashed interest.

"We—we are," Laura stammered, wishing there was an inconspicuous way she could ease off Devlin's lap.

"But you're just friends with Juan Carlos and Mr. Wiley, and you only kiss *them* on the cheek. You were kissing Devlin on the mouth."

"Well . . . yes . . ."

No sense denying the obvious, she thought, lowering her gaze.

"Are you and Devlin gonna make a baby?"

Her face burning and her mouth agape, Laura stared at her son again. Talk about cutting to the chase. And, of course, as was usually the case when Timmy chose to be precocious, she had no idea how to answer him.

"Not today," Devlin replied for her, a hint of laughter evident in his husky voice.

"Then can we go swimming again?"

"You bet."

Whooping with joy, Timmy jumped to his feet and wriggled out of his T-shirt.

With a murmured apology Laura slipped off Devlin's lap, avoiding his gaze, but he caught her by the hand before she could scoot away from him.

"We'll finish this tonight, all right?" he asked, tipping her chin up so that she had to meet his gaze.

She could have pretended not to know what he was talking about, and he would probably have let her get away with it. But Laura knew exactly what he had in mind.

They'd been tiptoeing around each other for a week. But now the time had finally come for them to be honest with each other. He'd started the ball rolling by telling her about his wife and daughter. And, as far as Laura was concerned, there was no going back.

"All right," she agreed with a tremulous smile.

He nodded once, leaned forward and claimed another quick kiss, then pulled her to her feet as Timmy began hopping around impatiently.

They lazed in the pool for the remainder of the afternoon, content to watch Timmy paddling around them. For a while Laura wondered if her son would ever wear himself out. But as the sun began to dip behind the mountain range to the west, they finally managed to coax him out of the water, promising to return again one day soon.

They changed into dry clothes so they wouldn't catch a chill from the cool evening air, then drove back to San Pedro. Since Devlin had told Mrs. Santos not to worry about preparing dinner, they stopped at a small restaurant on the outskirts of town that specialized in American-style pizza.

When they finally arrived back at the house there was no sign of Mrs. Santos or Alex. However, a light had been left burning in the kitchen and Bitsy was there to greet them.

"Guess they decided to make an early night of it," Devlin said as he set the picnic basket on the counter and bent to scratch the dog's ears.

"Sounds like a good idea to me, too." Laura smiled at him, her heart pounding with sudden anticipation.

Each time he'd touched her, and he'd found many opportunities to do so throughout the afternoon and evening, she'd thought of the moment when they'd be alone at last in his old-fashioned brass bed, the linen sheets cool against their heated skin.

"Why don't you go up and get Timmy settled?" he suggested, his eyes glimmering with sensual promise. "I'll be along in a few minutes."

"I'll be waiting," she murmured, then turned to Timmy, who was now fading fast. "Come on, buddy, let's get you tucked into bed."

"No bath?"

"Not tonight." She lifted him into her arms and nuzzled his neck. "After all the swimming you did today, I'm afraid if you get wet again you'll start to grow fins. And we don't want that to happen, do we?"

"Oh, Mommy, you're so silly."

"Oh, Timmy, I know."

Feeling younger and more vibrantly alive than she had in years, Laura headed toward the staircase, the sound of Devlin's laughter echoing with promise deep in her soul.

Chapter 9

His body taut with desire, Devlin stood by the counter, listening as the sound of Laura's footsteps faded up the staircase. Soon, *very* soon, they'd finally be together as they were meant to be. He'd answer all the questions she hadn't been able to bring herself to ask that afternoon. And once her fear and uncertainty had been laid to rest, he'd make love to her... slow, sweet, yet undeniably sensual love.

But first...

Seeing Bitsy sitting patiently by the kitchen door, Devlin moved to let him out into the garden. Then, aware that the dog would want to come inside again almost immediately, he emptied the picnic basket and put it away.

As he did so, his thoughts drifted back to the moment he'd told Laura about Carly and Melissa. He hadn't really intended to, and at first he'd been sorry he had. The time hadn't been right to elaborate, and as a result, all he seemed to have done was upset Laura.

But she'd let him know that wasn't strictly the case. She had been disturbed by what he'd told her, and she'd definitely wanted to know more. Yet, instead of pressing him for details or explanations, she'd offered him the sympathy and understanding he'd needed most at the moment.

If he hadn't already realized he was in love with her, he would have done so then. As it was, he'd found himself more determined than ever to make her a permanent part of his life.

Hearing Bitsy whimpering by the door, Devlin went to let him in. He bolted the locks, then crossed to one of the cabinets and took out a bottle of brandy and two snifters. After pouring a small measure for himself and drinking it down, he switched off the light above the sink and headed for the hallway, finding his way easily in the shadowy darkness.

From long habit rather than any real intention of allowing himself to be diverted, he glanced down the hallway toward his office as he started up the staircase. Then, eyes narrowed, he paused.

A slim beam of light spread across the tile floor along the bottom edge of the closed door. Devlin hadn't been in the room since late yesterday evening, and he distinctly recalled turning off the light when he left. So Alex was either in there now, or had been earlier.

Devlin didn't have any problem with that. Since *he* had been gone all day, he appreciated the fact that his friend was keeping tabs on what was going on in their corner of the world. After all, that was what Uncle Sam paid them to do. And if anything of vital import had come across the wires, Alex would have made sure he was advised of it.

Wouldn't he?

The younger man had ears like a bat. He'd have known the moment they'd returned home. And if he'd had any information to impart, he'd have done so as soon as he could get Devlin alone.

So why was he still standing in the hallway so indecisively, staring at the closed door of his office with a mounting sense of alarm? Why didn't he just continue on his way up the staircase?

Because something's not right here.

With a muttered curse Devlin strode down the hallway, his sneaker-clad feet making no sound on the tile floor. Transferring the snifters to the same hand that held the brandy bottle, he reached out and tested the doorknob.

It turned easily and the door swung inward with a quiet whoosh. As he stepped across the threshold he caught sight of Alex, standing at the desk, fiddling with the specially outfitted briefcase that held Devlin's automatic pistol as well as a neatly broken down long-range rifle.

"What the hell are you doing?" Devlin demanded as he crossed the office, his gaze flicking to the faxes scattered next to the briefcase.

Turning slowly, almost nonchalantly, Alex leaned a hip against the edge of the desk, his body blocking the briefcase and one hand spread across the sheaf of papers, and met Devlin's gaze.

"I don't suppose there's any way I could talk you into going upstairs and just forgetting you ever came in here, is there?" he asked in a deceptively mild tone of voice.

Alerted by the other man's stance as well as the words he spoke, Devlin eyed him even more suspiciously as he replied, "None at all."

"And you wouldn't believe me if I told you nothing out of the ordinary is going on?"

"No," Devlin snapped, his patience wearing thin.

Alex had never been one to play games. Not where their business was concerned. That he was doing so now, with what seemed to be the sole intent of keeping him in the dark, had started warning bells going off in Devlin's head.

"That's too bad." As if sensing his ploy wasn't working, Alex pushed away from the desk with obvious reluctance, allowing Devlin the access he wanted. "Another fifteen minutes and I would have been out of here. But you just had to come nosing around, didn't you? You couldn't go up-stairs to your wife like any normal, red-blooded—"

"Shut up, will you?" Devlin barked, not the least bit amused by his friend's prattling.

He set the brandy bottle and snifters on the desk, then picked up the faxes and swiftly skimmed through them, aware almost at once of the significance of the information contained in them.

A failed assassination attempt had taken place at a polit-ical rally in Honduras. And according to the reports he held in his hands, the modus operandi of the perpetrator—a bomb blast followed by sniper fire—pointed unequivocally to one Drago Espinosa.

After years living underground, the bastard had finally surfaced, just as Devlin had hoped he would only last night. But talk about rotten timing.

What was that old saying about being careful what you wished for because you just might get it?

Devlin had spent the past four years preparing himself for an opportunity like this, studying his prey until he knew his habits almost as well as he knew his own.

First and foremost, Drago prided himself on never leav-ing a job unfinished. So, ten to one he was still lurking somewhere in the shadows of Tegucigalpa's back streets— back streets Devlin had once haunted himself—biding his time until his quarry got within reach again.

Devlin had no doubt that if anyone could track Drago down in the Honduran capital, he could. But he'd have to do it alone, and he didn't have a minute to waste. He had to leave *now*.

For several agonizing moments he thought of Laura waiting for him upstairs, and considered going to her and telling her what he had to do. There was a very good chance she'd understand. She already knew about Carly and Me-lissa.

But if she didn't, if she begged him to stay—

"Let me go, Devlin," Alex urged. "I swear I'll get the bastard for you."

Devlin was ashamed of how tempted he was to accept his friend's offer. He'd certainly earned the right to stay here with Laura and Timmy, and send Alex to do his dirty work. But he simply couldn't bring himself to do it.

Drago Espinosa was *his* nemesis. And he owed it to Carly and Melissa, as well as to himself, to personally see to it that the monster never had another chance to destroy the lives of any more innocent people.

"With that leg? The odds of your coming back alive are zero to none," Devlin chided.

"The leg's almost as good as new," Alex retorted. "And I don't have a wife and kid to leave behind, so if I did slip up..." He shrugged and shook his head. "No big deal."

"You're staying here," Devlin ordered, folding the faxes and stuffing them in the back pocket of his jeans, then pulling the briefcase closer so he could make sure his weaponry was in order. "I want you to look after Laura and Timmy for me while I'm gone. From the information I've gotten, I don't think Giovanni's coming after the boy, but stay close to them all the same."

"Yes, sir. Anything you say, *sir.*" His tone sardonic, Alex snapped off a smart salute. "But what, exactly, am I supposed to tell your *wife* when she demands to know where you've gone and when you'll be back as you damn well know she will?"

"Just say I was called away on business and I'll be back as soon as possible."

"Like she's really going to buy that," Alex scoffed.

"Just smooth things over with her the best way you can for the time being, and tell her I'll explain everything when I get back."

For just an instant Devlin thought of Laura again. She was going to be furious when she found out he was gone, and he didn't blame her. But he had a job to do, one that would free him, once and for all, from the past. Having dealt with Drago, he'd finally be able to give Laura and her son the kind of life they deserved. If, he could only hope, she'd still let him.

Snapping the locks on his briefcase, Devlin nodded toward the far side of the room where a black leather duffel bag, always packed and ready to go, sat on the floor.

"You want to hand me that?"

"Sure." Alex picked up the duffel and slung it toward Devlin. "You want me to drive you to Leon?"

The town about fifty miles west of San Pedro had a small airfield where Devlin kept his Cessna.

"I've got a motorcycle stashed in the workroom off the garage. I'll take that." He started toward the door, which was slightly ajar, then paused and turned back to Alex. "Don't let them out of your sight under any circumstances while I'm gone," he warned.

"I won't," Alex replied, his gaze steady.

"You know where my personal papers are?"

"Top drawer of your desk."

"Right." He hesitated a moment, reluctant to admit the possibility that *he* might not come back alive, then added, "If anything happens to me, make damn sure McConnell looks after them."

"I will."

Knowing he couldn't have left Laura and Timmy in better hands, Devlin nodded once, then turned toward the door again.

"Take care of yourself."

"You, too, Dev. You, too."

If anything happens to me... happens to me... happens to me...

Devlin's words echoing in her mind, Laura stood in the shadows just outside his office, one hand pressed against her lips, the other knotted in the soft fabric of her robe.

She'd put Timmy to bed, then taken a quick shower, brushed her hair and donned a fresh nightgown. She'd turned down the satin coverlet and plumped up the pillows, and with only one small lamp burning, had climbed into bed and waited and waited for Devlin to join her.

He'd said he would be along in a few minutes, but well over thirty minutes had passed when she finally slipped into her robe and padded downstairs. She'd assumed he'd been waylaid by Alex or maybe Mrs. Santos, and she'd had every intention of extricating him from whatever was inadvertently delaying him.

Even when she'd noticed the slice of light escaping through the narrow opening of his office door, she hadn't been unduly concerned. They'd been gone all day, so he'd have wanted to check on...whatever it was he regularly checked on in his office.

It wasn't until she'd come close enough to glimpse the guns packed neatly into what appeared to be a normal black leather briefcase and hear bits and pieces of Devlin's conversation with Alex that her heart had begun to race.

The odds of your coming back alive are zero to none.

What, exactly, am I supposed to tell your wife?

Called away on business...smooth things over...if anything happens to me...

He was going to Leon on a motorcycle with a briefcase full of guns and he wasn't going to tell her why, much less take time to say goodbye. And there was a good chance he might not ever come back.

Through the opening in the door she saw Devlin walking toward her. She was tempted to stand her ground and confront him, but she was afraid the hurt and anger welling up inside her would render her incoherent.

Hoping she hadn't hesitated too long, she spun on her heel and ran toward the staircase. She was halfway down the hall when the office door swung wide and the light from within caught her in midflight.

"Laura, wait." Devlin's voice rang out urgently right behind her.

Pausing, she glanced over her shoulder at him. His face was drawn, his eyes shadowed, his mouth set in a narrow line. Whatever he was up to, he certainly didn't seem to be enjoying it, but that realization gave her no comfort at all.

"Why?" she demanded, trying unsuccessfully to keep her voice from quivering. "So you can tell me about your 'business' trip?"

"I don't have time to go into the details now, but as soon as I get back—"

"Of course. We can talk then," she said, cutting him off as she turned away again, then adding as she continued down the hallway, "I know you're in a hurry, so don't let me keep you."

Foolishly, she hoped that he'd come after her, that he'd drop the briefcase and duffel bag, sweep her into his arms, carry her into their bedroom and swear that nothing, *nothing,* was more important to him than she was.

As she started to climb the stairs she risked a look back. The door to Devlin's office was now closed, the hallway empty, and from the kitchen she heard the faint sound of masculine voices, the click of another door closing, then silence.

He was leaving, really leaving, without so much as a backward glance, damn his rotten soul.

Never in her life had Laura engaged in a temper tantrum. Not when she'd come home from school to find her mother dead of a heart attack. Not when word had reached her that her father had died of pneumonia. Not even when Johnny was killed in a drive-by shooting outside his restaurant.

But tonight it seemed as if something deep inside her had finally snapped. Devlin was going heaven only knew where, to do heaven only knew what, and she could very well never see him again.

With an agonized cry she stormed up the stairs and into their bedroom, strode to the nightstand, picked up the small crystal vase holding a cluster of Devlin's pink-tinged cream roses and hurled it onto the floor. Then, staring in horror at the bits of shattered glass, the scattered rose petals and the puddle of water splattered across the tile floor, she sagged onto the bed and started to sob.

She couldn't recall ever feeling quite so hurt or so angry in her life. Yet, at the same time, she was truly terrified that she'd never see Devlin again. And not just because she needed him to protect her from Giovanni.

She was in love with the rat—head over heels, heart and soul in love with him—despite the fact that she'd known all along he was more than likely involved in something shady.

One of his iniquitous schemes must have somehow gone awry in such a way as to demand his immediate attention, and off he'd gone, carrying a briefcase full of guns, as if nothing else, or *no one* else, mattered to him in the least.

Realizing she'd begun to feel awfully sorry for herself considering she'd known all along exactly what she was getting into, Laura swiped angrily at the tears on her cheeks with the back of her hand. Devlin was gone and there was nothing she could do about it. Nor did she have any control over whether he eventually came back to her in one piece. All she could do was wait and hope and—

The sharp rap of knuckles against the wood of her bedroom door startled her out of her maundering. Alex, she assumed, blotting her eyes with the tissue she took from the pocket of her robe.

"Go away," she ordered, not wanting to be caught in the midst of such a self-indulgent display of unwonted misery.

As if she hadn't spoken, Alex opened the door and stepped into the room. Tucking his hands in the back pockets of his jeans, he surveyed the mess on the floor, then finally met her gaze.

"Have a little accident, did you?" he queried breezily.

"Go away," she repeated more vehemently, her voice still thick with tears.

"I will, but first—"

"If you're here to try to 'smooth things over,' don't waste your breath. I don't give a damn where Devlin's gone, and I don't care if he ever comes back," she said. Then, unable to help herself, she immediately burst into tears again.

"Of course you don't," Alex soothed, moving across the room to offer her a clean handkerchief.

Laura took it from him grudgingly, wiped her eyes and blew her nose rather indelicately. Then, clutching the now crumpled square of linen in her hands, she looked up at him and smiled bleakly.

"Actually, I lied."

"I know."

"Can you tell me *anything?*"

"Gone off on business. Back as soon as possible. Details upon his return," Alex replied. "But I guess you already know that, since you were lurking in the hallway outside his office eavesdropping."

"I wasn't *lurking,*" she protested. "I was just—"

Looking to get him into bed so I could jump his gorgeous bones.

"What?"

"Nothing," she muttered, her face flushing.

She was such a fool, such a hapless, hopeless fool.

"He'll be back, Laura," Alex said. "Believe me, he will."

"How can I when I have no idea where he's going or what he's doing and you won't tell me?" she retorted, her anger surging to the fore once again.

"Listen, I don't like keeping you in the dark, but orders are orders."

"Yeah, sure, like you'd jump off a building if he told you to."

"Believe it or not, I did once. It was quite an experience."

"I'm sure it was," she sniffed, not the least bit placated.

"Are you going to be all right now?"

"What if I said I'm not?"

"I'd stay and hold your hand a while longer."

"In that case, I'm just fine."

With a snort that sounded suspiciously like a laugh, Alex turned and walked back to the door.

"You want me to clean up this mess?" he asked, glancing back at her.

"I'll take care of it."

"Then I'll see you in the morning."

"Yes, I suppose you will," she replied with a sigh of resignation.

"Hey, look at the bright side. Now that you're stuck with me for a few days, I'll finally have a chance to teach the kid how to cheat at poker."

"You're a prince, Alex, a real prince."

"Yeah, I know."

Flashing her a wicked grin, he slipped out the door, leaving her alone at last, still hurt and angry and afraid, yet oddly encouraged, as well.

Devlin would return, and when he did, she had every intention of making him wish he hadn't. At least for the first five minutes or so. . . .

"Do you think he'll come home tomorrow, Mom?" Timmy asked Saturday night as he poked lethargically at the chicken-and-tortilla casserole Laura had made for dinner in Mrs. Santos's absence.

"Honey, I don't know," she replied, just as she had each of the many times he'd questioned her about Devlin's return over the past two days. "Now, finish eating, please."

"Okay," he mumbled, his lip quivering as he lowered his gaze.

"I'm sorry, Timmy. I didn't mean to snap at you. But I really don't have any idea when he'll be back."

Feeling like an ogre, she reached out and ruffled her son's dark curls contritely. It wasn't his fault that after two restless days and virtually sleepless nights she was literally worn to a frazzle; she had no right taking her resultant ill humor out on him.

"We'd tell you if we did," Alex added, pushing his empty plate away.

Glancing at him, Laura saw that he was watching her, his eyes filled with concern, and knew his words had been meant as much for her as for her son.

She'd tried to put up a good front the past couple of days, talking about Devlin's business trip as if he were off somewhere taking meetings and doing lunch. But she'd seen the headline on the front page of the newspaper Alex had bought yesterday when he'd taken her and Timmy to the market. Later she'd read the accompanying article about a terrorist attack that had taken place Thursday afternoon at a political rally in Honduras. And, knowing how Devlin's wife and daughter had died, she'd been seized by the horrible suspicion that Devlin's hasty departure had had something to do with the attack.

She'd broached the subject with Alex last night after Timmy had gone to bed, but he'd simply stared at her with a blank look on his face. Her blood boiling, she'd found the paper in the living room and shoved it under his nose. He'd glanced at the article, then dismissed her notion so condescendingly that he'd almost convinced her she was mistaken. Almost.

"I really miss him a lot," Timmy stated softly.

"Me, too," Laura admitted, avoiding Alex's gaze as she stood and gathered up their plates and silverware.

While she appreciated his help with Timmy, she was still angered by his continued refusal to tell her what he knew. Especially since she'd done everything she could think of to weasel the information out of him.

She doubted even Chinese water torture would get him to talk, but if Devlin didn't turn up soon, she might just have to give it a try. She couldn't go on much longer not knowing where he was or what he was doing, without turning into a real basket case.

"Want to take a walk up to the square?" Alex asked, as if reading her mind and deciding a little outing might buy him some time.

Hearing the word *walk*, Bitsy clambered to his feet and stood by the kitchen door expectantly as Timmy scrambled off his chair, opened the pantry door and grabbed the leash.

"Looks like a yes to me," Laura said.

"We don't have to go if you don't want to."

"Oh, Mom, please, can we?" Timmy begged.

She'd much rather curl up in a little ball and cry, but she'd already done enough of that the past couple of days. A walk would probably do them all good. Timmy was bouncing around energetically once again, and Alex obviously needed to stretch his bum leg. As for her, maybe the fresh air and exercise would help her sleep tonight.

"Of course," she agreed, flashing the most enthusiastic smile she could muster. "Just give me a minute to put away the leftovers while Alex loads the dishwasher."

As was usual on Saturday nights in the summer, San Pedro's main square bustled with activity. As a mariachi band played on one corner, groups of young men and women walked around and around the park area, eyeing each other covertly. Married couples strolled hand in hand, their children frolicking around them, while the elderly crowded together on the dark green wrought-iron benches, nodding and smiling as they chatted with one another.

Laura had hoped the air of gaiety would lift her spirits, but she only missed Devlin all the more as she walked along among the seemingly carefree crowd.

She wanted to believe that one day they, too, would have that kind of peace in their lives and that they, too, would share that kind of happiness. But how could she when the little she knew about him scared her half to death? Was he really living a life of crime as he'd led everyone in San Pedro to believe? And if he wasn't, what in the world was he doing with a briefcase full of guns?

If only she had a few answers, but she didn't.

As the twilight deepened and the tiny, twinkling white lights strung through the tree branches began to glow, Timmy's feet began to drag. Hoisting the boy into his arms, Alex suggested they go back home, and Laura readily agreed.

All the way there, she found herself hoping that Devlin would be waiting for them. But the house was just as deserted as they'd left it.

Thanking Alex for the outing, she took Timmy from him and slowly climbed the stairs. She gave her son a bath, tucked him into bed, then slipped quietly across the hall.

Alone in her bedroom, she walked to the window and stared out into the darkness.

"Come home to me," she whispered, her heart aching with loneliness. "Please, come home to me."

Hurting more than he thought any human being could hurt and still ride a motorcycle, Devlin guided the Harley through the night, slumped over the handlebars, his teeth clenched, groaning when the bike hit a bump in the narrow, winding road that comprised the last leg of his journey home.

He should have gone to the embassy in Tegucigalpa, flashed his credentials and gotten medical attention. But he wasn't hurt that badly.

No broken bones, although he could possibly have a cracked rib or two. No serious bleeding, internal or otherwise, although he was going to have some awfully ugly bruises in some very private places. And no gaping wounds, although the cut on his forehead probably could have used a few stitches.

Still, they would have insisted on putting him in the hospital, and once there, he wouldn't have been allowed out again until McConnell gave clearance for him to be released. Since the last thing he could have tolerated right then was having someone delay his return to San Pedro, he'd drawn upon what little willpower he had left and headed for home instead.

He had done what he'd set out to do in Tegucigalpa. On his own, as he'd known he'd have to be in order to maintain the necessary element of surprise, he'd cornered Drago Espinosa in a dirty back alley in the Honduran capital. Then, fair-minded, moral, upright, decent man that he was, he'd tried to take the bastard into custody.

Had he shot him in the back as he'd had the opportunity to do, he would have saved himself a world of hurt. But that kind of "elimination," satisfying though it would have been, had never been his style.

In the end, Drago *had* died, but only because that's what he chose to do. Devlin would have much preferred to see him rot in prison. Drago, on the other hand, had opted for a fight to the finish rather than allow himself to be taken alive. That the bullet from the gun Drago had fired during their struggle had hit him rather than Devlin had actually been a minor miracle... one Devlin had accepted without question.

Wanting nothing to do with the red tape that reporting Drago's death personally would involve, Devlin had left an anonymous message with the appropriate authorities about where to find Drago's body. Then he'd retrieved his gear and headed for the small field outside the city where he'd left his plane. Even without the red tape, the trip home would take him anywhere from twelve to twenty-four hours.

He'd come close to dying before. But never had he been so glad to be alive as he'd been when he finally walked away from Drago's still form. And deep in some primitive part of him, he wanted to celebrate his victory over death in the most life-affirming way a man could.

The sooner he got back to Laura, the better. She was all that mattered to him now. She was everything good and true, and if he had to beg her on his hands and knees to forgive him for deceiving her, then leaving her, he would.

As he turned onto his street he switched off the Harley's engine, letting the motorcycle roll quietly the last few hundred yards to the carport. His legs trembling, he managed to kick down the stand and dismount. He unlashed his duffel bag and briefcase from the rack and, leaning heavily against the adobe wall, keyed in the code to open the sliding door.

His head suddenly spinning, he stepped into the garden, keyed in the reverse code to close the door, then stood where he was for several seconds, willing the dizziness to go away. Finally, drawn to the house and the woman waiting there for him, he started up the walkway, weaving drunkenly, stumbled into one of his rose beds and promptly passed out cold.

No more able to sleep than she had been the past couple of nights, Laura gave up trying. The clock on the nightstand read eleven-thirty. Not that late, but considering she hadn't gotten much rest in the past forty-eight hours, she should be totally zonked out. Instead, she was so restless she was ready to crawl out of her skin.

Thinking that a glass of milk might help, she slipped into her robe and headed for the hallway. She started toward the staircase, then paused, turned and padded into Timmy's room.

She saw at once that he was sound asleep, lucky boy. As she sat on the edge of his bed, her heart swelled with love. She'd tried her best to give him a good life, and she didn't think she'd done too badly so far.

But if they stayed here with Devlin permanently, would she end up doing her son a grave disservice?

Devlin had made it apparent that he cared quite a bit for Timmy. In fact, he treated him as if he were his own son. Since not all men were capable of displaying that kind of affection for another's child, that counted for a lot as far as Laura was concerned.

Yet she couldn't help but wonder what would happen when Timmy got older and began to demand concise answers to the questions he asked. He was only five now, and already she'd found it hard to put him off. What would she tell him when he was eight or ten or twelve and Devlin left them as he had Thursday night? Would she have answers then, the kind of answers she could give an impressionable young boy, or would she still be wondering—

From outside the open window came an odd thunking sound, followed by a muffled groan. Startled, Laura stood and hurried across the room. Staring down at the garden below, she saw nothing but shadows at first. Then, in the wavering moonlight, she spied the crumpled form lying half on the walkway and half in the flower bed by the fountain.

Devlin . . .

With a soft cry she whirled around and raced into the hallway, nearly colliding with Alex as he stepped out of his room.

"Whoa, take it easy. It might not be him," he warned, catching her by the shoulders as Bitsy's fierce snarls echoed up the staircase.

"It is," she insisted, vaguely aware that he held a revolver in one hand. "It has to be. And he's hurt, Alex. He's *hurt.* Now let me go."

She tried to wrench away from him, but he refused to release her.

"Only if you promise to stay behind me until we're sure—"

"I promise," she cried, willing to sell her soul to the devil if that was what she had to do to get to Devlin.

One hand wrapped around her forearm, Alex led her down the stairs, moving swiftly yet surely through the dark house despite his limp. In the kitchen Bitsy was clawing at the door, his snarls replaced by whimpers of excitement and expectation.

"He knows," Laura whispered, her heart thudding. "He knows Devlin's out there."

Wordlessly Alex unlocked the door, then held Laura back as the dog took off into the garden.

"Please, let me go," she begged again, then went still as a familiar voice rang out from the shadows.

"Damn it, dog, stop slobbering on me."

Freed at last of Alex's hold on her, Laura ran down the walkway and fell to her knees beside Devlin. Pushing Bitsy out of the way, she slid her arms around him and cradled his head in her lap.

"Devlin." She hugged him close, tears in her eyes, her hurt and anger forgotten. "Oh, Devlin, what's happened to you?"

"Laura, sweetheart, don't cry. I'm going to be all right. Just give me a minute or two and I'll be on my feet again."

Across from her, Alex hunkered down, tucking his revolver into the waistband of his jeans. "Are you lucid?" he asked, his tone matter-of-fact.

"Barely," Devlin replied, trying unsuccessfully to lever himself up on his elbows.

"Any bones broken?"

"No."

"Internal bleeding?"

"No."

"Concussion?"

"Naw." He closed his eyes and lay back again. "But I do have one hell of a headache."

"So, you're gonna live?"

"Yeah, I'm gonna live."

"Well, then, let's get you in the house."

Throughout their exchange, Laura stared at the two men as if they were aliens from another planet. Devlin was lying in her lap, obviously in pain, and they were bantering back and forth about broken bones and internal injuries, about *life and death,* damn it.

"We can't move him," she shrilled, her nerves just about shot. "We've got to call the ambulance service and have him taken to the clinic. Juan Carlos will know—"

"Laura, I'm going to be all right," Devlin repeated. He reached up and cupped her face in his hand, threading his fingers through her hair. "Just help Alex get me into the house, okay? All I need is a hot bath, a couple of painkillers, which I just happen to have on hand, and about twelve hours' sleep, and I'll be good as new. I swear."

Her panic eased by his calm assurance, Laura covered his hand with hers and nodded. Then, shifting her gaze to Alex, she asked quietly, "How do you want to do this?"

"I can take most of his weight. You just hang on to him for balance."

Somehow they managed to get Devlin on his feet again without seeming to do him any more damage. From his occasional groans as they maneuvered him into the house and up the staircase, Laura knew he'd made light of how badly he'd been hurt. But it wasn't until they settled him on the edge of the bathtub and she switched on the overhead light that she saw the true extent of his injuries.

"Oh, Devlin," she murmured, her eyes welling with tears again.

There was a wicked gash on the left side of his forehead while a livid bruise discolored the skin under his right cheekbone and along his jaw. There were also bruises at the base of his throat, as if someone had tried to throttle him, and his knuckles were scraped raw. His black T-shirt and jeans were torn and dirty, his dark hair matted with dried blood.

"Hey, it looks a lot worse than it is," he said, hunching over, his elbows braced on his knees.

Reaching around him, Alex turned on the tap, sending a rush of steamy water flowing into the tile tub. As he straightened, he eyed Laura narrowly.

"You're not going to pass out on me, are you?" he demanded.

"No," she retorted with as much vehemence as she could muster, afraid that he'd send her away.

"Good." He nodded approvingly as he knelt in front of Devlin and began to untie his sneakers. "Get the scissors out of the medicine chest for me."

"The scissors?" She stared at him blankly.

"So I can cut off what's left of his clothes."

Of course. So he could cut off Devlin's clothes. Why hadn't she realized that?

Because she'd never been in this kind of situation in her life, she thought, barely controlling the urge to laugh hysterically.

"Just cut the shirt," Devlin instructed, sounding somewhat stronger than he had a few minutes earlier. "I can manage the jeans on my own."

As Alex wielded the scissors, then eased the strips of fabric off Devlin, Laura uttered another anguished cry. His chest and back were badly scraped and bruised, as well.

"Sure you're not going to faint?" Alex asked again, glancing over his shoulder at her.

"No, I'm not," she replied, taking the scissors from him.

"Thanks, Alex," Devlin muttered as he fumbled with the snap on his jeans, then added with a meaningful look, "I can take it from here."

"You sure?"

"I'm sure."

Sensing Devlin's increasing irritation at being forced to submit to his friend's ministrations, yet knowing he was in no shape to take care of himself, Laura nudged Alex aside and knelt in front of her husband. Then, brushing his hands out of the way, she unsnapped his jeans.

"We'll call you if we need your help," she advised, not quite meeting either man's startled gaze as she quickly dealt with Devlin's zipper.

"I'll be in my room," Alex replied as he backed out of the bathroom reluctantly.

"Laura, you don't have to do this," Devlin insisted, catching her hands in his as she reached for the waistband of his jeans.

"I'm your wife, Devlin." She looked up at him beseechingly. "Please, let me help you."

He hesitated for one long moment, then lifted her hands to his lips and gently kissed her fingertips.

"Thank you."

"De nada," she replied, a smile tugging at the corners of her mouth as she uttered his favorite phrase. "Now, if you'll just lift up..."

At her urging, he shifted first one way, then another, so she could slip his jeans and briefs over his narrow hips and down his legs.

"I'm sorry I left the way I did, but—"

"Not tonight," she interrupted, averting her eyes shyly as she tossed his clothing aside.

"Why not?" he asked, regarding her curiously.

"I'd rather wait until you're feeling better." She stood, then offered him her hand so he could turn and slide into the bathtub. "That way I can rant and rave all I want without feeling guilty about kicking you, at least figuratively, while you're down. Okay?"

"Okay," he agreed, a hint of amusement evident in his voice. Then, as the steamy water lapped up around his battered body, he moaned deeply.

"Lie back," Laura ordered, folding a towel over the edge of the tub to cushion his head.

He did as instructed, wincing slightly, then closed his eyes as the heat from the water began to penetrate his aching muscles. As he began to relax, Laura gently smoothed a soapy washcloth over his body, then shampooed his dark, shaggy hair.

When the water began to cool, she helped him out of the tub and toweled him dry, her gaze lingering here and there until she realized he was watching her, a faint smile tugging at the corners of his mouth. Her face flushing, she quickly knotted the towel around his waist and made him sit on the side of the tub again. She dabbed antiseptic on his cuts, bandaged the gash on his forehead, gave him two of the painkillers she found in the medicine cabinet just as he said she would, and finally helped him into bed.

She tucked the covers up around him, then switched off the lamp, slipped off her robe and climbed in beside him, curling as close to him as she dared considering the extent of his injuries.

With another moan Devlin turned toward her and slid his arm around her, drawing her hard against his chest. She went willingly, uttering a soft sigh as he rubbed his cheek against her hair.

"It's so good to be here with you again," he muttered, his voice husky. "So...damn...good..."

"And to be with you," Laura said, tears trickling down her cheeks.

"Stay with me, Laura. Always..."

"I will," she vowed, feathering her lips against the hollow at the base of his throat. "Always."

Though she had no idea how or why, Laura knew she'd come dangerously close to losing Devlin, and with that knowledge came the realization of just how much she loved him. No matter who or what he was.

Although she imagined she'd find out soon enough.

The moment Devlin seemed up to it, she was going to be asking him a lot of questions, to which she'd be expecting some honest answers, for Timmy's sake, if not her own. And if Devlin admitted that the rumors about him were true?

Well, then, she'd do everything in her power to get him to change.

She'd once believed her love was strong enough to change Johnny Buschetti. Unfortunately, she'd never had a chance to prove herself right. But she'd never proved herself wrong, either.

Thus, cockeyed optimist that she probably was, she couldn't help but believe the same might just hold true with Devlin.

If they cared for each other, truly *cared,* then they'd find a way to put the past behind them and start over together, to make a new, honest, upright life for themselves and their children.

They *would,* she swore with fierce determination.

Moments later, warmed by Devlin's presence and lulled by the rhythm of his quiet, even breathing, Laura found her eyes drifting shut as she finally eased into a deep and virtually dreamless sleep.

Chapter 10

Devlin awoke just as the sky outside his bedroom window began to fade from the black of night to the pale, pink-tinged gray of almost dawn. For a few seconds, before he threw off the last dregs of sleep, he wasn't quite sure where he was. But then the scattered bits of memory teasing his disordered mind came together.

His fight to the death with Drago, the mind-numbing flight back to Leon and the seemingly endless motorcycle ride to San Pedro that had finally brought him home to Laura.

Home to Laura. . . .

Savoring the warm, silky softness of her body nestled against him, Devlin recalled how she'd cared for him last night. She'd set aside her all-too-justifiable hurt and anger, ministering to his needs with a love and tenderness he hadn't deserved. Then she'd lain in his arms as if there were no-where else on earth she'd rather be, and vowed to stay with him always.

He'd had no right to extract such a promise from her, and he certainly wouldn't hold her to it. Not when she'd made it before she knew the truth about him.

However, very soon now, there would no longer be any lies between them. Then he'd ask her again, and hope against hope that she'd renew her vow once more.

Beside him, Laura murmured quietly, nuzzling her cheek against his chest as she slid her arm around his waist more securely. Aware that she was still asleep, Devlin shifted slightly, accommodating her gladly.

Though the movement set off several sharp twinges of pain, he was surprised at how much better he felt than he had last night. Soaking in the bathtub seemed to have relieved the worst of his muscle aches, while the painkillers had helped him sleep soundly enough so that his scrapes and bruises could start to heal.

He was going to be stiff and sore for a few days, but he was definitely well on the road to recovery. Especially if the way his body was responding to Laura's nearness was any indication.

Lying naked beneath the lace-edged linen sheet, Devlin was achingly aroused, as he had been from the instant he'd remembered where he was. And once again the urgency to celebrate life that had given him the strength he'd needed to make his way back to her rode through him hard and fast.

Instinctively he shifted again, turning toward her so that his erection nestled against the soft curve of her belly. Imperceptibly he tightened his hold on her, bent his head and brushed his lips against her cheek.

With another unintelligible murmur she arched into him provocatively, sliding her hand from his waist over his hip to the top of his thigh, then up again.

He groaned inwardly, barely restraining the urge to crush her beneath him and take what he wanted, what he desperately needed. He knew that in her present state she'd submit to his demands. But he wanted so much more than acquiescence from her.

He wanted her not only willing, but also fully aware, and as desperately *wanting* as he was.

"Devlin?" she whispered, tilting her face up so that she met his gaze.

"Yes, Laura." He smiled down at her reassuringly as he stroked her back.

"Are you hurting again?"

"Not in the way you mean."

She stared at him, her expression bemused. Then, as he moved his hips and pressed against her, understanding dawned in her pale green eyes. A faint blush stained her cheeks, but she didn't look away, and after a moment more, she smiled, too.

"So, does that mean you don't need another pain pill?"

"Ah, sweetheart, all I need right now is you," he muttered, his voice husky.

"Mmm, good." Sliding her hand boldly between their bodies, she teased him with the light touch of her fingertips. "I need you, too."

"Are you sure, Laura? Very, very sure? Because I don't think I'm going to be able to stop if we go any further."

"Yes, Devlin, I'm very, *very* sure." She feathered light kisses along his bearded jaw, then without the least hesitation, offered the invitation for which he'd been waiting. "Make love to me. Please."

Her simple request was all the encouragement he needed. He threaded his fingers through her wildly tousled curls, tipped her face up and kissed her with a fierce possessiveness that she matched in her own sweetly feminine way.

As he groaned again, this time with implicit longing, she smiled inwardly, delighting in the obvious depth of his desire. Her tongue darting over his, she smoothed her hands over his chest and across his shoulders, gently mindful of his scrapes and bruises, then arched against him tantalizingly.

Responding to her silent entreaty, Devlin cupped her breast in his hand, tugging at her nipple with his thumb and forefinger through the fine fabric of her gown. When she whimpered softly, he fumbled with the tiny buttons down the front of her gown. Then, after several unsuccessful moments, he murmured an apology, ripped them open, stripped the gown off her and tossed it aside.

In the faint predawn light he gazed at her as he ran his hands over her tenderly, sculpting the curves of her breasts and the slight swell of her belly with his fingertips, then delving through the dark curls at the juncture of her thighs to dip inside her welcoming warmth.

"You are so beautiful," he muttered, bending to draw her nipple into his mouth as she lifted herself against his hand, opening to his gentle exploration.

Shifting restlessly under the masterful touch of his hands and mouth, Laura trailed the tips of her fingers down Devlin's chest and over the flat plane of his stomach. Then, with a teasing impudence that seemed to surprise him, she took him in her hands, stroking him in a wantonly needful, womanly insistent way.

She wanted to feel him inside her, filling her, touching her very core.

"Now, Devlin," she pleaded.

He'd wanted to go slowly this first time, lingering over her as he touched and tasted every part of her. But her sudden urgency only served to heighten his own primitive impulse to mate with her.

Rolling her onto her back, he positioned himself between her thighs, then braced himself on his elbows and smoothed her hair away from her face. A moment later, holding her gaze, he entered her in one swift, sure stroke.

With a low moan of pleasure she lifted her hips and wrapped her legs around him, delighting in their joining. Then, instinctively, she moved under him, pressing up, trying to take him even more deeply.

Sliding an arm under her, Devlin thrust into her again, giving her what she wanted, then held her still as he savored the totality of his possession. Finally, unable to restrain himself any longer, he began to move, his rhythmic strokes taking them closer and closer until together they catapulted over the edge, her soft cry mingling with his guttural moan.

Long afterward they lay together, still joined intimately, though Devlin had rolled to his side to relieve her of his weight. Nestled against him, Laura luxuriated in the warmth emanating from his body, the gentle whisper of his breath against her hair and the tickle of his fingertips along her spine, wishing they could stay just as they were forever.

Finally, and with seeming reluctance, he eased out of her and lay back, though he still held her close. Glancing up at him, Laura saw the strained look on his face and frowned.

"Are you all right?" she asked, unable to hide her worry as she reached up and touched his cheek.

Considering how badly he'd been hurt, maybe they shouldn't have—

"I think I'm the one who should be asking you that," he replied, catching her hand in his and nibbling at her palm. "A true gentleman wouldn't have rushed you quite the way I did."

"And here I thought *I* was the one in a hurry," she teased, somewhat relieved by his lighthearted tone.

"Seriously, Laura, are you all right?" he persisted.

"I'm fine, really."

"You're sure?"

"All right, I *am* a little sore, but only in a few places," she admitted laughingly.

"Mmm, me, too," Devlin agreed with a slight smile, then closed his eyes.

No matter what he said, Laura knew he had to be more than a little sore. In the dim light of early morning his face appeared pale and drawn beneath the shadow of his beard, while his scrapes and bruises looked much uglier than they had the night before. Yet his major concern had been for her.

Levering herself up on her elbow, she kissed him gently on the mouth, then slipped from the bed.

"Don't go," he protested, reaching out as if to stop her.

"I'm not." She hurried into the bathroom, grabbed the bottle of pain pills, filled a cup with water and returned to the bedroom. "Here, take these," she said, opening the bottle, dumping two pills into her palm and offering them to Devlin along with the cup of water.

"Just one." He swallowed the pill, then chided gently as he lay back again, "Don't look so worried. Give me another hour or two and I'll be almost as good as new."

"How about four or five hours?" she insisted, setting the pill bottle and cup on the nightstand.

"Only if you'll stay here with me." Smiling, he held out his arm to her.

"Gladly." Curling close to him, she rested her head on his chest. "But when Timmy wakes up—"

"Then we'll both get up," he cut in firmly.

Rather than argue with him, Laura kissed him on the chin, then settled down beside him, willing him to fall asleep again.

"How's he doing?" Devlin asked.

"Timmy? He's fine," she assured him, then added after a moment's hesitation, "but he really did miss you."

"I missed him, too. And you." He tightened his hold on her. "We have to talk, Laura."

"We will . . . later."

"I meant what I said about wanting you to stay with me."

"And I meant it when I said I would."

"I'm not—not what you think," he muttered, his voice beginning to slur.

"Later, Devlin. You can tell me everything later. Sleep now," she urged, knowing that was what he needed more than anything at the moment.

They'd have time to talk when he was rested. All the time in the world. She wasn't going anywhere, not ever. She was staying right here with him, for better or worse, for the rest of her life. She'd made her decision last night, and their lovemaking had only deepened her commitment to him.

He was her husband in every way now, and she was determined to see to it that they, along with their children, had a good life together.

Smiling to herself, Laura curved her hand over her belly. Neither one of them had thought to use any protection, and she was in midcycle. She could already be carrying Devlin's child in her womb. A new life to bond them even more closely in the days and weeks ahead.

She wondered if he'd be pleased. Then she thought of how he'd talked about his daughter and of how he'd treated her son, and knew in her heart that his pride and joy would easily equal her own.

When she was sure Devlin was sound asleep again, Laura pulled the sheet and coverlet up around him, then quietly slipped out of bed. Timmy would be awake very soon now, and she didn't want him disturbing Devlin for at least three or four hours. While he seemed well on the way to recovery, she knew he needed to rest so that he'd have a chance to heal.

She put on her robe, took clean underwear from the dresser, her kelly green knit dress and sandals from the closet, and crossed to her son's room. Finding him still asleep, she hurried into his bathroom where she washed and dressed. She was brushing the tangles out of her hair when he finally joined her, rubbing his eyes sleepily.

"*Buenos días*," she greeted him, smiling as he stared at her in surprise.

"What are you doing in here, Mom?"

"Devlin came home last night—"

"He did?" Whirling around excitedly, her son headed for the bedroom door. "I want to—"

"Whoa, not so fast." She caught him around the waist and turned him to face her. "He's really, really tired, so we need to let him get some sleep."

"But I want—"

"I know, honey. He wants to see you, too. But he has to rest for a while first."

"How long is 'a while'?" he asked, his lower lip jutting out unyieldingly.

"A few hours, at least."

"A few *hours?*"

"Yes," she stated succinctly in her because-I-say-so tone of voice.

"All right," Timmy replied, thankfully choosing not to argue anymore.

Laura helped him wash and dress, then they went down to the kitchen, where Bitsy greeted them with his usual early-morning exuberance.

Hoping to placate her son, she made his favorite breakfast, pancakes and bacon. He gobbled up his serving as quickly as he could, then asked if he could wake Devlin yet. When she told him that he couldn't, he slumped in his chair, scowling at her angrily.

Glancing at the clock above the refrigerator, Laura shook her head ruefully. It was only eight o'clock. She wanted Devlin to sleep until at least ten or eleven. But what was she going to do with Timmy in the meantime?

He was such a good child. However, when he set his mind on something, his persistence could be maddening. Normally, she had no problem summoning enough patience to deal with him in an equable manner. But she was rather weary herself at the moment, and she didn't want to end up snapping at him again as she had last night.

She could only hope that Alex would put in an appearance sometime soon, and help her keep him entertained. For now, however...

"Why don't you take Bitsy out in the garden and play with him for a while?" she suggested as she started to clear the table.

"Okay," he muttered dejectedly, dragging his feet all the way to the door.

Ten minutes later he was back in the kitchen, asking about Devlin yet again.

Handing him several of Bitsy's dog biscuits, she sent him out to the garden once more. Then she ran upstairs and knocked softly on Alex's door. When she got no response she turned the knob, opened the door and looked inside the room.

Not at all to her surprise, but much to her dismay, he wasn't there.

After two full days of keeping her and Timmy company, she couldn't blame him for taking off on his own as soon as he had a chance. Devlin had said he was a loner who liked to come and go as he pleased, and while he hadn't visibly chafed at the restrictions imposed on him in his boss's absence, Laura knew he hadn't exactly been thrilled with them, either.

Now that Devlin was home, he'd probably considered himself relieved of duty. More than likely he'd gone out at first light, and unfortunately, there was no telling when he'd return.

Hearing footsteps on the stairs, Laura backed out of Alex's room and closed the door, then hurried down the hall to waylay her son.

Halfway up the staircase, Timmy paused and looked at her expectantly.

"Is he awake yet?"

"No," Laura replied, trying with little success to contain her growing exasperation as she took him by the hand and led him back to the kitchen.

"Where's Alex?"

"I don't know."

As she returned to the sink to finish washing their breakfast dishes, her son shuffled over to a chair and threw himself into it. Risking a glance at him, Laura saw the mutinous look on his usually cherubic face, and knew she was going to have to think of something fast. If she didn't distract him soon, both of them were going to end up in tears, and she didn't want that to happen on Devlin's first day home.

She glanced at the clock again, wishing they could get out of the house for a couple of hours. Her initial impulse was to reject the idea altogether. However, on second thought...

Ten days had passed since Vincent Petrano had caught sight of her and Timmy outside the cathedral. But neither Giovanni nor any of his emissaries had yet shown up in San Pedro.

As a result, Laura had begun to believe that she'd misjudged the old man. For whatever reason, he no longer seemed to have any interest in his grandson.

Of course, she could be jumping the gun. But hadn't she overheard Devlin say almost the same thing to Alex Thursday night when she'd eavesdropped on their conversation?

Still, she didn't think it would be wise for them to wander too far from home. But Annie lived only three blocks away. They could take Bitsy with them, walk the short distance there, leave the dog at the Morenos' house, then go on to mass at St. Rita's with Annie and Juan Carlos.

They'd be gone long enough for Devlin to get the rest he so desperately needed, and they'd be doing something that Timmy should find agreeable.

Drying her hands on a towel, Laura stepped into the hallway, picked up the telephone and dialed Annie's number. When her friend answered, she quickly explained the situation.

"Unless you have any objections, we'll leave in the next ten minutes or so," she added.

"None at all," Annie said. "But are you sure you want to walk? We could come by in the car and pick you up."

"I'm sure we'll be okay. It's only three blocks and we'll have the dog with us. And maybe the walk will improve Timmy's mood."

"We'll be waiting for you, then."

Smiling to herself, Laura cradled the receiver, then returned to the kitchen.

"Why don't you get Bitsy's leash?" she suggested as she glanced at her son.

"Are we going somewhere?" he asked with not only interest but obvious enthusiasm, as well.

"Over to Annie's, then on to St. Rita's with her and Juan Carlos."

He frowned for a moment, obviously torn between his desire to stay home and bug her about Devlin and his equally strong desire to visit the Morenos.

"Can we stay at Annie's for a while after church so I can play on the swings and the slide?" he asked at last.

"Yes, of course," she readily agreed.

"Okay."

While Timmy went to get the leash, Laura found paper and a pencil in one of the drawers and wrote a short note telling Devlin where they'd gone in case he awoke before they returned. Then she took one of the two sets of keys to the front door from the tray on the counter, lured Bitsy out from under the table with the word *walk*, and helped her son fasten the leash to her collar.

Just outside the front door she hesitated for several moments, glancing up and down the street. To the right an elderly woman dressed in black shuffled along the sidewalk, heading away from them, while off to the left, in the direction they'd be going, a family of four dressed in their Sunday best paused at the corner to allow a car to pass, then crossed the street.

She saw nothing out of the ordinary. Nor did there seem to be any suspicious characters lurking about. Still—

"Come on, Mom. Let's go," Timmy urged, tugging on her hand.

"Okay."

Shrugging off her sudden uncertainty about the wisdom of what she was doing, Laura locked the front door, then stepped onto the sidewalk, keeping Timmy close beside her while allowing Bitsy to trot several paces ahead of them.

At the corner she stopped and looked both ways, but again didn't notice anything unusual. The family of four was now some distance ahead of them, obviously heading in the general direction of St. Rita's, as well. And though there was a car parked halfway up the cross street, she saw that it had a local license plate. Since it also appeared to be unoccupied, she thought nothing more of it.

They were almost at the end of the second block when she heard swiftly moving footsteps behind her. At the same instant Bitsy spun around, growling low in his throat.

"Mommy, what—" Timmy began.

Her heart racing, Laura glanced over her shoulder. Two men were running toward them. Two men she recognized even though she'd seen them with Johnny only a couple of times.

"Oh, no," she whispered. *"No."*

She'd wanted to believe that Timmy was safe simply because it had suited her purpose. But she should have remembered how implacable Giovanni could be, and never taken such a chance. Not even for Devlin's well-being.

Letting go of Bitsy's leash, Laura scooped her son into her arms and started to run. Snarling viciously, the dog hurled himself at their attackers. From behind her she heard one of the men curse, then a loud thunk sounded, followed by a yelp.

Glancing back, Laura saw the dog topple onto the street as the two men continued on, circling around her, one on either side.

"Come on, Laura, honey. Give me the kid," the one to her left coaxed, waving his club at her menacingly. "Save yourself some pain."

"Get away from us," she cried.

"Mommy, Mommy!" Timmy wailed.

"The old man wants him, and the old man always gets what he wants," the one to her right taunted.

"No," she shrieked, clutching Timmy to her, trying to evade them as they drew closer and closer.

Surely someone had to see what was happening and would come to their rescue. Surely. But there was no one anywhere nearby.

Suddenly, from the corner of her eye, she saw the man to her right lunge for Timmy. Instinctively she whirled away from him, only to come up against the man to her left as he lifted his club.

"No," she screamed, ducking away from the thick black stick as it whooshed toward her. *"No!"*

An instant later the club cracked against her skull as her son was wrenched from her arms. Pain shot through her head with a sickening intensity, sending her crashing to her knees, then crumpling into a heap as the bright pinpoints of light whirling before her eyes faded into deadly darkness.

Although he was groggy from the pain pill he'd taken, the moment Devlin drifted out of sleep the second time Sunday morning, he knew exactly where he was. Still, he was plagued by a vague sense of confusion.

As he rolled onto his back and stared at the ceiling, he had the strangest feeling he'd been awakened by a woman's scream. Not close by, but a little distance away. Somewhere outside his bedroom window. From about the same direction as Bitsy's barking.

Bitsy's barking?

Recognizing the hysterical barking he heard coming from down the street as that of his dog, Devlin shot out of bed and stumbled across the room. What was Bitsy doing out on the street? Ignoring the twinges of pain shooting through various parts of his body, he braced his palms on the sill and leaned out the open window.

Two blocks away a small group of people had gathered around a ferociously barking, snarling rottweiler. *His* rottweiler. And near the dog was a bright patch of kelly green . . . the same kelly green he'd seen Laura wearing only last week.

Filled with a sudden sense of alarm, Devlin turned away from the window.

"Laura," he shouted as he pulled shorts and a T-shirt from the dresser and struggled into them. *"Laura!"*

Only Bitsy's barking, coupled with the sudden shrill of the telephone in the downstairs hallway, disturbed the silence surrounding him.

Throwing open the bedroom door, he headed for the staircase, calling out for Alex. Again he got no answer. With Devlin home, he'd probably assumed, and rightly so, that he could again come and go as he pleased.

Fear clawing at his gut, Devlin ran down the stairs, skidded to a halt by the telephone and yanked the receiver from its cradle.

"Yes?" he snapped in lieu of a greeting.

"Devlin, it's Annie Moreno—"

"Is Laura there?" he demanded.

"She should have been by now, but—"

"Aw, hell."

Dropping the receiver, Devlin raced into the kitchen and reached for the front door keys. As he pulled them from the basket, he saw the note on the counter.

She'd gone to Annie's so he could rest.

Cursing under his breath, he glanced at the clock above the refrigerator, comparing the current time to the time she'd jotted down on the note, and realized she'd left no more than fifteen minutes ago.

Fifteen minutes.

What could have possibly happened to her and her son in that short length of time?

More than he wanted to imagine, he thought, as he flung open the front door and ran toward the growing crowd of people halfway up the next block.

It had taken Drago Espinosa only five minutes to kill half a dozen people including Carly and Melissa.

As he drew near, the others made way for him, and his worst fears were realized. Laura lay on the sidewalk, eyes closed, blood oozing from a nasty gash on the left side of her head. Bitsy's head was bloodied, too, yet the dog stood over Laura, guarding her valiantly, snapping and snarling at anyone who dared get too close. As for Timmy...

Scanning the crowd, Devlin saw at once that the boy wasn't there. But then, he'd feared that would be the case from the instant he'd realized Laura had taken him out of the house on her own.

Giovanni, you bastard, when I get my hands on you...

Somehow, some way, the old man and his cohorts had slipped into Mexico and, biding their time, had waited for Devlin to let down his guard.

And he'd done just that, in spades.

If only he hadn't been gone the past couple of days, maybe he would have noticed that strangers were lurking around the neighborhood as they must have been to pull off such a brazen attack in broad daylight. Then again, maybe not.

When several days had passed with no sign of Giovanni, he'd no longer considered the man a threat, and he'd said as much to Alex Thursday night when Laura had been standing outside his office.

He wasn't sure why he'd been so damned complacent. Although it *had* been easier for him to go after Drago thinking that Laura and Timmy would be all right on their own in San Pedro.

Just as it had been easier for him to delay leaving the embassy thinking Carly and Melissa would be all right on their own at the airport.

Obviously he hadn't learned from his mistakes. But it was too late to go back and do things differently. Right now he had to see to Laura, and then he'd go after Timmy.

"Bitsy, down," he ordered.

As the dog crouched down and quieted, Devlin knelt beside Laura and reached for her wrist. Her face was deathly pale and she'd lost more blood than he'd first thought, but thankfully, her pulse, while slow, was strong and steady.

"Laura," he urged, easing her onto her back and smoothing her hair away from her face. "Laura, sweetheart, wake up."

She stirred at the sound of his voice and her eyes fluttered open. As he swiftly checked for broken bones, she stared at him blankly. Gradually, however, recognition dawned in her pale green eyes.

"Devlin?"

"Yeah, it's me." He took her hand in his and brushed his lips over her fingertips. "Can you tell me what happened?"

Again she stared at him blankly. Then, her hand tightening in his, she remembered.

"Two men...Johnny's friends. They had clubs. They hit Bitsy and...and me." She paused, closing her eyes for a moment, then met his gaze again. "Where's Timmy?" she whispered, her voice filled with fear. "Devlin, where's Timmy?"

When he couldn't bring himself to answer her, she struggled to sit up, only to fall back again with a sharp cry of pain.

"Laura, be still," he ordered, vowing to tear Johnny's friends limb from limb when he got his hands on them.

"But I have to—"

"I'll get Timmy back. I swear I will. But right now I've got to get you to the clinic."

Having assured himself that she didn't have any broken bones, he lifted her into his arms.

"I didn't think Giovanni was interested in Timmy, after all," she murmured, tears trickling from her eyes.

"I didn't think so, either," he admitted. "And apparently that's exactly what he was hoping we'd do."

"I should have known."

"No, I'm the one who should have known," he said. "But I was so damn busy getting myself beaten to a pulp—"

Biting off his words angrily, he stood, and as he did so, the crowd shifted again, allowing Juan Carlos and Annie to come forward.

"Oh, no, I was afraid something like this had happened," Annie cried.

"Now, Annie, calm down," Juan Carlos chided, then eyed Devlin sternly. "Do you have any idea how long she was unconscious?"

"My guess is about ten minutes."

"Broken bones?" he continued, lifting Laura's eyelids.

"I don't think so."

"Bleeding?"

"As far as I can tell, only from the head wound."

"Let's get her to the clinic, then." Juan Carlos started to turn away, then paused and took a good look at Devlin. "What about you?"

"Bruised and battered, but otherwise, none the worse for wear."

Much to Devlin's relief, the Morenos had driven the short distance from their house, making the trip to the clinic much faster than it would have been on foot. He sat on the back seat of their car, cradling Laura in his lap while Bitsy lay on the floor by his feet, and answered Annie's questions as best he could.

Though not unconscious, Laura lay still, her eyes closed, obviously in pain from the blow she'd taken. There was a good chance she had a concussion. He could only hope she didn't also have a fractured skull.

At the clinic he carried Laura into one of the examining rooms. Then, at Juan Carlos's insistence, he returned to the waiting room.

Pacing from one end of the otherwise deserted room to the other, he tried to decide what to do next. He didn't want to leave the clinic, but there were some things he was going to have to do in order to ensure Timmy's safety.

He was in the midst of silently cursing Alex for disappearing when the waiting room doors opened and his friend limped into the lobby.

"Where the hell have you been?" Devlin snarled, making no effort to draw rein on his roiling emotions.

"You want to just hit me and get it out of your system so we can concentrate on finding the kid?" Alex snapped back, jutting his chin out challengingly.

"Don't tempt me." Clenching his fists, Devlin shoved his hands into his pockets. Then, realizing Alex knew what was going on, he looked at his friend questioningly. "How...?" he began.

"Obviously you didn't notice, but I was working the crowd while you were making sure Laura was still alive. There were two of them—*norteamericano* gangsters, according to one of the kids. One of them whacked Laura over the head while the other one grabbed Timmy. They drove off in a late model car with Illinois plates. Want the license number?"

"Not right now," Devlin replied, then acknowledged his appreciation. "I owe you big time."

"Yeah, I know." Alex grinned wickedly. "Want to hear the rest?"

"What do you think?"

"I went back to the house to see if anything had come in for you since yesterday afternoon. Sometime last night you got a fax from your contact in Chicago. Rico Loya and Charley Gonzo, trusted employees of Giovanni Buschetti, crossed the border at McAllen, Texas, four days ago. They were driving a late model car with Illinois plates. License number...ditto. Sounds like the ones who nabbed Timmy."

"Yeah, it sure does."

"So, do we go after them ourselves, alert the Mexican authorities, the U.S. border patrol, or what?"

"I doubt we'll be able to catch up with them on our own. They've got too much of a head start, and there's no guarantee they're going back across the border at McAllen. I don't think it would be wise to alert the Mexican authorities, either. They'd find them easily enough, but I can't see Rico or Charley surrendering without a fight. I don't want to risk a car chase or a shoot-out as long as they have Timmy with them."

"What about the U.S. border patrol?"

"I think they're our best bet." Crossing to the reception desk, Devlin pulled a pad of paper and a pen from one of the drawers and began to jot down names, job titles and telephone numbers. "I want you to go back to the house and contact these guys. Give them the information on the car, including the license number, tell them about Timmy and make sure no attempt will be made to try to stop them. Instead, I want them followed back to Chicago, and I want Giovanni under twenty-four-hour surveillance." He underlined the last name on his list. "Denny Gifford can handle that. Also, ask him to assemble a team of his best men and have them ready to go after the boy with me sometime in the next forty-eight hours."

Alex took the list from him and glanced at it, then met Devlin's gaze again. "I'm assuming your name alone will be enough to have your bidding done."

"More than enough." Leaning a hip against the desk, Devlin rubbed a hand across his bearded jaw as he regarded his friend ruefully. "Payback's gonna be hell, though."

"But worth it."

"Yes," Devlin replied without hesitation.

"Do you want me to talk to McConnell, too?"

"I'll contact him myself later today. I imagine he's heard about Drago by now. In fact, he's probably ready to blow a gasket wondering what the hell happened."

"He's not the only one."

"Let's just say Drago's luck ran out before mine did."

"That close, huh?"

"Too close," Devlin admitted.

"Close enough to convince you to ask McConnell for that job in D.C. so you can get Laura and Timmy out of here?" Alex prodded.

"After this I'm not sure she'd go anywhere with me. I was supposed to protect her son and look what a wonderful job I've done," he muttered.

"From what I gather, she took the boy out on her own—"

"Only because she thought it was safe, and I'm fairly certain she thought *that* because she overheard *me* say as much to you last Thursday night. If I hadn't been so anxious to clear the decks and go after Drago..." Shrugging angrily, Devlin turned away.

He could go over the errors in judgment he'd made all he wanted, but all the "if onlys" in the world weren't going to change what had happened.

He'd let Laura and Timmy down just as he had Carly and Melissa. The only difference was that at least *they* were still alive.

Laura was injured, but not dangerously so. And Devlin was sure Rico and Charley wouldn't let anything happen to Timmy as long as they weren't threatened. Granted, the boy was probably terrified, but he was a resilient child. Once he was reunited with his mother, as he would be very soon, he'd regain his equilibrium.

Together, the two of them would be able to get on with their lives. Devlin had every intention of making sure Giovanni knew his life would be a living hell if he ever came near them again, so they should be able to do so not only without fear of reprisals, but also without any need of *him*.

He'd get them settled somewhere in the States and make provisions for their financial well-being, then get out of their lives for good.

If that's what Laura wanted.

But then, why wouldn't she? She hadn't married him out of love, but rather out of a desperate need she would no longer have.

For the space of a heartbeat he thought of their lovemaking with something approaching hope. But he wasn't fool enough to believe that that alone was an adequate foundation on which to build a future. Not when he'd neither been honest with her nor kept his promise to keep her son safe.

How could she ever trust him again? More important, why would she want to try?

"Hey, man, I know you've made your fair share of mistakes. But you've done your penance, too," Alex drawled, interrupting Devlin's reverie as if he'd been reading his mind. "Seems to me you still feel the need to punish yourself, though, and you've decided to do it by walking away from Laura and Timmy. Why, I don't know. But don't you dare tell yourself you're doing it because that's what Laura wants. She loves you, and if you give her a chance, she'll prove it to you ten times over."

"What would you know about her loving me?" Devlin demanded, unwilling to believe what Alex was saying.

"Apparently a hell of a lot more than you, and I've only spent a couple of days with her," Alex retorted. "Give yourself a break, and give Laura one, too. Even if the end results weren't exactly what you'd intended them to be, you had good reasons for doing what you did, whether it was deceiving her about your identity or going after Drago. Since she's made mistakes, too, I have a feeling she'll understand." He hesitated, then, flashing a cocky grin, continued in a taunting tone of voice. "Of course, if you'd really rather she found someone else to warm her bed . . ."

"Get out of here, Alex. *Now,*" Devlin snapped, unable to bear the thought of Laura with another man, yet knowing he couldn't expect her to stay with him, either.

"I'm on my way," Alex assured him, still grinning, his tone nerve-janglingly mild. "I'll be at the house if you need me."

It was all Devlin could do to keep from heaving a chair at his head.

"Take Bitsy with you."

"Sir, yes, *sir.*"

Issuing a smart salute, he called to the dog as he limped out the door.

One of these days, Devlin vowed, clenching his fists again, he and Alex were going to have a little session, one-on-one, in the boxing ring at the "company" gym, gloves optional.

But for now...

He wanted nothing more than to make sure both Laura and Timmy were all right. Once that was a certainty, and they were together again, then maybe he'd give some thought to what Alex had said. And maybe he'd find the courage to ask Laura to give him another chance. Maybe.

Chapter 11

Alone in the waiting room once again, Devlin resumed his pacing. Hands shoved in the side pockets of his cutoffs, he stalked to the glass doors that led out to the driveway, turned and stalked back to the reception desk, his mind spinning and his heart aching as his concern for Laura increased with every moment that passed.

Though it seemed much longer, less than thirty minutes had gone by since he'd left her with Annie and Juan Carlos in the examining room. Still, he'd hoped by now one of them would have come out to tell him how she was doing.

If she was more badly hurt than he'd thought...if she did, indeed, have a fractured skull or internal injuries, they'd have to get her to the hospital in Leon without delay or she could easily—

"She's going to be all right, Devlin," Annie murmured, resting her hand on his arm.

He glanced at Laura's friend in surprise, so lost in his own thoughts that he hadn't heard her come into the waiting room.

"She has a mild concussion, and thus, one heck of a headache, and she needed several stitches in that gash, but otherwise, aside from a few scrapes and bruises, she's okay."

"Can I see her?" Overwhelmed with relief, he moved away from the desk.

"Yes, of course." Annie led him toward the examining room. "She's still kind of out of it. But that's normal, so don't be alarmed."

Laura lay on the examining table, her face still deathly pale, her eyes closed. But as he crossed to her side, she opened her eyes and reached out to him.

"Devlin."

"I'm here, sweetheart."

"We have to get Timmy…"

"We will," he assured her.

"He's going to be so afraid."

"He's a smart boy. He'll know we're coming for him."

"How soon?"

"You're not going anywhere for at least twenty-four hours," Juan Carlos interrupted, his tone implacable.

"But I can't—" Laura protested.

"You can and you will unless you want to risk orphaning your son."

She sank back and closed her eyes, obviously too exhausted to argue with him.

"Can I at least go home?"

"As long as Devlin promises to keep an eye on you and makes sure you do as I say." Juan Carlos looked at him questioningly.

"Whatever you say, Doc."

"I want her to stay in bed the rest of today and tomorrow. She's not to have any stimulants or any analgesics. You can put a cold cloth on her forehead to relieve the pain if it gets too bad. Also, I want to know immediately if she's nauseous or if her pupils fail to react to a change in light.

You'll have to wake her every few hours through the night to make sure they do. Understood?''

"Yes."

"If you have any concerns at all, call me."

"I will," Devlin agreed.

"Then, if you'll carry her out to the car, I'll drive you home."

"I can stay with her if you'd like," Annie offered.

"That won't be necessary," Devlin replied. "But thanks anyway."

He lifted Laura into his arms as gently as he could and walked toward the waiting room, wanting to get her home. He knew she was hurting, but there was little he could do for her except tuck her into bed. And the sooner he could do that, the better it would be for her.

For the remainder of the day Devlin divided his time between their bedroom and his office, alternately tending to Laura and checking with Alex to make sure his orders were being carried out.

He also had a long, relatively low-key conversation with McConnell. Hostilities were exchanged a couple of times regarding Devlin's tendency to bend the rules. However, upon hearing about Timmy's kidnapping and Devlin's plan to rescue him, his boss had immediately offered his full support as well as the use of one of Uncle Sam's Learjets for their flight from Mexico City to Chicago.

Just after eight o'clock Sunday night word came in that Giovanni's men had crossed the border at Laredo, driven to the local airport and boarded a private plane bound for Chicago. And sometime around midnight another message advised that the plane had landed. A sleeping child had been carried off, then handed into a limo, which had been tailed to Giovanni's mansion in the suburbs.

Relieved that Timmy's harrowing journey was over, Devlin left Alex in the office and climbed the staircase for what he hoped would be the last time that night. He doubted Giovanni would be foolish enough to try to take Timmy out of the country, but if he did, he'd be stopped by the federal agents who now had him under surveillance.

For a few hours at least, he could rest easy. Then, tomorrow, he could work out the last details of the plan he'd already set in motion.

He wasn't sure why the old man had thought he could get away with kidnapping his grandson, but Devlin had a feeling Giovanni was going to be awfully surprised when he realized his former daughter-in-law hadn't married a common criminal, as his henchmen had probably reported, but rather a government agent with no qualms at all about coming after him.

If Giovanni was as involved in underworld dealings as Devlin's sources had indicated, the last thing he'd want was to have Devlin and his associates breathing down his neck. And that was exactly the threat Devlin intended to pose to guarantee Laura's future peace of mind. Whether he remained a part of her life or not, she and Timmy would be protected.

After checking on Laura and finding her asleep, he slipped into the bathroom and took a shower. For most of the day, he'd been running on pure adrenaline, but now he was exhausted, physically and mentally. And as Alex had so bluntly pointed out, if he didn't get some rest he wouldn't be any use at all tomorrow or the next day when Laura and Timmy would need him most.

Back in the bedroom he sat on the edge of the bed and, hating to do it, switched on the lamp on the nightstand so he could wake Laura once more before he slept.

She responded to his gentle urgings with a murmured protest, stirred restlessly, then finally gazed up at him, her pale eyes reacting as they should in the lamplight.

"How are you feeling?" he asked, brushing her tangled curls away from her face, careful to avoid the bandage covering the gash on the side of her head.

"Head still hurts," she admitted. "But not quite so bad anymore."

"Any nausea?"

"No."

"Good."

Satisfied that she was as well as could be expected, he switched off the lamp, then crossed to his side of the bed and lay down.

Murmuring his name, Laura scooted across the space he'd purposely left between them for her comfort, and he gladly drew her into his arms.

"I just got word that Timmy's all right. He was taken to Giovanni's house about an hour ago."

"How... how do you know that?" she asked, tilting her face up to gaze at him in the darkness.

"I asked some friends of mine in the area to keep a lookout for him," he explained as simply as he could.

There would be time enough to go into details tomorrow. For now, however, he'd just wanted to put her mind at ease.

"We have to get him back," she murmured, her growing desperation evident in her voice.

"We will," he assured her. "I promise you, we will."

As if his word were all she needed, she relaxed against him trustingly, and within minutes slept again.

Holding her to him, Devlin thought of how close he'd come to losing her. Had she been hit any harder, any number of complications could have caused her death. And though he tried not to dwell on the possibility, he couldn't quite forget that he could still lose her in another, equally untenable way.

Once she had Timmy back again, she could very well choose to be done with him. And he couldn't see any way that he could bring himself to stop her. If she honestly thought she'd be better off without him, who was he to argue with her? Considering his track record, he had no right to even try.

Still, Alex's words teased through his mind, raising his hopes in a dauntless way. He knew he was crazy to allow himself to be heartened by the advice of someone who'd made such a mess of his own personal life. But then, his friend did have a proclivity for being right where other people were concerned.

Aware that he was grasping at straws, yet wanting to believe there was hope for them, Devlin settled Laura more firmly in his arms, closed his eyes and finally slept, as well.

When Laura awoke again, she did so on her own, albeit rather unwillingly. For a while now, sleep had been a safe haven from the wicked pounding in her head as well as... What? She couldn't quite recall, and somewhere in the back of her mind she knew better than to force herself to try.

Opening her eyes, she saw a splash of sunlight on the blue-and-white-striped satin coverlet. Though she wasn't sure why, she had an idea the day was already well advanced. Yet she made no move to turn and look at the clock on the nightstand, much less to get out of bed.

Sometime during the night the sharp, stabbing pain shooting through her skull had diminished. But she was afraid the dull throbbing that remained would all too easily turn into agony again if she didn't remain absolutely still.

But how could she when she had to— What? Again she shied away from the thought that seemed to hover on the edge of her mind. She had to remember and she would. She—

Timmy.

With a soft cry she pushed up on her elbows, then fell back again as one memory toppled onto another and the throbbing in her head intensified with blinding ferocity.

The two men with clubs...Bitsy's yelp of pain...Timmy's terrified sobs...then her descent into darkness. A darkness that now threatened to drag her down once more.

Only she couldn't give in this time. She had to get up, get dressed and go after her son.

"*Señora,* please," Mrs. Santos pleaded, hurrying over to the bed as Laura tried to sit up again. "The *señor* said you must stay in bed."

"But Timmy. . ." Fighting the pain, she finally levered herself into a sitting position. "I have to—"

"I know, *señora*, and you will. But Señor Gray wants you to rest now."

"Where is he?" she asked, beating back a sudden wave of panic.

What if he'd gone off on his own after Timmy? What if he had tried to cross into the United States and had been stopped? If he really was wanted for some crime he'd committed—

"He had to go out for a while, but he'll be back very soon," Mrs. Santos assured her.

Slumping against her pillow, Laura shoved a shaky hand through her tangled hair, then winced as her fingers trailed over the bandage on her left temple. At least Devlin hadn't done anything foolish yet. But if she didn't get away before he returned, he'd insist on going with her, and she couldn't let him take that risk. Not when she'd been the one to give Giovanni's men the chance to kidnap her son.

Looking back, she had no idea what had possessed her to go out alone with him. But she didn't intend to allow Devlin to pay for her mistake.

"Can I get you anything, *señora?* Some juice and a little something to eat, maybe?"

Even though she hadn't eaten in the past twenty-four hours, Laura wasn't hungry. But with Mrs. Santos busy in the kitchen, she'd have a chance to wash and dress, then slip away.

"Yes, please. Juice and scrambled eggs and . . . and some toast."

"Would you like me to help you to the bathroom before I go downstairs?"

"Oh, no. I can manage. I'm feeling much better."

The housekeeper regarded her skeptically, then turned and left the room.

Throwing back the top sheet and coverlet, Laura swung her legs over the side of the bed and stood. Instantly the throbbing in her head began to beat a wilder tattoo, and she swayed dizzily, clutching the nightstand for support. After a minute or two her vision cleared and somehow she managed to stumble into the bathroom. Once there, she had to sit on the edge of the bathtub for several minutes until she marshaled enough strength to stand again.

She would have liked to have taken a shower, but she was afraid she'd pass out. Washing her face and brushing her teeth were about all she could manage before she had to sit down again.

Aware that she'd never be able to dress, much less walk down the staircase and out of the house on her own, she crept back to bed, tears of frustration trickling down her cheeks.

How was she ever going to get Timmy back when the slightest effort left her weak as a kitten? And her head...

As long as she was still, the throbbing seemed to lessen, but when she moved around, it became excruciating again.

Curling onto her side, she buried her face in her pillow and sobbed softly. Poor Timmy. He had to be terrified, and here she was—

"Laura, sweetheart, don't cry. Everything's going to be all right."

In the space of a heartbeat Devlin was there beside her, gently easing her into his arms. Unable to stem her tears, she leaned against him, wanting to believe what he said.

"I'm—I'm so worried about Timmy. I never told him about Giovanni. I didn't want to frighten him. And now...now he's..."

"Only until tomorrow," Devlin said, his tone matter-of-fact. "I've made arrangements for us to fly to Chicago in the morning. By afternoon we'll have him back again. We will. I swear."

"But you can't go with me," she protested as another rush of tears filled her eyes. "What if we're stopped going through customs? I can't let you take that risk. I'm the one who—"

"I won't be taking any risk, Laura," he stated, his quiet voice laced with surprising certainty. "None at all." He eased away from her, piling the bed pillows behind her and settling her against them, then offered her his handkerchief as he added, "I'm not what you think I am."

Blotting at her eyes, Laura recalled that he'd said much the same thing after they'd made love Sunday morning.

"What do you mean?" she asked, then frowned as she looked at him, really looked at him, for the first time since he'd come into the bedroom and taken her in his arms.

He'd not only shaved off the scruffy beard he'd grown over the past several days. He'd had his long, shaggy hair trimmed into a shorter, much more conservative style, as well. And the expression in his eyes was so... reserved.

Her Devlin, the man she'd come to love, seemed to have disappeared. In his place was a cool, aloof, rather authoritative stranger. A stranger who had something to tell her that she was afraid she wasn't going to like hearing.

Not because her wish that he really wasn't a criminal would be granted, but because she'd know, once and for all, how deeply she'd been deceived ... again.

What was it about her that made it so easy for men to lie to her? First Johnny, and now Devlin Gray, each in a different way, it seemed. But deception was deception. And even if the "real" Devlin, whoever he turned out to be, could do more to help her get her son back than the Devlin he'd led her to believe he was, she wasn't sure she'd be able to forgive his duplicity.

"I haven't been living in San Pedro the past three years because I'm wanted for a crime I committed in the States. I know that's the impression I gave, but in reality I work for the United States government. With the help of a team of agents out in the field, I collect information, analyze changes in the political structure of Mexico and the rest of Central America, and advise my superiors in Washington accordingly."

Laura stared at him in silence, considering the obviously prepared speech he'd delivered and doing a little analyzing of her own, then stated rather baldly, "You're a spy."

"You could say that," he admitted, holding her gaze unwaveringly.

She understood now why he'd fostered such a bad reputation for himself around town. Not so that he could carry on criminal activities, but so he could prowl around as he wanted, collecting information for the United States government, without having to explain his comings and goings to anyone.

But surely he had to have known she'd keep his secret. And telling her early on would have afforded her some much needed peace of mind, as well. Although now that she thought back, she was surprised she hadn't figured it out on her own, feeling almost as angry with herself as she was with him. Talk about a total dupe!

"Why didn't you tell me sooner?" she demanded. "Afraid I'd blow your cover?"

"I never thought that for a minute," he denied.

"Then *why?*"

"At first, it just seemed easier to keep you in the dark, especially since our arrangement was supposed to be only temporary. And I had a debt to pay. I figured that if we didn't get too...close, I wouldn't be distracted," he began, choosing his words with evident care. "Then, that day we took Timmy to the hot springs, I realized I wasn't being fair to you. I'd intended to tell you the truth that night. But unfortunately, my debt came due before I could."

"The terrorist in Honduras," she murmured, all the bits and pieces finally starting to fall into place. "He was the same one who killed your wife and daughter, wasn't he?"

"How did you know?"

"There was an article about the attack in Tegucigalpa in the local paper on Friday. I just put two and two together." She hesitated, then continued quietly, "Did you...did you...?"

"His gun went off while we were wrestling over it. By some miracle the bullet hit him instead of me. So, yes, in a way I did make sure he wouldn't be able to kill any more innocent people."

She could understand why he'd been so determined to deal with the terrorist on his own, and she admired him for it. She could also rejoice in the successful completion of his mission. Yet she couldn't help wondering if Timmy would have been kidnapped if Devlin had been with them in San Pedro, instead.

But no, that wasn't really fair of her, she grudgingly admitted. Devlin had done all he could to ensure her son's safety, especially while he was away. And though his being hurt had influenced her decision somewhat, *she* had been the one who'd ignored her own very real misgivings, choosing instead to take her son out alone.

"I suppose Alex is a spy, too," she said at last.

"Yes."

"Does he work for you?"

"He has in the past, but he's affiliated with another section of the agency now."

"I see."

She looked away from him, plucking at the lace edging the linen sheet, trying to sort through all he'd told her despite the throbbing in her head.

He wasn't a criminal, after all, but an agent of the United States government, and, as such, ready, willing and able to confront Giovanni on her behalf. Right now, nothing else really mattered to her.

Once she had Timmy back again, she'd have more than enough time to deal with the tumultuous emotions his lack of honesty had stirred up in her. That he'd deceived her so completely hurt more than she could ever say. In fact, had never seeing him again been a reasonable option, at that moment she'd have gladly chosen it.

For now, however, she couldn't afford to dwell on her personal feelings. She had to focus on the fact that Devlin not only could, but would get her son away from Giovanni. He'd vowed as much over and over again since yesterday, and while her faith in him had been deeply shaken in some respects, she still believed he'd keep his word where Timmy was concerned.

Glancing at him warily, she saw him watching her, a distant look in his eyes, as he seemingly waited for her to say something more.

"The friends you mentioned—the ones you asked to be on the lookout for Timmy—they're agents, too, aren't they?" she stated.

"Yes."

"Are they still . . . ?"

"They have orders to keep him under surveillance until we arrive."

"Tomorrow."

He nodded.

"How—?"

"We'll drive to Leon in the morning and fly from there to Mexico City, where a Learjet will be waiting to take us to Chicago. Some of my associates have agreed to accompany us to Giovanni's house to help allay any possible problems. However, I doubt he'll put up any resistance once he realizes he's dealing with federal agents."

"So, we're just going to knock on his door and ask him to give up my son?" she asked, unable to hide her incredulity.

"More or less," he admitted, a sardonic smile twisting his lips. "Considering some of the shady dealings he's been involved in lately, he can't afford to have any federal agency looking at him too closely for any reason. And that's exactly the threat I'm going to pose.

"He had Timmy kidnapped because he didn't think you could come after him, either on your own or, thanks to my reputation, with me. When he finds out who he's really up against, he'll back off in a major way."

"Too bad he didn't know who you were in the first place," she retorted, her anger at him coming to the fore again, though she tried hard to keep it tamped down. "Then maybe Timmy wouldn't have had to go through all this."

"Believe me, Laura, if I could have prevented your son's kidnapping, I would have. But unfortunately, national security precluded advertising my real reason for being in San Pedro," he reminded her quietly. "However, Giovanni will find out all he needs to know tomorrow to guarantee you'll never have to worry about him hassling you again." He paused, then shrugged with seeming nonchalance as he added, "So I'll have served my purpose in the end, won't I?"

Hearing the faint hint of bitterness in his voice, Laura eyed him with sudden dismay as she remembered why she'd sought him out in the first place. To use him to thwart Giovanni.

She'd made that clear to him from the first, and now he was letting her know that he, too, remembered, and would not disappoint her in that respect.

But she'd long since realized she wanted so much more from him than to simply avail herself of his... services. Or she had until she'd found out he'd been less than honest with her.

"Oh, Devlin, I'm sorry," she murmured, tears welling in her eyes again as she tried to grapple with her warring emotions.

She was hurt, and her first instinct had been to hurt back. But hurting someone you loved only seemed to make your own pain that much worse, she thought.

"I'm sorry, too, Laura. More sorry than I can say."

He touched her cheek, drawing her gaze back to his, and for one long moment she saw the anguish in his eyes. She thought he would say more, but Mrs. Santos bustled into the room just then, bearing a tray with the breakfast she'd asked for and still didn't want.

"Ah, *señora,* here you go."

As the housekeeper set the tray in her lap, Devlin stood and moved toward the door, his expression shuttered once again.

"Since we have a long trip ahead of us tomorrow, I think it would be a good idea if you rested as much as possible today. Later, when you're feeling a little stronger, Mrs. Santos can help you pack a change of clothes for you and Timmy. I have several errands to run, so I'll be in and out for the rest of the afternoon. If you need me for any reason, tell Mrs. Santos."

"All right," she agreed, wishing she could tell him that what she needed most was to be held in his arms.

But how could she when he'd become a stranger to her again? A stranger who had concealed the truth about himself from her, even though he'd known how badly she'd been hurt by another man's lies.

Determined to regain her strength, Laura ate the food Mrs. Santos set before her. And, except for the short time she visited with Juan Carlos and Annie out in the garden, she stayed in the bedroom.

She had no desire to see Devlin again that day. Nor did she allow herself to think about him. Instead, she thought about her son, praying he was holding up as well as Devlin had insisted he would.

Once they were together again, she'd sort out her feelings for her husband. Until then...

Standing by the window that evening, watching the sun dip behind the mountains to the west, Laura twisted her wedding band around and around, and tried not to cry again.

When he could put it off no longer, Devlin finally walked up the staircase and into his bedroom. Though he'd considered spending the night elsewhere, in the end he couldn't seem to make himself stay away. Not when tonight might be the last night he spent with Laura.

He half expected her to order him out, but as he crossed to the bed after finishing in the bathroom, he saw that she was sleeping, though not very well. As he looked down at her, she tossed restlessly, muttering under her breath.

Afraid that she might be ill, he sat beside her and touched the back of his hand to her forehead. Though her skin was warm, she didn't seem to have a fever.

Murmuring again, she turned and reached out to him.

"Devlin?"

"I'll go if you want," he offered softly.

"No, please, stay."

He lay down beside her, drawing her into his arms, and as she had every other night they'd spent together, she curled against him trustingly.

Had she been fully awake, he doubted she'd have come to him so willingly. He'd seen the hurt and anger in her eyes and heard it in her voice after he'd told her the truth about himself. And he'd known she'd felt betrayed by him in a justifiable way. He'd offered her what little defense he had, but seemingly to no avail. She'd let him know she wanted nothing from him except his help in getting her son back. And once that goal had been accomplished...

Knowing he'd probably never have another chance to hold her again, he drew her closer still, stroking her curls as he gazed down at her in the moon-shadowed darkness.

He loved her more than life, but how could he ever expect her to believe that now? He'd doomed any chance he had of doing that the moment he'd said "I do," then chose to go on deceiving her.

Better to let her go so that she'd have an opportunity to find someone she *could* trust instead of trying to hold her with words she'd always be bound to doubt.

Much better, he thought, staring into the night. Much better for her, by far.

As for him, he'd survive. And, all things considered, that was probably more than he deserved.

Chapter 12

Although she was alone when she awakened the next morning, Laura had the strangest feeling she'd spent the night in Devlin's arms. But how could that be possible? she wondered, watching the faint beams of sunlight that played across the tile floor. Considering the way he'd deceived her, surely she would have turned away from him, even in her sleep.

More confused than ever, she swung her legs over the side of the bed and stood. At least the worst of her headache was gone, and she no longer felt dizzy when she went from lying down or sitting to standing. For a while yesterday she'd been afraid she wouldn't be well enough to make the trip to Chicago. But she felt almost normal again.

Except for the lingering ache in the vicinity of her heart, and that would disappear just as soon as she was reunited with her son.

She gathered fresh underwear and the simple, softly skirted yellow knit dress she'd chosen for the journey, then headed for the bathroom. She wasn't sure what time they would be leaving. Devlin had only said early morning, and she didn't want to be the one to delay their departure because she wasn't ready to go.

Hearing the bedroom door open, she paused and turned as Devlin walked into the room. For several moments she couldn't seem to do anything but stand and stare at him. Dressed in a gray suit, starched white shirt and dark red tie, and with his hair neatly trimmed, he resembled the powerful corporate CEO she remembered wishing he was much more than he did the rather disheveled ne'er-do-well she'd so foolishly fallen in love with. Especially when he gazed at her so warily, his gray eyes cool and distant, his mouth set in a grim line.

"Is something wrong?" he asked at last, breaking the silence stretching between them.

"Not really. I was just thinking that I don't know you anymore," she admitted, smiling sadly.

"Oh, but you do, Laura. Only my label has changed. I'm still the same man who made love to you a few nights ago. And there was nothing false about what we shared then. *Nothing*. However, considering I haven't been completely honest with you in the past, I doubt there's any way I can convince you of that now." Pausing, he glanced at his watch; then, meeting her gaze again, he continued hurriedly, not giving her a chance to respond. "I'd like to leave no later than eight o'clock. Unless you'll need more than an hour and a half to dress."

"I'll be downstairs at eight," she replied as she turned back to the bathroom, his reminder of their lovemaking sending her thoughts careening all over again.

He was right. There had been an innate honesty to the intimacies they'd shared. Labels hadn't mattered. They'd simply been a man and a woman loving each other with heartaching tenderness and soul-searing passion.

One could argue that all that had really changed since then was his job description, and she hadn't suffered from that in a tangible way. Her faith in him had been shaken, but not totally, and her pride hurt, yet not devastatingly so. Unlike Johnny, Devlin hadn't made her vulnerable. Instead, he'd afforded her a position of power from which she could fight Giovanni. And that was exactly what she'd sought from him in the first place.

With a quiet sigh she turned on the tap and shrugged out of her nightgown, telling herself yet again that she'd deal with her feelings for Devlin another time.

Immediately her thoughts turned to Timmy. He'd be waking up for the second morning in a strange bed in a strange house. But tonight she'd be with him again, and tomorrow morning... Well, they'd just have to see what tomorrow morning brought, wouldn't they?

An hour later, bathed and dressed, she walked downstairs, her hair freshly shampooed and a touch of make-up covering the worst of the shadows under her eyes. She carried her canvas bag in one hand, Timmy's floppy-eared stuffed rabbit in the other. As she crossed the hallway she caught a glimpse of Devlin and Alex in Devlin's office, but she went on to the kitchen without stopping.

After greeting Mrs. Santos, she filled a mug with coffee and wandered out to the garden; Bitsy, home again after spending all day yesterday under observation at the vet's, wriggled over to her and snuffled happily at her hand. Glad to see the dog had recovered from the knock in the head he'd had, Laura scratched his ears, telling him what a good boy he was. Then, moving down the walkway, she turned her face to the morning sun as she inhaled the scent of Devlin's roses.

She had the oddest feeling that she wouldn't be coming back there again. But then, once Giovanni was no longer a threat, she and Timmy would be going back to their own house, wouldn't they? She'd have no reason to stay married to Devlin. He'd have served his purpose, as he'd so succinctly put it yesterday, and having fulfilled his promise to her, she imagined he'd be glad to be finished with her. Only *she* wouldn't be glad—

"Are you ready to go?" Devlin asked, his husky voice cutting across her thoughts.

She hesitated a moment, taking one last look around the garden, her gaze lingering on his roses, not wanting her interlude with him to end, yet knowing in her heart that it must. Timmy was waiting for her, and he was all that really mattered to her now.

As for her and Devlin, they'd been forced together by unusual circumstances and, as they'd agreed at the outset, they'd soon be free to go their separate ways.

"Yes, I'm ready."

Turning, she followed him into the house, collected her bag and Timmy's stuffed animal, and said a fond farewell to Mrs. Santos.

Along with Alex, they drove to Leon as planned in Devlin's Jeep. At the airport there, all three of them boarded the Cessna and, with Devlin at the controls, took off for Mexico City.

Laura sat behind the two men, holding Phil in her lap, saying nothing during the relatively short flight. Devlin and Alex were quiet as well, exchanging only a few comments, mostly about the plane's handling.

However, from the little else they said, Laura gathered that Alex would be flying back to Leon and more or less holding down the fort in San Pedro, at least temporarily. She also got the impression that Devlin wasn't planning on returning to the town after he dealt with Giovanni.

Somehow, she'd taken for granted he would. But once she really thought about it, she realized he probably couldn't. Not after making this trip on her behalf. He was using his authority as an agent of the United States government to get them out of Mexico without any hassles, thus blowing the cover he'd maintained for almost three years.

For the first time, she considered all that he was jeopardizing for her and her son. All along, he'd bent over backward to accommodate her needs, going out of his way to see that she got whatever she wanted. And while she'd been grateful, she hadn't truly appreciated the price he might eventually have to pay until now.

At the airport in Mexico City the Cessna was shuttled over to a far runway where a jet waited, door open and engine humming. With practiced skill Devlin guided the small plane off to one side. Then, leaving Alex to unload their bags and give Laura a hand, he crossed the tarmac and climbed aboard the jet.

"Almost there," Alex said as she hopped to the ground. "Flight time to O'Hare in that baby is under three hours."

She nodded wordlessly, standing aside as Alex grabbed her carryall and the bag Devlin had packed for himself. For a fleeting moment she wondered if his specially outfitted briefcase was tucked among his clothes, then shook her head, amazed at the things she found herself thinking of.

But if she dwelled too long on Timmy, and what he must be going through, she'd never be able to hold herself together.

The poor child had seen her beaten and left for dead. Then he'd been whisked away by the thugs who'd done it. He'd been driven through Mexico, flown to Chicago and delivered to an old man who'd never been known for his sympathy or understanding.

There was no telling what kind of shape her sturdy, independent, normally happy little boy would be in when she finally got to him. All she knew for sure was that he'd need her to be strong, not only this afternoon but in the days and weeks ahead when the nightmare he'd lived through would still be fresh in his mind.

"He's going to be all right, you know," Alex said, shifting her carryall and Devlin's bag to one hand, then taking her arm with the other and leading her to the jet. "He's a tough little guy, and a damn fine poker player. I bet he's dealing his grandfather a real fit. In fact, my guess is the old man will be glad to get rid of him."

"Oh, Alex." She smiled tremulously, grateful for his encouragement.

"And you're going to be all right, too," he continued, holding her back a moment at the foot of the stairway leading up to the jet's open door. "As long as you don't let Devlin walk away from you. Do that and you'll both live to regret it."

Puzzled, Laura glanced up at him and saw him watching her, a stern look in his eyes.

"Why are you telling me that?" she asked.

"Because I've already told Devlin the same thing several times, and it doesn't seem to be sinking in. He has some altruistic notion that you'll be better off without him because he screwed up and lost your trust. But you and I know that isn't true. Don't we?"

"Maybe he's the one who'd be better off without *me*," she replied, looking away again. "He didn't really want anything to do with me and my predicament when I first came to him, but he let me use him anyway. And now look what it's costing him."

"Believe me, honey, no one *uses* Devlin Gray. He helped you because that was what he wanted to do. And considering he'd lie down and die for you, this isn't costing him much at all."

"How can you be so sure?" she demanded, wishing what he was saying was really true.

"I'm psychic," he said, a teasing glint in his eyes.

"Yeah, sure," she muttered.

"Take care of yourself, Laura." He dug in his pocket and produced a worn deck of cards, the marked cards he'd taken such delight in showing Timmy how to use while Devlin was away. "Give these to the kid for me, and tell him I'll see him next summer."

"You will?" She stared at him curiously.

"At his brother's christening." Bending, he kissed her on the cheek. "I'm going to be the baby's godfather."

"Unless the men in white coats get hold of you first," she retorted, tucking the cards into the little purse she carried, then brushing at the tears in her eyes. "Thanks, Alex."

"You're very welcome, Laura."

"What's going on?" Devlin demanded, standing at the doorway, looking down at them, a frown creasing his forehead.

"Not a thing." Alex handed him their bags as Laura started up the stairway. "Have a good trip."

Her thoughts whirling all over again, Laura sat in one of the passenger seats and fastened her seat belt. After securing the door and speaking to the pilot again, Devlin sat across the aisle from her and did likewise. A few minutes later the jet taxied down the runway, then soared into the sky.

As soon as they were airborne Devlin released his seat belt, indicating she could do the same, and slipped out of his suit coat.

Seeing that he wore a leather shoulder holster and gun, Laura stared at him askance. An instant later she turned away, chiding herself for not realizing he'd be armed. They were going to be confronting a ruthless man who'd thought nothing of having his grandson kidnapped, and they had to be prepared for the worst. Still, the thought that guns might be drawn terrified her.

What if Timmy were to get caught in the cross fire?

"I'm not wearing a gun because I honestly think I'll need it," Devlin said, reaching across the aisle and taking her hand in his. "But, just in case..." He squeezed her hand reassuringly.

"I understand." She met his gaze again, willing him to know that she trusted his judgment.

He nodded, then let go of her hand, settled back in his seat and closed his eyes, effectively shutting her out.

Clutching Phil in her lap, Laura sat back, too, and tried not to think any farther ahead than she had to.

Upon landing at O'Hare, she and Devlin were met by four men whose dark, conservative suits, short haircuts and cool, authoritative demeanor mirrored Devlin's in an overwhelming yet oddly reassuring way.

He introduced them to her, then the men led them through customs with no more than a cordial nod from the officials manning the desks, and out to a couple of black, late model sedans parked at the curb.

After helping Laura into the back seat of one of the cars, Devlin huddled with the other agents for several minutes, apparently going over the final details of their showdown with Giovanni. Finally he joined her as two of the agents climbed into the front seat and the others walked back to the second car. Within minutes they were on the freeway heading toward the exclusive suburban neighborhood where Giovanni lived.

Even after five years away, Laura remembered the route well, and as they turned off the freeway, onto the quiet road that led to the community's gated entrance, a shiver of uncertainty raced up her spine. Digging her fingers into the furry stuffed animal she held almost as a talisman, she willed herself to be calm.

Devlin's plan had sounded so simple yesterday, and she'd seen for herself that he'd gone to great lengths to ensure everything would go smoothly. He was a highly trained professional, used to dealing with men like Giovanni Buschetti, as were the other agents who'd met them at the airport. She couldn't be in better hands. Nor could she have asked for anyone more qualified to come to her son's rescue.

Still, the thought of actually bearding the old lion in his den scared her half to death.

As if sensing her fear, Devlin reached out and drew her into his arms. After the distance he'd maintained between them through the early part of their journey, his gesture came as a surprise, but one Laura gladly and gratefully accepted. Unable to still her trembling, she leaned against him and rested her head on his shoulder.

"Everything's going to be all right," he assured her. "An hour from now it'll all be over. You'll have your son back, and you'll never have to worry about Giovanni again."

"I'm just so afraid something will go wrong," she admitted.

"Giovanni isn't going to do anything to put Timmy at risk. And he isn't going to try to harm us, either. He'll rant and rave, but once he realizes what he's up against, he won't fight us. He's a businessman, and as such, can't afford any gangster-style shoot-'em-up theatrics." He paused, then added quietly, "Trust me on this, at least."

"I do." She tipped her face up and met his gaze, but couldn't tell if he believed her.

Though he held her in the protective curve of his arm, his expression was as reserved as it had been since he'd come to her in their bedroom that morning. As if he were simply doing his duty, nothing more.

At the entrance to Devonshire Place, the driver of their car showed his identification to the uniformed security guard, and as they had been at customs, they were waved through without further question. A few minutes later they pulled into the long, winding driveway leading up to Giovanni's elegant Mediterranean-style mansion.

"I think it might be a good idea if you waited in the car," Devlin said, moving away from her and straightening his tie.

"No."

Obviously surprised by her refusal, he glanced at her and frowned. "I'm not expecting any trouble, but—"

"After everything Timmy's been through, I want to be there for him," she insisted. "*Especially* if there's trouble."

Something in her tone must have convinced him, because he nodded once, then said, "Just stay close to me."

Together they walked to the front door, Devlin's associates following a few paces behind them. Devlin rang the doorbell, then pulled a flat leather wallet from the inside pocket of his suit coat.

After what seemed like a long time, but couldn't have been more than a minute or two, a middle-aged man dressed in a white knit shirt and dark trousers opened the door and stared at them suspiciously.

"Yeah, what do you want?" he demanded.

"Several things," Devlin drawled, opening his wallet and holding it up so the man could get a good look at his identification. "But Mr. Buschetti will do for starters."

The man studied Devlin's identification, glanced at Laura, then turned his attention to the other agents. He seemed to be weighing his options, and for a moment or so Laura thought he'd slam the door on them. Finally, however, he stepped back and opened the door wider, allowing them to enter.

"Wait here while I get him," he instructed none too cordially as he closed the door. Then, leaving them standing in the foyer, he disappeared down a hallway that Laura remembered led to Giovanni's study.

The house was deadly quiet, and as they waited, Laura eyed the grand staircase that swept up to the second floor. Timmy was up there somewhere. She knew it.

Wanting to go to him, she started to move away from Devlin, but he caught her by the arm, bringing her back to his side.

"I thought I told you to stay close to me," he muttered.

"But I know Timmy's—"

"Who do you think you are, coming into my home?" Giovanni demanded in a loud voice as he stormed into the foyer, his anger almost palpable. "I'll have my lawyers—"

"And I'll have every agency of the federal government picking your bones from now till the day you die, old man," Devlin interrupted, his deceptively mild tone serving to underscore his intent to do exactly as he said.

"*You*—" Ignoring Devlin momentarily, Giovanni glared at Laura, his face red, his hands balled into fists. Instinctively she shrank away from him. As she did, Devlin put his arm around her and drew her close. "You cheap little—"

"Don't insult my wife," Devlin warned, his tone still mild but infinitely more menacing.

"Your wife?" The old man spat. "She's married to some common criminal—"

"Your boys got their wires crossed, old man. She's married to me, and as you can see, I'm not a criminal."

Once again Devlin held out his identification. As his henchman had, Giovanni studied it, his anger increasing visibly as he began to realize exactly what was going on. Yet, when he gazed at them again, he had a sly look in his beady eyes.

"So, Mr. Gray, what do you want from me?" he asked.

"I want my son," Laura cried, suddenly afraid that Giovanni had somehow managed to spirit him away.

"Your son? My dear, I have no idea—"

"Mommy, Mommy!" Timmy's voice rang out from the hallway above, then he appeared at the top of the staircase, a harried young woman trailing after him. "I knew you'd come, Mommy, I knew you would."

As he ran down the staircase, Laura broke away from Devlin and went to him, catching him in her arms and hugging him close. Behind her she heard Giovanni's shout of rage, and from the staircase the young woman's whimper of fear.

"Oh, Timmy, are you all right?" she cried.

"I was kinda scared. But I knew you and Devlin would find me even though *he* said you wouldn't." He put his arms around her neck and held on tight. "He's not a very nice grandfather, Mom. He yells all the time. And she's a—a twit."

"Oh, Timmy, honey..."

Torn between laughter and tears of relief, she stood and held him in her arms. Devlin and Alex had been right. He was one tough little boy, and amazingly, he seemed none the worse for the traumatic experience he'd had.

"I'm going to fight you for him," Giovanni snarled. "My lawyers—"

"Are going to be awfully busy finding ways to keep you out of jail if you come anywhere near my wife or her son again," Devlin cut in, placing himself between her and Giovanni as the old man moved toward them. "Now, if you'll excuse us . . ."

He put his arm around her and started toward the door.

His rage seeming to soar out of control, Giovanni strode after them.

"I'll fight you—" he began, then moaned low in his throat. "Tony . . . get my—"

As Laura looked back, Giovanni grabbed his chest and crumpled to the floor, his face suddenly pale, his eyes rolling back in his head.

Despite the hell he'd put her through, Laura's first instinct was to go to him and try to help him. But Devlin hustled her out the front door.

"He's ill," she protested. "We have to—"

"Denny, call 911 and get an ambulance here," Devlin ordered. Then, still guiding Laura toward the car, he added, "I want you and Timmy out of here before the press gets wind of what's going on."

"Is he gonna die?" Timmy asked, his voice quivering.

"Maybe," Devlin replied. "But not because of us." As they came to the car, he took Timmy from Laura so she could climb into the back seat. "How are you doing, buddy?"

"Okay." He hugged Devlin, then added, "Really, *really* okay now."

"Good." Meeting Laura's gaze, he smiled as he handed over her son. "How about you, Mom? Are you okay, too?"

"Oh, yes. I'm really, *really* okay, too." Reaching out, she touched his cheek. "Thank you, Devlin. Thank you so very, very much."

"De nada."

He caught her hand in his and squeezed it gently. Then, letting her go, he backed away and closed the car door. After speaking to his fellow agents for a minute or two, he walked around to the other side of the car and joined them in the back seat as the wail of a siren cut through the suburban stillness.

"Let's get out of here," he ordered.

As the car sped down the driveway and onto the street, Laura made sure Timmy's seat belt was fastened, then plopped Phil in his lap.

"He missed you," she said.

"Thanks for bringing him, Mom." He cuddled the rabbit close and smiled up at her wearily, the strain of his ordeal showing in the shadows under his eyes.

"And these are from Alex." She dug the deck of cards out of her purse and handed them to him. "He said to tell you hello."

"Oh, boy. His special cards." Her son gazed up at Devlin, a mischievous twinkle in his eyes. "Did he ever show you how to use them?"

"Only after he won all my money," Devlin replied with a wry chuckle. Then, ruffling Timmy's dark curls, he asked casually, "Did anyone hurt you in any way over the past couple of days?"

"Just when they gave me the shot after they knocked my mom out. I fell asleep and woke up here."

Under Devlin's gentle questioning, Timmy related bits and pieces of his "adventure." As far as Laura could tell, he hadn't been mistreated physically either by his grandfather or the young woman who'd been hired to look after him. He'd also realized that Giovanni was his grandfather, and thus hadn't been too frightened of him.

Thirty minutes after leaving Giovanni's house the car pulled up in front of an elegant old hotel in the heart of downtown Chicago. After thanking his associates for their help, Devlin took their bags from the trunk, led them into the lobby, paused at the desk to pick up two keys, then escorted them to an elevator that whisked them up to a suite overlooking the lake.

They ordered an early dinner from room service, and with Timmy still chattering excitedly, they ate together at the small table in the sitting room.

When Timmy's eyelids finally began to droop, Laura led him into one of the two bedrooms. She gave him a bath and shampooed his hair, savoring the mundane chores as she'd never thought she would. After tucking him and Phil into one of the twin beds, she sat with him until he fell asleep. Then, leaving a light burning in case he awoke, she returned to the sitting room.

Devlin stood by the window, still wearing his suit coat.

"Is he asleep?" he asked, turning to face her.

"Yes." She hesitated, aware that his expression was much more reserved than it had been when Timmy had been with them. Then she started toward him. "I can't tell you how much I appreciate—"

"You don't have to thank me," he interrupted. "Getting Timmy back was the least I could do for you." He moved away from her, pausing by the chair across the room. "While you were with Timmy, there was a news bulletin on the television. Giovanni died early this evening of a massive heart attack."

"Oh."

Sinking onto the small sofa, she stared at Devlin, wishing she could feel something other than relief upon hearing of the man's death.

"He won't be causing you any more grief, although I imagine you'll have to deal with his estate since he's more than likely named Timmy as his heir."

"But I couldn't accept—"

"Keep enough to give Timmy the kind of life he deserves here in the States, and donate the remainder to charity," he suggested.

"But—" she began again.

"Since it will probably take some time for the will to go through probate, I've set up an account for you. The money should tide you over until you get settled." He took a bankbook from his pocket, crossed to where she was sitting and tossed it on the coffee table. "Let me know when you find a place to live and I'll have Mrs. Santos ship your things to you." He set a plain white business card atop the bankbook. "You can reach me at this address. You can also send me the annulment papers when you get them."

She stared at him wordlessly as he slipped his ring off and placed it on the table, but he refused to meet her gaze. She'd thought they'd at least talk about the future. But it seemed Devlin had already made up his mind about what he wanted to do.

"You can stay here as long as you want. I'll sleep in the other room tonight, but I'll be out of your way first thing in the morning."

"What—what are you going to do?" she stammered, finally finding the courage to speak.

"I'm supposed to be in D.C. Friday morning. Until then, I'm not sure."

"I see," she murmured, feeling more lost and alone than she ever had.

After the way she'd treated him, not only at the outset but throughout most of their relationship, she couldn't blame him for wanting to be done with her. She'd chosen to think the worst of him despite every indication to the contrary. Then she'd been hurt and angry when she'd found out the truth about him, though she probably wouldn't have believed him if he'd tried to tell her sooner.

And now...

Now he was walking away from her as Alex had warned he would. But was he doing it because that was what he wanted, or because it was what he thought *she* wanted?

"Take care of yourself, Laura. And Timmy," he said, glancing over his shoulder at her as he paused by the bedroom doorway, his eyes shadowed.

"Devlin, wait," she said, reaching out to him.

But he turned away again and continued into the bedroom, closing the door on her urgent entreaty.

She sat where she was for what seemed like a very long time, gazing at the bankbook and business card, as well as his gleaming gold wedding band, and thought that perhaps their parting really would be for the best.

But how could it be when she loved him with all her heart?

She'd never told him that, not once. Yet she'd known it was true almost from the moment she'd said "I do." So much that she'd been willing to stand by him even when she thought the worst of him. Because she'd believed that he loved her, too.

Had finding out the truth about him really changed all that? As he'd said, only his label had changed. He was still the same man who'd pulled her from a rain-swept gutter, the same man who'd offered to protect her and her son by giving her his name. He was still her Devlin, her husband, her love, and she intended to make sure he knew it.

And after that, if he still wanted her out of his life, she was going to force him to look her in the eye and say so.

With a determination born of desperation, Laura picked up Devlin's discarded ring, stood and crossed to his bedroom door. She knocked once. Then, not waiting for permission, she turned the knob and walked into the room.

Devlin stood by the window, much as he had in the sitting room earlier. He'd discarded his suit coat and shoulder holster and unbuttoned his shirt halfway down the front, but that was as far as he'd gotten before he'd paused to stare into the night.

He told himself he'd done what was best, not only for Laura, but for himself, as well. But somehow he was having a hard time believing it.

Her knock took him by surprise, as did her uninvited entrance. Turning, he eyed her warily as she advanced on him.

"Is anything wrong?" he asked. "Timmy—?"

"Timmy's sleeping." She met his gaze, tipping her chin up challengingly.

"Then what do you want?" he demanded, his tone gruff, trying his best to chase her away.

The longer she stayed in the room with him, the more he'd want to grab her and kiss her, and if he did that, he'd never be able to let her go.

She hesitated, momentarily put off by his unyielding manner, but then she seemed to regain her courage.

"I want what you gave me Sunday morning. I want your love, Devlin, and I want to give you my love in return," she stated simply, a shy smile edging the corners of her mouth.

He stared at her, stunned, then turned away again, trying desperately to regain his balance.

"We had sex Sunday morning," he replied. "Nothing more."

"Oh, no, Devlin, that's not true. Because you don't 'have sex.' You 'make love.'" She tossed his words back at him with just a hint of teasing laughter.

His body responded to the sound of her, the very scent of her as she moved closer, with an intensity that left him breathless. Bracing his forearm against the cool glass of the window, he closed his eyes, willing her to be gone while she still had a chance.

"I love you, Devlin," she murmured, putting her arms around his waist and resting her head on his shoulder. "And I'm fairly sure you love me. We both made some mistakes in the beginning, but we didn't do each other any serious harm. At least, not as far as I can see." She rubbed against him temptingly, then added almost as an afterthought, "Of course, if you can't forgive me for thinking the worst of you when I really should have known better, I'll try to understand."

"But you only thought that because I deceived you," he protested.

"Well, I'll tell you what. Why don't we call it even, and start over. Now..."

She trailed her fingertips over his belt buckle, then lower and lower still. Though he felt himself wavering, he caught her hand and held it away from him. She laughed softly, her breath warm against his back. Then, pressing her advantage, she raised up on her tiptoes and kissed him on the neck.

"Please, Devlin," she whispered.

Wondering if he'd ever be able to refuse her anything, then admitting he loved her too much to even try, Devlin turned and caught her to him. And, finally giving in to the need he'd tried so hard to deny, he kissed her long and slow and deep.

When he finally raised his head, she smiled up at him, her eyes gleaming with mischief.

"Was that a yes?" she asked.

He swept her off her feet and carried her to the bed. "That, Mrs. Gray, was definitely a yes." He set her down, then sat beside her. "As long as you're sure..."

Taking his left hand in hers, she slipped his ring onto his finger.

"I've never been more sure of anything in my life."

Epilogue

Pausing in the kitchen of the rambling two-story house they'd bought almost a year ago, Devlin looked out into the backyard. The once-neglected rose garden was now thriving under his tender, loving care. As he caught sight of his family, a smile tugged at the corners of his mouth.

Cradling their six-week-old son in her arms, Laura wandered slowly along the brick walkway he'd laid just last month, while Timmy capered across the lawn, laughing and chattering, as he played with Bitsy.

There had been a time when he'd thought this kind of happiness would never be his again. But Laura had made him realize that anything was possible with a little forgiveness and a heart full of love. Now, if only they could convince Alex of the same thing.

His smile widening into a grin, he walked out into the yard. Hearing him, Laura turned, her pale eyes lighting with pleasure.

"Dad's home," she announced, though Timmy was already hurling himself into his arms.

"Dad, Dad!" Timmy cried. "Guess what we did in science class today? We looked at bugs under a microscope."

"So, how did they look?"

"Ugh, gross," he replied, then immediately asked, "Wanna do my soccer drills with me?"

"You bet. Go get your ball."

As his son dashed into the house, Devlin slipped his arm around his wife and kissed her, then bent and kissed little Andrew's bald head.

"How was your day?"

"Not too bad. And yours?"

"Not too bad, either." He grinned again. "Alex called. He'll be in on the nine-o'clock flight Saturday morning along with Annie and Juan Carlos."

"Oh, good." Laura smiled with genuine pleasure, then asked with a hint of wickedness, "What about your sister?"

"Kari's plane gets in at noon."

"And the christening isn't until two o'clock Sunday. Since they're both godparents, they can't leave before then. So, they'll be here together over twenty-four hours." She hesitated, then looked at him uncertainly. "I hope we're doing the right thing."

"I hope so, too." He hugged her close and kissed her cheek. "We definitely owe Alex one."

"Yes, we do," she agreed as they walked toward the house.

"And it's about time Kari came to her senses."

"Mmm, yes." She glanced at him, smiling again. "Tell me something, will you?"

"What?"

"Is Alex psychic?"

"Where did you ever get that idea?" he hedged.

"Is he?" she pressed, knowing he would answer her honestly.

At that moment Timmy burst through the door, soccer ball in hand.

"Later, okay?" he asked.

"Okay." Her smile widening, she kissed him on the chin. "I love you."

"I love you, too."

* * * * *

INTIMATE MOMENTS®
Silhouette®

COMING NEXT MONTH

RITA Award Winning Author
Emilie Richards
presents

Emilie Richards' "The Men of Midnight" miniseries continues in June 1995 with IAIN ROSS'S WOMAN, IM #644.

Iain Ross had no idea that the woman he'd saved from drowning was the embodiment of his own destruction. Billie Harper seemed harmless, charming...too good to be true. And maybe she was. Because an age-old curse had rendered her Iain's sworn enemy, but still he was powerless to resist her—and their destiny....

Don't miss MacDOUGALL'S DARLING, featuring Andrew, the last of "The Men of Midnight." His story is coming your way in August 1995, only in—

He's Too Hot To Handle...but she can take a little heat.

SILHOUETTE

Summer Sizzlers

This summer don't be left in the cold, join Silhouette for the hottest Summer Sizzlers collection. The perfect summer read, on the beach or while vacationing, Summer Sizzlers features sexy heroes who are "Too Hot To Handle." This collection of three new stories is written by bestselling authors Mary Lynn Baxter, Ann Major and Laura Parker.

Available this July wherever Silhouette books are sold.

SS95

Within a few lost souls,
the *Heart of the Wolf* beats fierce
and wild. Feel them, fear them, tame them....

Don't miss SECRET OF THE WOLF (SS #54), the
spine-tingling first book in Rebecca Flanders's terrific
new *Heart of the Wolf* trilogy.

After being struck down by a car, he remembered
absolutely nothing of who he was. But as pieces of
his shattered past returned, "Michael" was learning
what real fear was. He knew his family's secret could
threaten the very woman who had so graciously
taken him into her home. And he realized the
terrifying question they were about to face was
not who he was, but *what*....

Find out Michael's secret this July—only from

PRIZE SURPRISE
SWEEPSTAKES
OFFICIAL ENTRY COUPON

This entry must be received by: **JUNE 30, 1995**
This month's winner will be notified by: **JULY 15, 1995**

YES, I want to win the Panasonic 31" TV! Please enter me in the drawing and let me know if I've won!

Name_____

Address _____ Apt. _____

| City | State/Prov. | Zip/Postal Code |

Account #_____

Return entry with invoice in reply envelope.

© 1995 HARLEQUIN ENTERPRISES LTD.   CTV KAL

PRIZE SURPRISE
SWEEPSTAKES
OFFICIAL ENTRY COUPON

This entry must be received by: **JUNE 30, 1995**
This month's winner will be notified by: **JULY 15, 1995**

YES, I want to win the Panasonic 31" TV! Please enter me in the drawing and let me know if I've won!

Name_____

Address _____ Apt. _____

| City | State/Prov. | Zip/Postal Code |

Account #_____

Return entry with invoice in reply envelope.

© 1995 HARLEQUIN ENTERPRISES LTD.   CTV KAL

OFFICIAL RULES

PRIZE SURPRISE SWEEPSTAKES 3448

NO PURCHASE OR OBLIGATION NECESSARY

Three Harlequin Reader Service 1995 shipments will contain respectively, coupons for entry into three different prize drawings, one for a Panasonic 31" wide-screen TV, another for a 5-piece Wedgwood china service for eight and the third for a Sharp ViewCam camcorder. To enter any drawing using an Entry Coupon, simply complete and mail according to directions.

There is no obligation to continue using the Reader Service to enter and be eligible for any prize drawing. You may also enter any drawing by hand printing the words "Prize Surprise," your name and address on a 3"x5" card and the name of the prize you wish that entry to be considered for (i.e., Panasonic wide-screen TV, Wedgwood china or Sharp ViewCam). Send your 3"x5" entries via first-class mail (limit: one per envelope) to: Prize Surprise Sweepstakes 3448, c/o the prize you wish that entry to be considered for, P.O. Box 1315, Buffalo, NY 14269-1315, USA or P.O. Box 610, Fort Erie, Ontario L2A 5X3, Canada.

To be eligible for the Panasonic wide-screen TV, entries must be received by 6/30/95; for the Wedgwood china, 8/30/95; and for the Sharp ViewCam, 10/30/95.

Winners will be determined in random drawings conducted under the supervision of D.L. Blair, Inc., an independent judging organization whose decisions are final, from among all eligible entries received for that drawing. Approximate prize values are as follows: Panasonic wide-screen TV ($1,800); Wedgwood china ($840) and Sharp ViewCam ($2,000). Sweepstakes open to residents of the U.S. (except Puerto Rico) and Canada, 18 years of age or older. Employees and immediate family members of Harlequin Enterprises, Ltd., D.L. Blair, Inc., their affiliates, subsidiaries and all other agencies, entities and persons connected with the use, marketing or conduct of this sweepstakes are not eligible. Odds of winning a prize are dependent upon the number of eligible entries received for that drawing. Prize drawing and winner notification for each drawing will occur no later than 15 days after deadline for entry eligibility for that drawing. Limit: one prize to an individual, family or organization. All applicable laws and regulations apply. Sweepstakes offer void wherever prohibited by law. Any litigation within the province of Quebec respecting the conduct and awarding of the prizes in this sweepstakes must be submitted to the Regies des loteries et Courses du Quebec. In order to win a prize, residents of Canada will be required to correctly answer a time-limited arithmetical skill-testing question. Value of prizes are in U.S. currency.

Winners will be obligated to sign and return an Affidavit of Eligibility within 30 days of notification. In the event of noncompliance within this time period, prize may not be awarded. If any prize or prize notification is returned as undeliverable, that prize will not be awarded. By acceptance of a prize, winner consents to use of his/her name, photograph or other likeness for purposes of advertising, trade and promotion on behalf of Harlequin Enterprises, Ltd., without further compensation, unless prohibited by law.

For the names of prizewinners (available after 12/31/95), send a self-addressed, stamped envelope to: Prize Surprise Sweepstakes 3448 Winners, P.O. Box 4200, Blair, NE 68009.

RPZ KAL